# The Iron Road

# The Iron Road

### JANE JACKSON

ROBERT HALE · LONDON

© Jane Jackson 1999
First published in Great Britain 1999

ISBN 0 7090 6452 7

Robert Hale Limited
Clerkenwell House
Clerkenwell Green
London EC1R 0HT

Photoset in North Wales by
Derek Doyle & Associates, Mold, Flintshire.
Printed in Great Britain by
St Edmundsbury Press Ltd, Bury St Edmunds, Suffolk.
Bound by WBC Book Manufacturers Limited,
Bridgend, Mid-Glamorgan.

# *Chapter One*

Local dignitaries had been unanimous. The facts were plain. Navvies and decent society didn't mix. They might be necessary to build the line, but no one – certainly not fathers, husbands, or brothers – wanted them living too close. They were like a marauding army with their drinking and brawling. They caused trouble wherever they went. And no woman was safe from their lascivious attentions.

But they had to live *somewhere* while they were building the new Helston to Penryn line. After intense discussions, agreement was reached. The best place for the shanty village would be out near Trewartha. After all, it was reasoned, Sir Gerald Radclyff must have made a packet out of selling land to the Railway Company. And it wasn't as if the shacks and huts would be visible from his house or the surrounding park. Yes, unfortunately, this site was five miles from the railhead and supply depot, but as the line progressed, moving closer to their encampment, the navvies wouldn't have to travel quite so far to begin the day's work.

So the squalid shacks huddled in a fold between two hills out of sight of all except the navvies who lived in them, and their women.

The aldermen and councillors congratulated themselves. All things considered, the chosen location, a few hundred yards from the route the line would take, was ideal. The river at the bottom of the valley offered an abundant supply of fresh water. True, the paths down to it were steep and lined with gorse and brambles, but in autumn blackberries were free for the picking and would surely make a welcome addition to whatever it was such people usually ate.

Of course, one couldn't stop them coming into town. On paydays when they had money they spent freely. Mostly on beer it was true. However, if local innkeepers were prepared to accept the risks in return for the extra cash who could blame them? Business was business.

None of them knew or cared what went on in the shanty village, or what life might be like for an eighteen-year-old girl alone in the world.

Veryan Polmear lifted the wet cloth and looked at the bloody welts on the back of the eight-year-old boy lying face down on her narrow bed. Swallowing a rage that threatened to choke her, she blinked hard. She had no right to weep. He hadn't made a sound. He had huddled in the shadowed doorway of her hut, waiting for her to come. And when at last she'd arrived, bone-weary from the day's work and desperate for sleep, he had struggled painfully to his feet. Just for an instant she'd been tempted to send him away. *Where to?* No one else would take him in. And she certainly couldn't send him home. True, William Thomas might by now have sunk into his nightly drunken stupor, but if he hadn't, Davy would get another beating.

So, she had held out her hand to him. And sliding his grubby little paw into it, he had turned his head away, not wanting her to see as his shoulders heaved soundlessly. Now he lay on her rough grey blankets, trembling with delayed shock.

She lifted a plate from off the top of a basin by her feet. Taking a large piece of flannel from a jug of steaming water she wrung it out, opened it on her lap, scooped handfuls of soaked bread from the basin and spread it evenly over the centre of the cloth. Then, folding the edges over, she laid it gently on the broken skin, biting her lip as he flinched.

'It'll feel better very soon, Davy. A bread poultice is magic. It sucks out all the pain.'

He lay there, pale and unmoving. She stroked the skinny bare calf that poked out from his ragged trousers. They were far too big: hand-me-downs hacked off at the knee and left to fray by a mother too often drunk to finish any job properly. Veryan wanted to hate Bessie Thomas for her cowardice in allowing this treatment of her son. But it was difficult to hate a woman whose own bruises barely had time to fade before fresh ones replaced them.

'Can you feel it working?'

He shifted carefully, and glanced sideways at her. 'Did your da ever beat you?'

She shook her head. 'No. I was lucky. My father was a kind

man.' She remembered his laughing eyes; his rust-coloured hair several shades lighter than her own thick curls. He had swung her high in the air and called her his treasure, and she had felt warm and loved and *safe*.

'Why did you run away then?'

'What makes you think I ran away, Davy?'

He started to shrug, and his small young-old face screwed up in pain. He sniffed. 'Dunno. I 'eard it somewhere. They said you must've run away, else what was someone like you doing on the works?'

'My father was a soldier. He went away to fight in a place called the Crimea.' She had missed him and longed impatiently for his return. To recall the sound of his voice and bring him closer she had read for herself the books he used to read to her: *The Count of Monte Cristo*, *The Last of the Mohicans*, *Rob Roy*: exciting stories, full of adventure, that he had brought to vivid life in her mind. Reading had been her only escape from her mother's strange moods. And now books were her only friends, apart from young Davy. Yet it hadn't always been like this. She could remember a different life. Not clearly, for she had been very young, *Davy*'s age. But she could still recall a large house, with gleaming furniture and pictures and ornaments, and a garden with towering trees, drifts of fragrant flowers, and grass like bright green velvet. There had been servants too, a cook and maids, and a gardener and groom.

'Did he kill lots of people?'

'I don't know, Davy. He didn't come back. A lot of the soldiers became very ill and died before they could fight anyone.' Her mother's grief and rage had frightened her. Then they had left the house. *So many moves. Each place poorer and dirtier than the last.* So much she was unable – could not bear to remember.

He searched her face, his eyes large and full of fear. 'You won't die, will you?' he whispered.

Aching for him, for all the hurt he'd already endured in his short life, she widened her mouth in a reassuring smile and smoothed the tangled hair back from his dirty face. 'No, Davy. I won't die, I promise. Now, is the magic working? Does your back feel a little bit better?'

He thought for a moment, then nodded. As she continued to smooth his forehead his eyelids flickered and closed. Gazing at the small boy, she felt as if she was being torn in half. She was desperate to leave the works. But if she went, what would happen to Davy? She couldn't take him with her, nor could she abandon him to his father's brutality. *He wasn't her responsibility*. So how did she cut him out of her heart?

The following morning Veryan replaced one flatiron on the stand beside the fire and, after wrapping the holder around the handle, lifted the other. Licking her finger she touched the black surface to test the heat and turned back to the table and the last shirt. *Please don't let it rain again, not tonight*. It was pay-day, and if the men couldn't get into town there would be trouble.

She had lived on five different lines and on each one public response had been the same. Initially, local inhabitants had talked of the new railway with a mixture of amazement and apprehension. But once they became used to the earthworks and the sight of the little engine trundling along the newly laid line towing flat-bed wagons loaded with rails, sleepers, and ballast, their attitude had changed. Though some apprehension remained it was joined by excitement as they began looking ahead to the day a proper train would arrive, a huge black locomotive hissing clouds of steam as it thundered through the countryside carrying people and goods at speeds undreamed of.

Recognized as a necessary evil, the navvies were tolerated. They had money and enjoyed spending it. And, it was grudgingly admitted, they were more likely to fight amongst themselves than with the locals. But for navvy women it was a different story: they were treated like vermin, refused service in shops, their children chased away.

In all fairness, Veryan admitted, some deserved it. But what of the others? The ones struggling against impossible odds to live decent, orderly lives? They didn't deserve such scornful contempt. The injustice fuelled Veryan's deep anger, increasing her determination to escape. *She didn't belong here*.

'Dear life, girl,' Queenie huffed irritably from her sagging, dirt-encrusted armchair, eyeing the flatiron. 'Why don't you just spit on it?'

'She wouldn' do that,' Bessie Thomas jeered. 'She idn like the rest of us.' Emerging muffled from her cut and swollen mouth, the words held hopeless envy.

Glancing at the woman whose careworn face was distorted with the livid bruises of last night's beating, Veryan bent her head, saying nothing as she pushed the iron over the coarse material.

'You got a drop of something to put in this tea, Queenie?' Bessie wheedled. 'Help keep out the cold?'

'Never mind the bleddy cold, I can see you're hurting.' Queenie shook her head. 'Dear life, Bess, whatever did you do to get William so riled up?'

'I dunno. I don't reckn he need a reason.'

'Well, I wouldn't stand for it, I tell you that fer nothing.'

'I know, Queen.' Bessie gave a shamefaced shrug. 'But I aren't you. C'mon, you must 'ave a drop you can spare.'

Veryan glanced at Queenie, hoping, *willing* her to say she didn't have any. After the last riot, local magistrates had forbidden whisky on the works. Although he had complained bitterly about the loss of revenue, Horace Pascoe, the contractor, had reluctantly obeyed the ruling. But the previous day, when the brewer's carts had braved the deeply rutted muddy track to bring up fresh barrels, Veryan had noticed among them several smaller kegs, improbably marked *paraffin*. Anxiety had slithered between her ribs and settled in cold heavy coils in the pit of her stomach.

Queenie rummaged among the cushions at her back then hitched herself forward. Pulling the cork out with a grunt, she tipped the smeary bottle over the two steaming mugs.

'Does Pascoe know?' Veryan asked uneasily.

The old woman squinted round at her. 'Know what?'

'About the whisky.'

'Daft question. 'Course he does. Nothing comes on the works without that man knowing about it and taking his cut. He wouldn' let me have more'n one keg. And I had to pay over the odds for that. But if it comes in wet again tonight,' she grinned, 'I'll get my money back *and* make a tidy profit.' She recorked the bottle. 'Here, stir that fire up a bit. My joints is paining me something awful today.'

Setting the iron down, Veryan shovelled coal onto the glowing embers. The tongues of flame and sharp smell of whisky jolted her memory. Her mind flew back four years to another shanty on another works. She saw men hot-eyed with lust and alcohol, and her mother, equally drunk and laughing insanely as she was pawed and tossed from one to another.

Hiding in the shadows, too frightened to move, she had watched her mother – a woman of breeding and education and self-destructive wildness – stagger about then, arms flailing, stumble backward over the fire. The flames had licked hungrily at her whisky-soaked skirts. And before Veryan could utter a sound, the flames had leapt, blossoming with eye-searing brilliance into a huge flaring ball. They had swallowed her once-pretty mother and spat out a shrivelled, blackened *thing*.

'You going to stand there all day?' Queenie demanded. 'The fire won't burn no hotter with you staring at it.'

Veryan turned the shirt. The iron clattered as she picked it up. *It couldn't rain. It mustn't.*

Queenie's chair was positioned close to the beer barrels. The keys were chained to a man's broad leather belt she wore over a brown serge skirt stiff with food and beer stains. Her grubby blouse was covered by a man's shirt over which she had draped a tattered shawl. She had worn the same clothes for a fortnight. Beneath stringy, greying hair scraped into an untidy bun, her greasy skin shone. A wide mouth and heavy jowls increased her resemblance to a fat, pale toad. But her small eyes were as sharp and bright as a bird's.

She slurped the strong tea and sighed with satisfaction. 'Warms the cockles, that does.' She frowned at her companion. 'So what made him mad this time?'

Bessie sipped carefully, wincing. 'Pascoe's been going on to the gangers and they been pushing the men. But William says they can't work no faster. All this rain 'ave made it a mud bath down there.'

'The word is a new engineer's coming,' Queenie announced. 'Pascoe isn't going to like that. I don't think the other one 'ave set foot on the works more'n a couple of times in the last twelve months.' She looked over her shoulder at Veryan. 'You'd better shift yourself, girl. The men'll be steaming if their dinner isn't there when the hooter goes.'

Veryan had been up since six, tackling the endless washing produced by nine men returning every night drenched to the skin and caked in mud. 'I've only got one pair of hands.'

'And I'll have less of your lip, miss. Just remember who took you in, who fed and clothed you—'

'As if I could ever forget,' Veryan muttered.

'See what I have to put up with, Bessie? Is that gratitude? After all I've done for her?'

'That temper matches 'er hair. You know what's wrong with 'er,' Bessie confided. 'She need a man.'

Veryan would have laughed only there was nothing funny about the battered woman's unquestioning acceptance that this was the only way a woman could live. 'No I don't,' she replied firmly.

Bessie ignored her. 'Both my girls had a man and a couple of kiddies by the time they was her age.'

Setting the iron on the hearth, Veryan quickly folded the last of the shirts. 'I'll *never* be a navvy woman.'

'Oooh, listen to you, Miss airs-and-graces,' Bessie mocked, adding spitefully, 'Your mother wasn't so fussy.'

Veryan's head jerked up, anger and still-sharp grief bringing a torrent of scathing words to her lips. But at the sight of the bruised face, hunched shoulders, and shaking hands desperately clutching the whisky-spiked tea, she bit them back, unable to kick someone already so far down, even if they did deserve it.

'I'm not my mother and I won't live like that.' *Or die the way she did.* Making room for the shirt on one of the slats she hauled on the rope. The pulley creaked as she hoisted the heavily loaded clothes rack above the glowing coals. Then, crossing to the rickety dresser, she picked up a large wicker basket.

'What have you put up for them?' Queenie demanded.

'Bread, cold meat and cheese, and a jar of pickled onions.'

'Don't forget their beer.' Queenie pointed to a cask. 'You turn up without that and there'll be hell to go.'

'I 'eard the boy Edyvean moved in with Maisie Mitchell yesterday,' Bessie said, tentatively pushing her mug forward, trading information for the deadening effects of alcohol. 'Old enough to be 'is mother she is. And her chap not even cold in 'is grave. Maisie idn one to go 'ungry. If you get my meaning.' She flashed Queenie a loaded glance.

Tying the ends of her woollen shawl behind her back, Veryan tucked the cask under one arm. With the basket on the other she walked out into the pale March sunshine.

After the long wet winter everyone had been hoping the change of season would bring respite. And, at last, this morning had dawned fine and clear. *If it would just stay dry for twenty-four hours: long enough for the men to get paid, get changed, and get into town.* But as she glanced at the filmy sky, screwing up her eyes against the sun's glassy brilliance, anxiety pricked like a thorn.

Rarely used before the navvies arrived, the path had been widened and churned into deep soft, water-filled ruts by hundreds

of feet tramping to and from the line. The clay-like mud built up
on the soles of her boots and with the awkward weight of basket
and cask, Veryan found it hard to keep her balance. The path joined
another winding through the wooded valley. Layers of leaf-mould
made the mud even deeper, and dense undergrowth between the
trees shut out the light making the path feel like a ravine. She heard
a drumming sound and stopped, looking uncertainly around.

The sound grew louder, bouncing and echoing off the trunks so
it was impossible to tell which direction it was coming from. She
tried to run, to reach the open ground beyond the trees. Stinking
mud spurted up her legs and splashed over her skirt. But with a
ground-shaking rumble half-a-dozen riders rounded the bend
behind her.

'Get out of the way, you stupid girl,' the leader, a bulky man in a
top hat, bellowed. A thin beam of sunlight flashed off his spectacles.
*How? There was nowhere to go.* Stumbling and skidding to the edge
of the path, she flinched away from the panting, foam-flecked animals that filled the path, the deafening tumult of hooves, creaking
leather, and jingling harness. A couple of the other men shouted too,
angry that her unexpected presence might scare the horses. She had
seen them once or twice before, on the works. Well-dressed, well-
fed, arrogant men: directors of the Railway Company.

She half-turned, making herself as small as possible, trying to
protect the precious food. One rider's boot caught her hard on the
shoulder. She staggered, dropping the cask, and fell to her knees,
still desperately hanging onto the basket as they hurtled past.

Shaken and furious, she struggled to her feet. The basket lay on
its side. Wiping muddy hands on her skirt she reached for it, pray-
ing the men's dinner was still safe inside. If it weren't. . . . They
wouldn't beat her. No man laid a hand on Veryan Polmear. But
they would certainly make her pay one way or another, and her life
was difficult enough already.

'Are you all right?'

Looking up she was astonished to see that the last rider had
reined in and turned back. He was having difficulty controlling his
horse. Tossing its head it danced sideways, anxious to be with the
others.

'What are you doing?' one of his colleagues shouted impatiently. 'For heaven's sake don't touch her. Navvy women are very free
with their favours. God knows what diseases she's carrying.'

Ignoring his colleague, the first man urged his mount towards her. 'Are you all right?' he repeated.

She straightened up, her face burning with furious embarrassment. What did he expect her to say? *Yes, sir. Thank you, sir. My clothes are wet and dirty, my shoulder feels as if it could be broken, but don't you concern yourself, I'm fine.*

'I am no threat to your health, sir. But should you have cause to shake the hands of those with whom you ride, you would be wise to wash afterwards.' As his expression reflected shock followed by swiftly controlled amusement she turned away, reaching awkwardly for the muddy cask, catching her breath as the weight pulled on her throbbing shoulder. She heard his horse prance restlessly.

'They probably didn't expect anyone else to be on the path.'

It wasn't an apology. Men never apologized. 'Indeed?' she commented acidly. 'Yet this is the only path to the works.'

'Ah. I didn't know that.' Reaching into his pocket he held out his hand. 'For your trouble.'

Stunned – for this was wealth – she gazed at the silver coin on her muddy palm and looked up, her anger smothered by amazement and a feeling she had all but forgotten, *delight*. 'Th—thank you.'

Momentary surprise crossed his sun-darkened features then, with a brief nod, he wheeled his restless horse and galloped after his friends.

As she walked past abandoned fields and demolished cottages whose rubble made a wasteland of gardens that had once grown rows of tasty vegetables, she held the coin so tightly it dug into her fingers. She could visit Aggie's second-hand shop in Penryn. The temptation was strong. She had few clothes. And the daily tramp to the line through endless mud and rain had weakened the leather and rotted the stitching in her boots. They wouldn't hold together much longer. But to leave the works would be impossible without money, and this would double her meagre savings in the Penny Bank. She'd hold on a bit longer. Surely the rain would stop soon? She thought of her benefactor and felt her mouth soften in an unaccustomed smile.

The hooter blew just as she reached the works and she had to endure catcalls from several other gangs before she came to the men who lodged in Queenie's shanty. Throwing down picks and shovels they came towards her, the smell of them overpowering.

'What you been up to then, girl?' Paddy McGinn grinned, looking her up and down as she handed him the beer cask and a tin mug from the basket.

With no choice but to answer, she said briefly, 'I slipped.'

'I've 'eard that before.' A brawny navvy with a wide toothless grin nudged his neighbour, a swarthy, wiry man the men called Gypsy Ned. Ever since he had arrived the previous week she had felt his eyes on her like sticky fingers. She had tried to ignore him as she did all of them. But somehow he made it more difficult than usual.

As ganger, Paddy slaked his own thirst first before refilling and passing the mug to each man in turn while Veryan handed out the food. She tried to block out the sniggers and crude remarks inspired by her muddy dishevelled appearance. And her flush, which sprang as much from renewed anger as embarrassment, provoked even more comment.

Did Queenie send her to the works as a way of making her pay for being *different*? Or was it punishment because she refused to give up her dream? Both, probably. But there was another, much simpler, reason: Queenie sent her because she was too fat and too lazy to get out of her chair and come herself.

Ned sidled up and stood too close. 'I been watching you.' His breath was foul. He flicked a coated tongue over his lips. 'I know what you want. And I'm the man—'

She glanced at him in contempt. 'Over my dead body.' Then, with the icy disdain she used to keep them all at a safe distance, she turned her back. *She had to get away. She couldn't reclaim her old life. But anything was better than this.* Three blasts on the hooter signalled the return to work.

'Move yourselves, boys,' Paddy growled, jerking his head towards the top of the shallow cutting. 'We're being watched.' The navvies picked up their shovels and began trudging back to the embankment. Paddy hung onto the cask. 'I'll keep this. We'll need it this afternoon.'

Starting back the way she had come, Veryan looked in the direction Paddy had indicated. The directors sat astride their horses at the top of the slope, grouped in a semicircle around the man who had given her the silver coin. Who was he? Then, suddenly, it came to her: this was the new engineer.

# Chapter Two

JAMES Santana stood in the stirrups, his gaze following the wide canyon that gaped like an open wound in the landscape, and hid weary disgust behind an expression of interest. Another rescue job. He should have stayed in Spain and to hell with the agreement. He could have convinced other wealthy landowners of all the advantages a private railway line would bring, but he'd given his word.

How had it happened? He'd gone over and over it in his mind, and was still convinced he hadn't given Natalia any reason to believe. . . . Maybe that was it. Maybe she had thought to precipitate matters, and persuade her father at the same time. But surely she *must* have known Don Xavier was not a man to be coerced. Or had it been an act of pique? Not knowing was what rankled. Not knowing made it so much harder to put the episode down to experience and consign it to the past. Someone coughed, and he was suddenly aware of the directors watching him, waiting.

'Well, Mr Santana.' Adjusting his top hat with a gloved hand, Ingram Coles beamed. 'As chairman of the board, I'm sure I speak for my colleagues when I say how delighted we are that you will be joining our venture.'

Glimpsing the other men's expressions, James doubted it. They needed him, but they didn't really want him there. He was an outsider. Moreover, an outsider who was bound to ask questions they would rather not answer.

'As you know,' Ingram Coles continued, 'Mr Smallwood has an excellent reputation and we considered ourselves fortunate to have secured his services. However, he didn't inform us of his numerous other commitments.'

As he looked down into the works James could see, even from here, all the signs of poor organization and neglect: wheel-less wagons and broken tools abandoned and ignored; earth churned to glutinous knee-deep mud; standing water with no drainage channels to allow run off, lumber for walk-ways and rails for the temporary track carelessly dumped. The horses were limping, which signified disease in their feet, and the men moved with sullen slowness.

James sat back in the saddle. Because all the main lines had been completed, more and more railway engineers were being forced to look abroad for work. There would have been several applicants for this job, many with far more experience. Yet he had been given the post. He was glad to have the work, and it was well within his capability, but a tiny part of him remained wary.

'Smallwood hasn't attended a directors' meeting for months,' Victor Tyzack sniffed in disapproval.

James glanced at the deputy chairman. A tall man in his late forties he looked uncomfortable, and James guessed he was on horseback only because the terrain precluded use of a carriage. Next to him, astride a sleepy-eyed grey gelding, sat Clinton Warne, his forehead a map of anxiety. Stocky, with dark hair and bushy sidewhiskers, the general manager had a nervous habit of stretching his clean-shaven chin as if to escape his upright collar. Like the others he wore a braid-edged frock coat over a matching waistcoat and check trousers. And like theirs, James noted, the watch chain draped across his paunch appeared to be solid gold.

'Nor has he visited the line. Of course we didn't know that. At least, not until—'

'The point is—'

James turned. The snapped interruption came from Harold Vane, the company solicitor. A bulky man with an egg-shaped face he frowned through his pince-nez.

'Work on the line has fallen behind schedule. A situation I consider totally unacceptable, particularly in view of the restrictions and penalty clauses we were forced to concede.'

As anger tightened the solicitor's cherub lips so they looked like a fleshy drawstring purse, James felt a quiver of disgust. That kick had been deliberate. What kind of man did such a thing? He pictured the girl. He'd seen plenty of navvy women, but never one like her. She was neither coarse nor cowed. True, her clothes were little more than rags and she had called him sir. But there had been more spirit than subservience in her manner. The kick had obviously hurt. He had expected whining or curses. She'd given him neither. Her speech – the words she'd used, her phrasing was totally unlike that of any navvy woman he'd ever heard.

'I'm sure, once it's explained to him, Sir Gerald will—'

'My dear Ingram,' Harold Vane cut across the chairman, 'he will demand every last penny. Where money is concerned there is no man more acute or determined.'

'Yes, well,' Ingram Coles said, 'that is the whole purpose of engaging Mr Santana, is it not?' He turned to James. 'To shake things up, get them moving, and make up the lost time?'

'We are indeed most fortunate,' Harold Vane said. 'Mr Santana has a quite remarkable record of accomplishment.'

James smiled, calmly meeting narrowed eyes as hard as two black pebbles in the moon-like face. 'For one so young?' As he voiced what he knew they were thinking, he sensed rather than heard the collective intake of breath. 'Mr Brunel was but twenty-seven on his appointment as engineer for the Great Western Railway.'

Ingram Coles nodded as the men exchanged glances. 'Mr Brunel was a genius.'

'Indeed he was,' James agreed.

'I see you do not lack confidence,' Harold Vane observed.

'I have no reason to,' James responded evenly. 'And would be of little use to you if I did.'

'I say you are just the man we need, sir.' Ingram Coles patted his horse's neck. 'We were all most impressed by the reference from your previous employer.'

James's lips twitched in an ironic smile. Don Xavier was a man of honour. A glowing testimonial and full payment in exchange for James's immediate return to England. Young women, he'd explained, were impressionable, prone to exaggerating their feelings and imagining themselves in love. But regardless of James's half-Spanish ancestry, an alliance was unthinkable. Not, he had added as James stiffened in protest, that Mr Santana had ever harboured any such idea. But he would surely understand that as heiress to a considerable fortune it was important Natalia marry a man of equal standing. His daughter knew her duty. She would quickly forget her foolish notions once James was no longer around.

'I take it,' James said, 'that Mr Smallwood has officially vacated his position?'

'Indeed he has.' Harold Vane was grim. 'And he's damned lucky we decided not to sue.'

'That is all in the past.' Ingram Coles's voice held an unexpected hint of steel. 'We must look to the future. So, Mr Santana, what do you require of us?'

James scanned the works. 'Copies of the surveys and plans.' Then he turned his horse so that he faced them. 'Plus costings, and details of fees paid.' He saw the stiffening expressions, the swift secret glances.

Clinton Warne's chin shot forward. 'I really don't see—'

'Is that absolutely necessary?' another of the directors, silent until now, enquired. 'Surely it's privileged information?'

James simply waited, not justifying his request. He knew that at least half of them would have accepted bribes to ensure materials were purchased from particular companies. No doubt others had received a handsome commission for acting as agents in the purchase of land for the railway. But if he was to achieve what they wanted it wasn't enough simply to reorganize and speed up construction of the line, he needed a detailed picture of the company's finances.

Harold Vane's hooded gaze lighted on him like a bird of prey. 'As an employee of the company, Mr Santana is under an obligation to treat anything he may learn as absolutely confidential. Is that not so, Mr Santana?'

'Of course. My sole concern is to get the railway built.' He watched the directors visibly relax. 'However, I see one immediate problem: it appears the track is being constructed for a broad gauge line.'

'Naturally,' Ingram Coles replied. 'Broad gauge allows greater speed. More passengers and freight can be moved in a given time, which in turn generates higher revenue and therefore greater profit.'

'Indeed,' James nodded. 'But Great Western is the only major company using broad gauge. This inevitably means delays when transferring to standard gauge lines. As many stretches of Great Western track now have an extra rail to allow use by rolling stock of both broad and standard gauge, would it not be prudent to lay this line as standard right from the start?'

'I take your point, Mr Santana. Indeed I do, but—'

'That decision is not ours to make,' Harold Vane cut in once more, brusque and impatient. 'The Act specifies broad gauge. As you have been abroad, Mr Santana, you may not be aware of the difficulties we have faced from those in Parliament opposed to the railways.'

'They are making a great fuss over the fact that one in four members of the House of Commons holds a directorship in a railway company.' Victor Tyzack's sniff was belligerent. 'What's wrong with that, I'd like to know?'

James gave a small shrug. 'Perhaps they fear that, with such active involvement, the government might be influenced in favour of the railway companies?'

'So what if it is?' Victor Tyzack demanded. 'We are playing a major role in creating a powerful and forward-looking economy for this country. All businessmen understand that certain accommodations are a vital part of negotiations. Yet ignorant people have the impertinence to accuse us of corruption.'

'They also say' – Clinton Warne's jutting chin quivered with indignation – 'we have too little regard for the welfare of company employees. This is a gross injustice. While mines are closing all over Cornwall, *we* are providing work for two hundred men. And it is healthy outdoor work.'

'*And* they are paid three times the wage of a farm labourer,' someone else chipped in.

'You have joined us at a trying time, Mr Santana, but' – Ingram Coles's bright smile re-emerged like the sun from behind a cloud – 'the market is strong and I have no doubt that the Helston to Penryn line will provide an excellent return on our investment, and that of our shareholders, of course. Now, as we are so close to Trewartha, this would seem to be the perfect opportunity for you to visit Sir Gerald Radclyff. I'm sure you'll be able to allay his concerns.'

As the other directors nodded, James could see their relief at being able to transfer the responsibility from their own shoulders to his.

'And if there's anything else you need,' the chairman added, 'don't hesitate to ask. We will help in any way we can. Right, gentlemen, back to town I think.'

'You aren't going to tour the line?' James's surprised enquiry met with a unanimous shaking of heads.

'No point in confusing things,' Victor Tyzack said quickly.

'Too many cooks, and all that,' Clinton Warne agreed.

As they prepared to depart, Harold Vane brought his horse alongside James's. He leaned forward, deliberately intimidating, his voice soft and full of menace. 'We're paying you a lot of money, Mr Santana. Start earning it.'

Huge iron gates mounted on stone pillars topped by heraldic lions marked the imposing entrance to the Radclyff estate. The long drive wound across rolling parkland dotted with ancient oaks, towering copper beeches, and a canopy of broad chestnuts whose tightly folded leaves were just beginning to unfurl. The warmth of the sun released the scents of wet earth and primroses, the buttery perfume of gorse, and the sweet mustiness of leaf-mould. James closed his eyes as memories of Galicia broke over him like a curling wave.

Much of Spain was arid desert, but not Galicia. Frequent rain and hot summer sun made the north-west corner of Spain a rich and fertile region growing wheat, barley, oats, and rye, as well as potatoes, turnips, and orchards full of apples. On Don Xavier's estate outside Santiago, pigs rooted beneath oaks and chestnuts just like these, and cattle roamed the rich valley pastures.

Cushions of pink and purple heather and clumps of blackberry and gorse bushes were daubs of vivid colour on the high heath just as they were at Carn Brea and Goonhilly. And the rocky coastline; like that between Land's End and St Ives, offered sheltered bays and deep estuaries as safe havens from the thundering Atlantic Ocean.

James gave himself a mental shake. *Forget Galicia.* There had been little time to explore the region or to discover more about his Spanish ancestry. Perhaps once this job was completed he would go back.

Clicking his tongue, he urged his horse into a canter. Reaching the top of a knoll, his eyes shaded by the brim of his top hat, he saw a massive embankment of dark earth lying like a giant scab across the undulating hillside. It lay about half a mile away beyond the flags marking the boundary of the works and the scattered debris of felled trees.

How could the directors expect anyone to condone this wanton desecration? No wonder the chairman had preferred to send him to explain the problems to Sir Gerald. Still, much of his reputation

had been built on his ability to redeem apparently irreparable situ-
ations. How else, at twenty-seven, would he have gained such a
wealth of experience? And he was going to need every bit of it.
Instinct told him the battles hadn't even started.

A little further on, James caught his first glimpse of Trewartha.
A handsome country house built in the Georgian style, it had wide
shallow steps leading up to a white-pillared porch. New tendrils of
Virginia creeper had begun their annual pilgrimage across the stone
frontage and around the side. Tidy lawns edged the gravel drive,
and he could see the roofs of several outbuildings tucked away
behind neatly boxed hedges.

Dismounting, he handed the reins to a stableman with skin like
seamed leather and legs so bowed he rocked from side to side as he
led the animal away.

Removing his hat and gloves, James tugged the bronze bell-pull.
While he waited for someone to come he glanced around. Porches
were usually a haven for spiders, cobwebs, and dead leaves. This
one was spotless. Nor was there any trace of dried mud on the boot
scraper beside the bottom step, and the wide sweep of granite chips
in front of the house had been freshly raked. Sir Gerald Radclyff
maintained high standards. Little wonder the directors preferred to
delegate their excuse-making to someone else.

The glossy black front door opened and a butler, portly in
striped trousers and cutaway coat, raised an enquiring eyebrow.
'Sir?'

'Good afternoon. My name is James Santana. I'm the Railway
Company's newly appointed engineer. Would you ask Sir Gerald if
he could spare me a few minutes?'

The butler stepped back, both bow and expression a perfectly
judged blend of civility and aloofness. James bit back a smile. 'If
you'll step inside, sir, I'll see if Sir Gerald is available.'

The spacious hall smelled faintly of beeswax and lavender. On
twin marble plinths, matching porcelain vases were filled with dried
flowers and grasses. A red lacquered cabinet inlaid with ivory stood
between two panelled doors. And around the edges of a Chinese carpet dark wood gleamed with the rich patina of age and polish.

After showing him into a drawing-room the butler withdrew,
closing the door quietly. Sunshine poured in through tall windows
framed by moss-green drapes looped back by gold and green braided silk with tassels. James swiftly scanned the room. A man's pos-

sessions frequently revealed more of his character than he might choose to volunteer. The paintings, the delicate statues, the glass-fronted cabinet containing exquisite porcelain, and the Louis XIV furniture reflected the tastes of a connoisseur.

Wandering across to the nearest window James looked out. The earthworks scarring the landscape were clearly visible. Yet what had Sir Gerald expected? Building a railway meant altering geography. Hills had to be demolished, tunnelled under, or cut through; valleys bridged or filled in, swamps drained, inclines levelled. It was a colossal undertaking. And as well as having received a very good price for his land, no doubt Sir Gerald would be only too pleased to adopt a mode of travel faster, more convenient, and certainly more comfortable than any horse-drawn carriage. Progress meant change. A certain loss of privacy and a restructured view were small prices to pay.

Hearing the door open behind him, James turned, his mouth already stretching into the practised smile that tempered confident professionalism with courtesy.

'Mr Santana, I'm so sorry to have kept you waiting.' She was young, no more than twenty, and her low-pitched voice reminded him of a cool bubbling spring. Pale-gold hair was drawn from a centre parting into an elaborate coil at the back of her neck. As she closed the door and came towards him, her crinoline swayed gracefully. The fitted bodice of lace-trimmed cornflower silk curved from her bosom to define a delightfully slender waist.

She smiled, and he was suddenly reminded of Natalia. But that made no sense. They shared no physical similarity. Natalia was several inches taller and her hair raven-black. Natalia had brown eyes, while this girl's were as blue as her gown. So what was it? What had he recognized? Impatiently, he pushed the thought away. But, having expected to meet Sir Gerald, this additional distraction left him momentarily confused.

'My husband is engaged at the moment but will join you very shortly. In the meantime may I offer you some refreshment?'

*Husband?* James's confusion deepened. He had expected her to say *father*. From the directors' attitude when they spoke of Sir Gerald he had assumed the baronet was an elderly man. Yet with such a young wife. . . . James cleared his throat, relieved that with his back to the window she was unlikely to be able to read his expression.

'Thank you, but no.' He'd had no lunch, and would have given his right arm for a stiff drink. However, if Sir Gerald Radclyff was as astute as the company solicitor intimated it was wiser to decline. He needed all his wits about him. And Lady Radclyff's unexpected arrival plus his own reaction to her had already thrown him off-balance. 'I must apologize for calling unannounced.'

'Please, there's no need.' She sat down and indicated that he should do the same. 'My husband said you would come.'

'Oh?' James said carefully.

Her brief smile was impish. 'What he actually said was that Ingram Coles would be certain to send you instead of coming himself.'

Amusement battled with astonishment at her frankness. 'You've met the directors?'

She nodded. 'They came to dinner. They listed all the benefits the railway would bring and insisted we should be tremendously proud to be part of the grand march of progress.'

'As indeed we should.' James wondered how much longer Sir Gerald would be. He had little appetite for small talk. He was hungry and tired and had a great pile of paperwork waiting at an office he'd barely set foot in. Then, glancing up, he saw the glint of irony in her wide blue eyes and gentle smile. Awareness stirred, and beneath it. . . . *Was he mad? This was Sir Gerald Radclyff's wife, for God's sake*. Appalled at his own weakness he ruthlessly suppressed all feeling.

She tilted her head. 'And is this progress worth the cost, Mr Santana? I'm not referring to money. I'm talking about the hundreds of men who have been maimed or killed on Cornish lines alone.'

He cleared his throat again. 'Lady Radclyff, given the scale of the work involved—'

She raised a hand. 'Please, no clichés.' Again, her smile robbed her words of any offence. 'I've heard them all. Especially the one about it being impossible to make an omelette without breaking eggs. We are talking about *people*, Mr Santana. Men with wives and families.'

'Your concern does you great credit, but I assure you—'

'Forgive me, Mr Santana, but I am involved with several charitable organizations and I've studied reports of the conditions in which these men live and work. I found them most disturbing.'

James smothered a sigh. There was no doubting her sincerity. But why wouldn't women confine themselves to those aspects of life to which they were best suited, the running of homes and raising of children? Their increasing determination to involve themselves in matters they did not understand was growing tiresome.

'The work *is* dangerous,' he agreed. 'Which is why a navvy's wage is correspondingly generous.'

'Yes, the pay *is* good,' she nodded, 'while a man is able to work.'

James could see that, despite a nervousness that revealed itself in her right index finger digging at the broken skin around her thumbnail, she was determined to make her point and against his will felt a twinge of admiration.

'But if he's injured or killed, what then? There is no compensation. His family is left destitute.'

'Yes, that's true. And I'm sorry. But that's the way things are. The rules are not mine.' He had no reason to feel guilty. He didn't like it any more than she did, but it was a hard economic fact of life. The work was dangerous; inevitably men got killed.

'Imagine what would happen,' he went on, 'once a company or a contractor admitted the principle of liability. How many navvies would bother to work for their wages when they could stage an accident then claim compensation for their injuries? How many claims would it take before there was no money left to build the line? And if that happened all over the country then where would the remaining navvies find work so they could feed their families?'

As the blush climbed her throat, staining her cheeks a deep rose, he saw her raise one hand to the lace trimming on her bodice. Its rise and fall was a visible sign of her agitation. She bit her lip then smiled. 'You express yourself with admirable clarity, Mr Santana.'

Realization washed over him in an icy wave. The whole purpose of this visit was to placate Sir Gerald. Tact and diplomacy were essential. Yet he was arguing with the baronet's wife. *What had possessed him?* 'I beg your pardon. I didn't—'

'Please,' she interrupted. 'I'm not offended. You paid me a rare compliment.' Seeing his bewilderment she explained, 'You responded honestly, as you would have to a man.' Before he could comment she went on, 'And I do take your point. But surely there must be some way to improve conditions for those living and working on the line?'

Though intensely relieved, James didn't know how to reply or what to say. As an engineer his brief was to plan and survey the route a line would follow, specify the bridges, viaducts, cuttings and embankments required, and oversee the construction of the permanent way. The hiring of the men was left to the gangers who were accountable to the contractor. The conditions under which the navvies lived and worked were nothing to do with him.

'Well, I—'

'Perhaps – if you have no objection, of course,' – her mouth curved in a shy smile – 'I could come and see for myself how we might best be able to help?' She leaned forward slightly. 'The committee I sit on would truly appreciate such a humane gesture on your part. There are so many who will use the line when it is complete, yet have no care for the welfare of those involved in building it.'

Such earnest enthusiasm was difficult to refuse. Besides, accommodating Lady Radclyff's social conscience might improve his chances of appeasing Sir Gerald. And that would certainly raise his stock with the directors. Yet while these were perfectly adequate reasons for agreeing to her request, they would not have been sufficient to persuade him. The truth was he wanted to see her again. There was something about her, something that puzzled him. It was not conscious on her part. He had been flirted with by enough spoilt, bored women to recognize every ploy. She was different: obviously intelligent yet strangely naïve. There was no artifice or coquetry in her manner. He'd met other women of her station. Most viewed charity work as a necessary duty. She cared.

'Mr Santana?' Her colour had risen under his frowning scrutiny.

'Forgive me, Lady Radclyff,' he said quickly, furious with himself. 'I would be delighted—' The door opened and James received his second shock of the afternoon.

Sir Gerald Radclyff, for with that bearing it could be no other, was at least thirty years older than his young wife. James's surprise increased as Lady Radclyff rose, folding her hands in front of her. She remained standing, and James had to force his curiosity aside as he continued his swift appraisal of the man he had come to see. Now was not the time to speculate on this unusual pairing.

Perhaps a hand's span taller than his wife, which still left him several inches short of James's six feet, the baronet was of slight build, with fluid graceful movements that belied his years. This was a man who took care of his body. His hair, flecked with grey at the temples, curled forward from a side parting to blend with bushy side-whiskers. He was otherwise clean-shaven. His aquiline features revealed nothing, but James sensed himself assessed. And, watching the fastidious mouth thin into a smile, he was fleetingly reminded of a snake.

Approaching her husband, Lady Radclyff laid one hand lightly on his arm. 'Gerald, I've been telling Mr Santana about my charity committee and he has kindly agreed to let me visit the railway works to see what is needed and how best we may help.'

'Indeed, my dear.' The baronet covered his wife's hand with his own. But to James it appeared to be not so much a gesture of affection as a confirmation of ownership. 'That is most obliging of him. You'll take Polly with you, and one of the grooms?' It was clearly an instruction.

'Certainly.' Her smile was fond. 'I wish you wouldn't worry so.'

He raised her hand to his lips. 'You're very precious to me, my dear. I know how much your charity work means to you, but I will not countenance any risk to your safety.' His gaze flicked briefly to James who recognized the warning and wondered if he might have been wiser to refuse Lady Radclyff's plea. *Of course it would*. This job was turning out to be very much more complicated than he had envisaged.

'And now, my dear, you must excuse us. I'm sure Mr Santana is anxious to explain the reasons for lack of progress on the line.'

# Chapter Three

BY SEVEN that evening, rain was failing steadily onto already sodden earth. In the shanty, warm, humid air was thick with the smells of wet clothes, unwashed bodies, and boiled meat. Lifting the frayed hem of her apron Veryan wiped her damp forehead then turned to the stack of dirty plates and bowls. Cooking for nine men created interminable washing-up. Behind her, sprawled on benches around the table and cursing the weather, the navvies waited impatiently for the little engine that would take them, sitting on the flat-bed wagons, back into Penryn to spend their wages.

They had started drinking as soon as they returned from the works. And once the meal was finished they had begun drinking again. Normally they were long gone by now. The engine was late. *Let it come soon.*

Queenie's round cheeks were crimson from the heat and her small eyes glittered with satisfaction at the money she was making. 'Hark at that.' She cocked her head. Even with the noise the men were making Veryan could still hear the rain drumming on the tarred felt roof. 'Pissing down it is.' Queenie surveyed her lodgers. 'Their wages is burning holes in their pockets. And if that engine don't come they can't go nowhere to spend it. Oh well.' With a sigh of satisfaction she folded her hands under her sagging bosom and settled more comfortably in the chair. ' 'Tis an ill wind as they say. Here, girl! Got mud in your ears have you?' As Veryan started, rising wearily to her feet, Queenie held out her tin mug.

'Get me a drop more whisky – out of the keg,' she added, lowering her voice. 'No need for anyone to know about the bottle. Got to keep that for a rainy day. Ha! A rainy day.' Her voice caught on a hiccup then she belched. Veryan took the mug without a word. 'Have a drop yourself,' Queenie urged. Do you good it will.'

Veryan said nothing. Silence was safer on nights like this. It gave her a kind of invisibility. Handing back the mug with its measure of spirit she turned away. But Queenie grabbed her skirt.

'Listen, it's time you gave up these daft ideas about leaving the works. Staying in one place and having a cottage and a garden is for ordinary folks, not for the likes of us.'

Blank-faced, wishing she had never clothed her dream in words, much less confided it to Queenie, Veryan silently screamed her denial. She would *never* accept that. She wasn't *us*. Eyes lowered, she simply waited. Impatiently, Queenie pushed her away.

'You're some stubborn maid. No one can say I haven't done my best. I've treated you like you was my own.'

Veryan bit the inside of her lip, not sure whether to laugh or cry, and too tired for either. She was little more than a slave. Yet Queenie's laziness had been her protection. For if Queenie had not taken her in after her mother's death, her only means of survival at fourteen would have been living with one of the navvies.

Ten men lived in the shanty: nine since Cider Joe had broken his leg four days ago and been carried off the works tied to a gate. Seven shillings a week bought each man three meals a day, his washing done, and sole occupancy of one of the bunks which filled the far end of the shanty from floor to roof.

But while Queenie took the money and ruled from her armchair, it was she, not Queenie, who hauled water from the stream to fill the two coppers, one in the wash-house, the other in here next to the hearth. It was her hands, not Queenie's, that were constantly cracked and sore from scrubbing sweat-stained shirts and mud-caked breeches. It was she who cooked the often fly-blown meat and shrivelled vegetables Pascoe sold in his tally shop, the men's only source of food unless they could catch a rabbit or poach game from a nearby estate. She walked to the works each day with bread, cheese and beer for their dinner. She carried coal from the tip, chopped wood for the fires, and tipped the ashes down the privy to deaden the stench.

And over the last four years she had learned to be ever more wary of pay-days.

Once they had paid Queenie – who always insisted on money in advance – the men invariably made for the nearest town. On this line it was Penryn. There they stayed, drinking, gambling and whoring until they ran out of money, or were released from jail.

On other occasions when the engine had been late, or had broken down, they had walked. But this time the rain was too heavy. They would be soaked to the skin before they even reached the road.

For Pascoe, as for Queenie, the men's confinement was a blessing. Bringing whisky onto the works guaranteed he would recoup the money he had just paid them in wages.

Drying the last of the plates and bowls, Veryan stacked them on the rickety dresser. Her bruised shoulder was stiff and aching. And, as the men bawled at one another – laughter punctuated by curses, shoving and scuffles more frequent – every instinct urged her to leave. Trouble was imminent and she wanted to get away before it erupted.

Drying the crude cutlery she put in the drawer. All except her special knife, the one she used for cooking. Worn away to a thin curve half its original width, its short blade was razor sharp. She had seen both Paddy and Nipper eyeing it. If she left it in the drawer it would have gone by morning. Slipping it into her skirt pocket she hung the cloth over a line at one side of the fire. Then, trying to be inconspicuous, she edged between Queenie and the broad backs of the men at the table towards the door.

'Where do you think you're going?' Queenie demanded.

'It's all done. I haven't left anything.'

'I never said you did. I asked where you was going,' Queenie's voice was slurred, her tone belligerent.

Veryan's wary sidelong glance towards the men caught a bloodshot stare in which curiosity was stirring. She looked swiftly away. 'To my hut.'

'How am I supposed to deal with this lot on my own?' Queenie whined. 'I only got one pair of hands. No, you stay here. And you needn't look like that. *Smile*. Think of the money. I'll see you right. You'd like a new dress, wouldn't you? Or some new boots? 'Course you would. And so you shall. All you got to do is be a bit more friendly. Have them eating out of your hand you will.'

Shaking her head she turned to the door but found her way blocked by a swaying figure. She moved to one side. He did the same. She took a step the other way and he followed. She saw the beer in his nearly full mug slop over one dirt-engrained hand. As she glanced up he grinned, revealing a mouthful of decaying teeth.

' 'Ere, look at Ned,' Nipper shouted. ' 'E's dancing.'

'He cannae dance,' Mac scoffed, his accent broad Glaswegian. 'Not wi' two left feet.'

Aware of men turning to look, Veryan felt heat flood her face. She swallowed, then spoke with quiet firmness. 'Let me pass.'

He blinked, his face slackening in surprise. As he hesitated, one of the others said something she didn't catch, causing a burst of laughter. Her tormentor grinned.

'Hark at the *madam*,' he mocked. 'Woss it worth, then?' Leering, he reached for her. She reacted instinctively, pushing him hard in the chest. Eyes wide with surprise he stumbled backwards and crashed against the door. The mug flew from his hand, bounced on the earth floor, and rolled to a stop among the feet of the nearest men.

'Hey! Tha's my beer. I paid for that beer.' As Veryan tried to slip past him he seized her arm, frowning. 'You owe me for that. I reckon—' He belched loudly and grinned. 'I reckon you owe me a kiss.' He pulled her towards him.

Deafened by the chorus of whistles and catcalls, and the thud of benches overturning as the men scrambled for a better view, Veryan struggled desperately, warned by some sixth sense not to scream. Wrenching free she lunged for the door but he was surprisingly quick and snatched at her blouse. Weakened by age and too many washes, the faded material tore.

At the sharp dry sound the men fell silent. Instantly the atmosphere changed. What had been merely a rough game became suddenly dangerous. Clutching the ripped material to her breast, Veryan looked round wildly at Queenie.

Enthroned in her armchair, her expression an odd mix of shame and excitement, the old woman held out the mug, her hand weaving unsteadily. 'Have a swallow, girl. You might as well get used to it.'

Veryan stared at her, not believing. 'No.' She shook her head. 'You can't let— I won't— not—'

'Look, it's the way things are. Time you faced up to—'

'*No!*' Veryan's scream held all the hurt and fury of ten lonely frightened years. The men froze. But only for a moment. No longer individuals they were now a pack.

'Go on, Ned, she owes you for that beer.'

'I reckon she owes me too.'

'And me.'

They edged towards her. She could hear them breathing. Holding her blouse together with one hand, she fumbled with the other among the folds of her skirt, found the pocket.

'Stay away.' Despite her trembling it was a warning, not a plea. Her fingers tightened round the knife's handle.

'Listen to her,' one of them sniggered.

'I like 'em with a bit o' spark.'

'Ach, she'll nae be any fun. I'd rather go to Miz Treneery's.'

'There's always a bleddy queue on pay days. An' Ned idn in the mood to wait.'

'I reckon she needs tamin'.'

'She'll be a easier ride once she've been broke.'

Her eyes fixed on the gypsy; Veryan tried to ignore the comments and suggestions that were becoming coarser by the second.

Glassy-eyed, a half-smile on his slack mouth, Ned made a lunge.

She jerked backwards, filled with a rage as bright and sharp as summer lightning. It smothered her terror and infused her with strength. Whipping out the knife she held it in front of her, the blade pointing upwards.

'Stay away,' she repeated. 'Leave me alone.'

There was a moment's total stillness.

'Ach, I warned ye,' Mac spat in disgust. 'I said she'd no' be any fun. I want another drink.'

The tension broke and the men turned away, grumbling, as they crowded around Queenie.

Veryan felt behind her for the latch and slipped out quietly, pulling the door shut behind her. She stood for a moment, her heart thudding against her ribs, and sucked cool fresh air into her lungs. The rain had eased for a moment and a brassy moon played hide and seek behind dark rags of cloud. She started towards her hut, picking her way around silvered puddles. A door slammed, making her jump. As she glanced round a stocky figure stepped out of the shadows.

'I been waiting for you,' William Thomas growled, grabbing her arms. 'Time somebody taught you a lesson. Who do you think you are? You got no business interfering.'

Veryan wrenched free. 'And you have no business beating an eight-year-old child.'

He grabbed her again. 'Want a kid to look after, do you? How about I give you one of your own, eh? Like that, would you?' His fetid breath made her gorge rise. Avoiding her flailing fists, he pulled her hard against him. He reeked of stale sweat and spirits.

'Let go of me!' Veryan fought furiously. She kicked out hard, and felt intense satisfaction at his grunt of pain.

'Bitch,' he spat. 'You'll pay for that.'

The shanty door opened spilling light and noise into the evening.

' 'Ere, what's going on?' Ned, drunk and furious, hurled himself forward. 'Gerroff,' he snarled, taking wild swings at William. 'She's mine.'

'You'll just have to wait your turn,' William panted, jabbing Ned viciously with his elbow then, fastening his arm so tightly around her she could hardly breathe, he began dragging her towards the narrow alley between two shanties.

Gasping and struggling, she felt for the knife. Ned flung himself forward fists flying. One struck Veryan a glancing blow, knocking her sideways. She dropped the knife. William doubled up, retching and winded. Head swimming, Veryan tried to get up. But Ned pushed her down again, his wet mouth fastening like a leech on her throat, his fingers scrabbling at her skirts.

Still fighting she was losing her strength. He had his forearm across her throat and was pressing down. She couldn't breathe, couldn't see. Terror lent her strength and she gave a last desperate heave. Jack-knifing her legs she kicked wildly. Ned gave a grunt and collapsed, twitching. He gave a strange sighing groan and was still.

'What the hell's going on? What's all the row about?' Queenie waddled forward as Veryan crawled away from the inert body, coughing and gasping.

'Dear life, girl. Woss the matter with 'e? Shaking like a bleddy leaf you are.'

'Fight. . . . Ned. . . . William.' The words emerged as a hoarse croak and were all Veryan could manage as Queenie helped her up. The men were carrying Ned back to the shanty. Veryan looked round for William Thomas. He was standing a few yards away. In the moonlight she saw his expression clearly, a gloating grin of pure evil. He moved, pulling Davy forward. The child's face was a mask of fear. William turned away, half-dragging, half pushing the boy toward their own shanty.

'C'mon,' Queenie urged. 'You come back wi' me. You need a drop of something to calm 'e down.'

Veryan shook her head. 'No.' She swallowed painfully. 'I'm all right. I just want to lie down.'

Queenie shrugged, tugging her grubby shawl across her bolster-like bosom. 'Please yourself.'

Sliding the bolt across, Veryan lit the lamp then sat on the edge of her bed, hugging herself as she waited for the queasy faintness to pass.

A sharp rap on the door sent shock tingling along her nerves and her heart gave a sickening lurch.

'Open the door, girl. C'mon, hurry up.'

Veryan didn't move. 'Won't it wait, Queenie? I just want—'

'No, it won't bleddy wait. Now you open this door, else I'll fetch one of the men.'

As Veryan slid back the wooden bolt, Queenie whirled in.

'He's only dead, isn't he.'

'Who is? What are you talking about.'

'Who d'you think? Ned. He's dead. Stabbed. With your knife.'

Veryan stared at her. He couldn't be dead. The blackness swirled across her eyes. Her head swam. She stumbled to the bed and dropped onto it.

'I didn't stab him.'

'Well, it was your knife Paddy pulled out of him. And we all seen you threaten him with it.'

'Yes, I know, but—'

'Look, I don't care one way or t'other. He idn no great loss.' Queenie tugged her shawl tighter. 'But we don't want no magistrates on the works. Not when all the men have been drinking, and spirits is banned. Wouldn't do us no good at all, that wouldn't. Getting rid of the body won't be no problem. He's stinking of drink so if he's put on the line 't will look like an accident.' She patted Veryan's face with dirty fingers. 'Don't you worry. I'll take care of it. I've looked out for you since your mother died, 'aven't I?' She put her hand on the latch.

'Just one thing: I don't want to hear no more about you leaving the works. Best to forget that. You'd always be looking over your shoulder; always wondering if someone would find out what you done. Best if you stay here with me and make the best of it.'

Later that night driven by a vicious wind, the rippling curtain of rain beat down on the lifeless body of Gypsy Ned. It pounded fallen leaves to mush and flattened rust-brown bracken. It gouged channels down the embankment, softened poorly compacted soil, and pooled in the new excavations.

And in the darkness, further down the track where the massive pillars of an almost-completed viaduct spanned the tree-lined valley beneath, it trickled into badly mortared cracks. Dripping and dribbling through the rubble, silently, unseen, it washed grit and dust from between the stones. A large boulder shifted imperceptibly, altering the load on a supporting baulk of timber.

Carrying the two brimming buckets, Veryan kept her eyes on the steep path and tried to avoid the muddiest patches. The dragging weight put even more strain on her aching shoulder, and her ankles were being rubbed raw by the wet slap of her skirt and petticoat hems. But these discomforts were nothing compared to her agony of mind. *She had killed a man.*

Normally she was the first up. But that morning she had been roused from a state far deeper than mere sleep by an irate Queenie hammering on the door.

'What's going on? Why aren't the fires lit? Why idn the porridge cooking?'

Startled awake, still trapped in her nightmare, she had staggered blindly across the tiny hut and pulled back the wooden bolt. The door flying open had knocked her against the wall as Queenie barged in.

'What time do you call this? Come *on*, will you? Bleddy day'll be half over by the time you stir yourself.' She stopped, her face changing. 'Oh my Lord, girl. What *have* you done?'

Pushing back her tangled hair, Veryan shook her head, her voice a dry rasp as she tried to excuse, to explain. 'I didn't mean— But I couldn't let him—'

'No, I aren't talking about that. What's wrong with your arms?'

Veryan looked down blankly. Then it all flooded back. Last night after Queenie had left her, she had stumbled into the lean-to wash-house next to the shanty and scooped a bowl of water from the still warm copper. Back inside the little hut, built with her own hands from salvaged planks and panels, she had bolted the door. Then, ripping off the torn blouse she had screwed it into a tight bundle and thrown it into the furthest corner. She possessed few clothes and that had been a favourite. But though she might mend the tear and wash out the mud, nothing would remove the memories. She could not bear to look at it, much less wear it again. When she lit the fires in the morning she would burn it.

Soaping a rough cloth she had scrubbed her face, arms and upper body: everywhere Ned's hands or even his breath had touched. Her gasps had deepened to shuddering sobs and she had rubbed and rubbed until crimson droplets had begun to stipple and smear her sun-browned skin.

Flinching from Queenie's accusing stare she pulled the sleeves of her darned nightgown below her wrists, hugging her arms protectively against her body. She hadn't meant – hadn't *intended*— How could she have stabbed a man, *taken a life*, and not even remember? She cleared her throat. 'Where—?'

'It's all been took care of. Don't you think no more about it. Least said soonest mended. Now, move yourself. The men is waiting for their breakfast, and I don't want no more trouble.' She waddled to the door. 'You can't blame the men. It was your own fault. It would never have happened if you was spoken for. But oh no, none of 'em was good enough, not with you being a Polmear.'

Veryan bit back the reminder that Queenie herself had also deterred any would-be suitors, not wanting to lose her skivvy.

'All that nonsense about leaving the line and living among good folk.' Queenie snorted. 'Well, you can forget that.' Triumph rang in her voice. 'You won't be going nowhere now, my girl.'

Halfway up the path Veryan carefully set the buckets down for a moment. As she uncurled her fingers and painfully flexed her shoulders, her thoughts fluttered like frightened birds in a cage. *She could not have let him* – she shuddered. But in defending herself she had inadvertently played right into Queenie's hands.

Until last night she had stubbornly refused to accept the hand fate had dealt her. Her dreams of escaping to a different life had given her the strength to keep going. Without those dreams, without even the hope of something better. . . . A yawning chasm of despair opened inside her. What was the point of fighting any more? *She was so tired.*

Resistance flickered, a candle flame in the darkness. And to bolster her courage, rekindle her determination, she reached for memories of her childhood. But they were so faint, so difficult to recall. It was like trying to grasp a handful of mist.

The sound of a bugle, the warning signal for blasting, floated toward her on the breeze. Lifting the buckets she resumed her trudge up the path. A few moments later she heard a dull *crump*, and felt the ground shiver. Breathless, her lungs on fire, legs trembling from the climb, she reached the top of the path. Shouldering through the bushes onto the rutted muddy track which led to the shanty village she almost collided with a burly figure. Her violent start slopped water onto her skirt and shoes, making them even wetter.

'Whoa!' he grunted. His surprise equalled hers, but knowing that didn't soften her fury. The grin spreading over his square, dark-stubbled face only made it worse. Though she had escaped violation the other night, this near-collision had triggered a vivid flashback. She wanted to scream at him, to lash him with words for frightening her when she was already suffering more fear than she could handle. But, already gasping for breath, she had no strength to spare.

'All right, then, maid? You gave me some start coming out like that.'

Ignoring the greeting that proclaimed him a Cornishman, she turned away and started walking. She could still see him in her mind's eye. The gaudy waistcoat and neckerchief, the velveteen square-tailed coat and sealskin cap, all marked him as a navvy.

'Hold on a minute!' He started running after her, cursing as his heavy boots slipped on the thick sticky mud. 'How far to the railway works?'

She was tempted to ignore him. But his rich Cornish accent hooked a fragment of memory buried deep inside. *My pretty little maid.* That's what her father had called her. With hands like shovels he had gently towelled her hair dry in front of the fire, enthralling her with stories of his adventures in far-off lands as he combed out the tangles. *Why had he abandoned her?*

'What's wrong? Cat got your tongue?'

Working in the shanty and living so close to men, she recognized the stranger as one who would consider silence a challenge and who would not give up until he obtained a response.

She stopped, glancing back. 'How should I know where the works are?'

' 'Course you know. It's where you're from and where you're going.' He ambled forward, solid and muscular, looking her up and down with cheerful insolence. 'There aren't no houses for miles.

Yet here's you carrying water, so you must live handy by. And if the shanties aren't far, then the works can't be more than a mile or two.'

A variety of comments sprang to her lips, ranging from *Aren't you clever?* to *Just go away and let me be.* But they remained unspoken. Instead she gave him a brief nod and continued on her way.

With his long loose stride he easily overtook her. 'My name's Tom, Tom Reskilly.'

Veryan stopped again, her impatience shaded with anxiety. 'What do you want, Mr Reskilly?'

Twin grooves appeared between his heavy brows and she knew he was confused by the contrast between her voice and her appearance.

As a child she had been tutored in grammar and correct speech. She knew her father, though proud of his Cornish heritage, had wanted her to feel comfortable among her mother's family, who had made no secret of their belief that their daughter had married beneath her. And though she could mimic the markedly different accents of west and north Cornwall, those lessons were too deeply engrained to be forgotten. And that was another reason for saying little. For all her attempts to remain unnoticed, others in the shanty village knew she didn't belong there. She might be *with* them, having no other place to go, but she wasn't *of* them.

Being able to read and write gave her a certain status. And her help was often sought, and willingly given, when letters needed to be read or written. But her only close friend was an eight-year-old boy. She knew why. She had not followed the accepted pattern. Most other girls of her age on the works were living with a navvy and had borne at least two children. Was her life better than theirs? Instead of cooking and washing for one man, she cooked and washed for ten. But at least her body was her own. *For how much longer?*

'I was told to ask for a ganger by the name of Maginn. Know him, do you?'

An image of Paddy, bold and clear, flashed into her mind. He was top man in the shanty. *He could have stopped them.* But, hot-eyed, he had shouted with the rest, urging the gypsy on, avid-faced and sweating. The memory was a sharp prod in a still-raw wound and she shied away from it.

'No.'

Tom Reskilly simply nodded. 'No matter. I'll find him. Take in lodgers do you?'

'No.'

'Well, you must know someone who do.'

Veryan thought of the shanty and the two empty bunks. 'Ask at the works.'

He looked at her, his gaze steady and speculative. 'Chatty little soul, aren't you? Well, I'd best get on. Can't hang about here burning daylight.' He raised a forefinger to the brim of his cap. Though the gesture contained a hint of mockery it held something else as well, something that shook her.

'I'll see you again.' It was both threat and promise. His quick grin revealed strong teeth with only one gap near the back. Against skin weathered to the same golden brown as the inside of oak bark, his eyes were the colour of violets.

While she stared at him, trying to identify a feeling she didn't recognize, a feeling bound up with his salute, he winked then loped away, whistling.

*He thought her worthy of courtesy?* Confused, disoriented, she trudged on with the buckets, deliberately keeping her gaze on the track. He certainly had a way with him. But the next time she saw him, *if* she ever did, there would be no smile, no casual teasing charm. *She had killed a man.*

What did she care for his opinion? Handsome he might be. And there was more to him than a roguish grin and a silver tongue. She wasn't sure how she knew, yet she would stake what little she owned that it was so. But what did it matter? He was a navvy. And that made him the last man in the world to interest her.

As she arrived back at the shanty village the sound of a woman's voice, shrill and pleading, made her stomach knot painfully. Setting the buckets down she massaged her cramped fingers. Drawn closer, she was wary of joining the other women watching in sombre silence. For them what was happening probably recalled all-too-familiar personal experience. She was merely an observer, envied because of Queenie's protection. *If they only knew.*

'Just a few more days, Mr Timms. Denny promised. He said as soon as he found work he'd be sending for me and the kids.'

'I'm sorry, Cora—'

Stick-thin and aged beyond her years, the young woman drew herself up angrily.

'That's Missus Pearce to you. I aren't no works woman. Denny and me was married proper in a church. He's a decent honest man, and—'

'That's as maybe, *Mrs* Pearce,' the timekeeper, a bluff stocky man, checked his ledger. 'But he isn't here now.'

'There's men coming in on the tramp all the time,' she cried desperately. 'One of them is bound to have seen him. I been going down the works every day asking. Just give us a couple more days. Please, Mr Timms. I'm begging you.'

A soft, barely audible sound rippled from the throats of the watching women.

The timekeeper shifted his weight from one foot to the other. 'You know the navvy law,' he insisted, dogged and determined. 'Only men working on the job, or their families, are allowed to live in the shanties. Your man's been gone three weeks now. You got to get out.'

'And go where? What am I supposed to do?' The young woman's anguished cry startled the baby in her arms who wailed in protest. Her other two children, both boys, one aged about five, the other a year or so younger, giggled as they pretended to fight, each clinging to her skirts with one hand, completely oblivious to their mother's distress.

The timekeeper's shrug implied that wasn't his concern. 'Go on the parish.'

Angry whispers rustled among the women.

'Lose my children? Give up my freedom? Be forced to wear workhouse clothes so everyone knows? Be treated like I'm some kind of criminal when I haven't done nothing wrong? Never! I'll *never* go on the parish.' Abruptly her voice changed again from defiance to entreaty. 'Please, Mr Timms. Just one more day?'

The timekeeper's gaze flicked to the watching women who stared back in silent hostility. He shifted again, clearly uncomfortable and losing patience. 'Look, one more day won't make any difference. Your man could be dead for all you know.'

Veryan knew Bernard Timms wasn't a cruel man. His brutal words were a simple statement of fact.

'I got my job to do. No way can I let you stay another night in that hut. Not unless. . . .'

Veryan saw the women exchange glances. They knew what was coming.

'What?' Cora Pearce demanded, hope battling with anxiety, itself tinged with suspicion and dread. 'Not unless what?'

Bernard Timms tapped his ledger. 'Beany Flynn says he's willing to pay your rent if you'll take him as your man.'

Cora Pearce's thin face turned chalk-white. 'But— I'm a married woman. What if my Denny comes back?'

'What if he doesn't?' The timekeeper was brusque. 'Come on. I haven't got all day. What's it to be? Yes or no?'

Veryan saw agonized indecision on Cora's pinched features as she automatically rocked the crying baby then looked down at her other two children.

When she raised her head her face was etched with shame and grief. 'Yes,' she whispered.

As Bernard Timms made a note in his ledger, the women turned quietly away to their shanties. But inside Veryan the guilt and fear and rage that had been draining her of purpose suddenly coalesced into a resolve as cold and clear as frosted starlight.

Newspapers constantly railed against the evils of slavery, condemning the southern states of America for inhuman behaviour. Yet what of the slaves in England? For navvy women were little better. Moving from line to line, they quickly lost touch with their families. All they had was their man and their children. But if he lost his job, or grew bored with the responsibilities of family life, he went on the tramp looking for new work, leaving her to follow when, *or if*, he sent for her. Thus, in order to survive, women like Cora Pearce could start the day as the legally married wife of one man, and end it, for her children's sake, living as the kept woman of another.

*Not me*, Veryan vowed. *I won't give up. Somehow I'll get away.*

# Chapter Four

Veryan felt every muscle tighten as she heard the men arrive back that evening. Before she had been wary, watchful. Now she felt vulnerable and afraid, and hated the feeling. She tried hard to shrug it off. But everything was different now. *They said she had killed a man.*

Grumbles and curses overlaid the squelch and suck of boots in the mud as the men tramped into the village and dispersed to the crude and sparsely furnished huts.

Veryan kept her back to the door and with shaking fingers dropped suet dumplings into the thick bubbling stew. The shanty was suddenly full of voices and thuds. Boots were kicked off, mud-soaked shirts and trousers thrown into a corner for her to collect later. Then, hauling on dry clothes over grubby and felted woollen combinations, the men crowded around Queenie who had tapped a new beer barrel.

'Who's this then?' Queenie demanded, her voice rising above the rest. 'You're some fine-looking feller. What's your name?'

'Tom Reskilly, ma'am.'

Though she'd expected it – he'd asked for Paddy after all – the sound of his voice caused a strange contraction deep inside her.

Confused and angry at her own reaction, she kept her head bent, refusing to look round.

'Listen to 'im! Ma'am is it? I know your sort, my lad: a silver tongue and itchy feet. I bet you've broken a few hearts. Where're you from?' Curiosity and amusement had replaced Queenie's habitual cynicism.

'Born at Treskillet. Just come from a branch line down west.'

Hearing him establish his Cornish origins as well as the fact that he'd not been out of work for very long, Veryan recognized Tom Reskilly was a lot more astute than his brash cheerful manner suggested. Had Paddy forewarned him? Suggested the best way to approach Queenie? Not that it would have made any difference. Queenie was a law unto herself when it came to lodgers. She had turned away a chirpy little man from Bristol. Yet she had accepted the dour Mac who grumbled incessantly, and Gypsy Ned. Veryan's head swam and the sweat bathing her was suddenly icy. Dropping in the last of the dumplings she replaced the heavy lid. It clattered loudly and she flinched.

'So what're you doing up here then?'

'C'mon, Queen,' Paddy Maginn groaned. 'How about our beer? Chacking, we are. I said Tom could have Cider Joe's bunk.'

'Oh you did? Well you had no business to. Not till I've seen the colour of his money.' Paddy might run the gang, but the shanty was Queenie's. Foul-mouthed and temperamental, she still provided better food and conditions than most of the other shanties. 'If you want to bunk here, my 'andsome, it'll cost you seven shillings week, in advance. Take it or leave it.'

'And what do I get for my money?'

Turning to set out bowls on the narrow folding table she used for preparing food, Veryan stole a glance. He was still smiling, but his tone made it clear that whether he stayed or not was *his* decision. The men caught it too, for the noise level fell as they stopped to listen.

'Three meals a day. It's good food too. Well, the best we can get from that cut-throat, Pascoe. You get your own bunk and locker, and your washing done.'

A spoon slipped with a metallic rattle from Veryan's clumsy fingers and her face flamed.

Tom Reskilly said, 'What more could a man ask?' And Veryan heard the clink of coins.

'Right then,' Queenie was brisk. 'Who's first for beer?'

'Bleddy mad you are, man,' Nipper jeered. But he was careful to keep his voice low. 'How didn't you go to Elsie Bray's? You'd have got more than food there. She'd 'ave warmed your bed all right.' His voice grew louder as discretion was overpowered by jealousy and grudging admiration. He turned to the other men. 'And she wasn't the only one. Did you see they women standing in their doorways? Near enough throwing theirselves at him they were.

And not just the young girls neither. Tidn' fair. How don't I get women chasing after me?'

' 'Cos you ain't as pretty as 'im,' Fen retorted.

'And you stink,' Yorky grimaced, his weathered face resembling crumpled brown paper.

'Veryan!' Queenie shouted above the roars of agreement and laughter, 'put some more dumplings in that stew. I got a new lodger. You hear me, girl?'

As Veryan looked over her shoulder and gave a brief nod, Tom Reskilly caught her eye. He touched his cap, a deliberate repeat of his gesture on the path. One of the men nudged him.

' 'Ere, you don't want nothing to do with 'er. She's trouble, she is.'

Turning away, her face burning as she struggled against a quicksand of shame and defiance, Veryan tried to block out the whispers and mutterings. *It had just been a bit of fun. All right, so Ned had had a drop too much. But there was no need to take a knife to the poor bugger, for Crissakes. She thought she was too good for the likes of us. Saving herself she was. She needn't bleddy bother. Who'd want her now after what she've done?*

Let them mock. Let him think what he liked. She had been attacked by two men, both had been drinking, and both were bigger and stronger than her. Yet they were saying it was *her* fault: *she* was to blame. She bent her head over the new batch of dough, hot tears of anger and helplessness sliding down her cheeks. She dashed them away with a floury hand.

The men moved with their beer to benches around the big table.

'What did ye do tae get yersel' sacked?' Mac demanded of Tom.

'The contractor wouldn't pay us what we were due. Said we'd have to wait. I told him there was no food and kiddies were starving. He said that wasn't his problem. So I broke the bastard's jaw. I had to get away quick then. So I thought I'd try my luck up this way.'

'I bet you've left half-a-dozen women weeping and wailing,' Queenie shouted over in dry accusation.

'I gave no promises,' Tom shrugged.

'Crafty bugger,' Nipper said gloomily.

The door flew open and Cora Pearce burst in. She looked wildly round, spotted the newcomer and rushed towards him.

'Mister? Have you seen my man? Denny Pearce?'

Veryan saw Tom Reskilly's gaze flick over Cora. He probably looked at a horse with the same practised objectivity. 'On the tramp is he?'

Cora nodded quickly: anxious, hopeful.

Tom shook his head. 'Sorry, my bird. I reck'n your man will be long gone from Cornwall. There's nothing down here for him. The Trewirgie line's in trouble. They're laying men off. And the gangs laying extra rails on the West Cornwall line aren't taking no one on. 'Tis a short contract, see, and they want to keep the work for themselves.'

Cora's thin shoulders drooped and, as hope finally died, she aged ten years in as many seconds.

'Cora Pearce,' Queenie snapped, 'it's time you stopped all this. Thanks to Beany Flynn you got a roof over your head and food on your table. It's not every man who'll take on someone else's kids. You're bleddy lucky, and don't you forget it.' She turned to the men, waspish and irritable. 'What's up with you lot? Something wrong with the beer?'

Cora was elbowed aside as the men crowded around Queenie and the barrels. Covering her mouth with a red-knuckled hand, she stumbled out.

As she hefted the heavy cauldron onto the small table Veryan saw Paddy, beer in hand, take Tom to the double row of lockers on the back wall and point out the one that had been Cider Joe's. After stowing his few possessions Tom came towards her, carrying two bowls.

'Told you I'd see you again, didn't I?' he said softly.

Head bent as she dished up the stew, Veryan didn't reply.

'You're not spoken for then?'

The full ladle tipped dangerously as her head jerked up. 'Didn't you hear what they said?'

'I heard.' His violet gaze was level. Then he grinned.

'Here, girl, keep your flirting for later,' Queenie shouted, raising hoots and laughter. 'These men been working all day. They want their food while it's still hot.'

Flushing scarlet, Veryan bent her head again. 'Go away,' she said with quiet force. 'Find your fun somewhere else.'

The men had collected their bowls of stew and were seated at the table when once again the door crashed open. A man lurched in, drunk and angry.

'All right, where is 'e?' he shouted, glaring blearily around.

'By all the saints,' Paddy grumbled. 'Can't a man have his tea in peace? All this coming and going and shouting, it's like Dublin market so it is.'

'I told you before, William Thomas,' Queenie snapped. 'You're not welcome in here. Now get out.'

'I'll go when I've spoken to *her*.' He stabbed a grimy finger at Veryan.

Flinching as vivid memories assailed her, Veryan ignored him and lifted two boiled suet puddings out of the copper.

'All right,' he snarled, coming towards her, shoulders hunched, head thrust forward. 'Where is 'e? Where's Davy?'

Losing interest, the men turned back to their food. A good fight was one thing, but no one with a lick of sense got involved in a family row. Hunched over their bowls they shovelled up the stew, slurping and chewing noisily.

'I don't know.' It was the truth. She hadn't seen him all day. She tugged at the knots, scalding her fingers. Fear shafted through her but she fought it. William Thomas had never been able to frighten her before. She would not let him frighten her now.

'Don't you give me that rubbish,' he bellowed. 'The boy follows you round like a bleddy shadow. Well, I won't have it. You and your bleddy books, filling his head with nonsense. You're turning him against us.'

Veryan's head flew up. 'You don't need my help for that. You're doing very successfully all by yourself.'

'You stay away from him, do you hear me?' Leaning over the flimsy table he stabbed his finger at her again. 'I'm warning you.'

Sickened by his drunken belligerence: remembering Bessie's bruised and swollen face, and her own terror, Veryan's fear was swept aside by angry contempt. 'Or what? Why does a man your size need to beat a small boy?'

'To teach him obedience and respect,' he snarled. 'I reck'n you could do with a lesson.' Grabbing the table he dragged it sideways. Startled, Veryan reared back. But before he could grab her, Tom Reskilly had sprung from his seat, seized a fistful of collar and, twisting it tight, hauled William towards the door. Crimson, choking, his eyes bulging, Davy's father thrashed his arms wildly.

'You don't raise your hand to a lady,' Tom said. A few of the men sniggered. But as he glanced round they quickly fell silent. Shoving the man out, Tom closed the door and wiped his hands on the seat of his trousers. Resuming their meal the men murmured among themselves. Veryan watched Tom come towards her, her head bursting. *He was a navvy*. The first man since her father to think her worth respect. *He was a navvy*. She was determined to escape from the works.

'Listen—' he started quietly, but she didn't let him finish.

'Leave me alone,' she whispered, half plea, half dismissal. 'I'm not— I can't— If there's any mercy in you, just let me be.' She turned away and, with shaking hands began cutting the puddings and spooning them into bowls. She could hear him breathing but he didn't speak. Then he loped back to his place at the table. He was met by noisy approval for having got rid of William, and further warnings about her.

After several moments, calmer now, driven by curiosity, she risked a glance. He was talking to Paddy, *and watching her.* As their eyes locked briefly she tensed, steeling herself for his grin of triumph. All she saw was a slight frown. She reached for the pan of watered-down syrup, trying to shut out the insistent echo, 'You don't raise your hand to a *lady*.'

Chloe Radclyff had drunk her morning tea out of bone china so fine it was almost transparent. She had taken her morning bath in water fragrant with attar of roses. And now she sat at the toilet table in her dressing-room wearing fresh, sweet-scented linen beneath her embroidered silk wrapper. Polly's sweeping strokes with the silver-backed brush had reduced her headache to a dull pressure at the base of her skull. She was desperately tired, yet jumpy as a cat.

She watched Polly dip her fingertips in a pot of pomade, rub it between her palms, and smoothed it lightly over her hair leaving a glossy shine. A fire burned brightly in the grate, and downstairs a variety of dishes were being prepared for breakfast. For the hundredth time that morning she reminded herself of how fortunate she was, how much she had to be grateful for.

Brought up a gentlewoman, marriage had been her destiny. But after. . . . Everyone said her father had done the honourable thing. There was no place in society for a man who couldn't settle his gambling debts. So he had taken his leave with characteristic flamboyance and a duelling pistol to the temple. And while his friends praised his sense of honour, she, with no mother to turn to for comfort and explanations, struggled to come to terms with his abandonment.

Well-meaning friends had lost no time in pointing out the precariousness of her own position, for there would be no dowry to compensate for the stain on her father's name. Their shock when Gerald married her had been profound. As her own had been the evening he proposed. They had dined early. He had returned that day from London having been away for almost a week. She had noticed immediately his pallor and the dark circles under his eyes.

'Gerald, are you ill?' she had blurted, concern overriding good manners. 'You look so tired.' If anything happened to him, what would become of her?

'I'm fine.' He had patted her hand and smiled reassurance, but his eyes had glittered strangely. That evening as they dined he had seemed preoccupied. Assuming he was still suffering the after-effects of the long journey she had taken the burden of conversation on herself, talking lightly of her activities during his absence, and relaying snippets of gossip she had heard at a committee meeting. He had not bothered with brandy, but had accompanied her to the drawing-room.

Seating herself at one side of the blazing fire she had felt an odd shiver of anticipation as he sat down opposite. She had taken extra care while pouring the coffee aware that her hand was less steady than usual, yet unsure why she should be feeling so nervous.

He had crossed one leg over the other and flicked a speck of ash from his immaculately pressed trousers. 'As you know, just before he ... died ... your father entrusted your welfare to me.'

Replacing the silver coffee jug on the tray she had clasped her hands in her lap.

'It's been two years. And in that time I have become very fond of you, my dear. You possess many admirable qualities. But the one I find most appealing is your gentle nature. I have noticed of late a growing stridency among women, a militancy which I find grating and unpleasant.' The down-turned corners of his mouth conveyed his distaste. 'Whereas you, my dear Chloe, are all sweet acquiescence: femininity personified.'

'Thank you, Gerald.' Relief had increased her delight at his compliment, for he demanded the very highest standards and quickly distanced himself from people or projects that failed to measure up. But that hadn't been the end of it.

'Chloe, my dear, I should like you to do me the honour of becoming my wife.'

She had been sixteen years old.

'Begging your pardon, ma'am, but are you all right?'

Suddenly aware that Polly's hands had ceased their coiling and pinning, Chloe looked up, saw her maid's anxiety reflected in the mirror, and felt a rush of affection. Polly clucked over her like a mother hen.

'Shall I fetch you something?'

'No. I'm all right.' If she said it often enough it would be so. Nervous afflictions were for other women, not for her. She did not want to be like them.

'Not that time again is it, my lady?' An expression of horrified guilt crossed the maid's face. 'You should have said. Look, don't you worry. When we were in Falmouth last week I got some more of those special pills from the apothecary.'

'No. It isn't. Polly, don't *worry* so.' Gerald worried about her. Polly worried about her. Yet she could not confide in either of them. She could not bear even to imagine the horror they would be unable to hide. She must turn her thoughts outward: away from the shameful fevered dreams, the yearnings she didn't understand. If she focused on her charity work, concentrated on helping those less fortunate than herself, then maybe. . . .

Seeing her maid's face in the mirror fraught with genuine concern, Chloe made herself smile. What would she have done without Polly? Having no close female relatives there had been no one to prepare her, no one to ask. Polly had explained to the terrified fourteen year old that she was now a woman, and that the accompanying pains would ease in time. Only they hadn't. In fact, over the last two years they had grown worse, confining her to bed for twenty-four hours where she curled in white-faced agony around a stone hot-water bottle sipping the hot gin Polly promised would help. And it did: though she loathed its perfumed taste, and shuddered violently as she forced it down.

There had been ten applicants for the post of lady's maid. Gerald had interviewed them in her presence, permitting her the final choice. She had chosen Polly, her pleasure at the prospect of a companion doubled by Gerald's approval. And in the ensuing six years Polly had proved herself utterly devoted. *And yet.* . . .

Chloe pressed her fingertips to her forehead. Such suspicions were wicked and unworthy. No one could have shown her more kindness or looked after her better than Polly. As for Gerald, she owed him everything. He was the kindest, most generous of husbands. He deserved her total loyalty. She must not even *think*—

'Ma'am?'

Aware she was in danger of betraying the turmoil that had kept her awake for most of the night, Chloe straightened her back and, clasping cold fingers more tightly in her lap, stretched her mouth into a smile.

'I was thinking about the next committee meeting,' she improvised. 'What do you think, Polly? My blue? Or the new lilac with my aubergine jacket?'

'The lilac is very becoming, ma'am.'

'It is certainly the more sophisticated.' Chloe made a wry face. 'Yes, the lilac, definitely. Who knows, it might even persuade Mrs Fox to stop talking over my head.'

She had been thrilled to receive invitations to join various charitable organizations. It hadn't occurred to her then that they were issued only out of deference to her husband. It was several months before she was informed, by one of her colleagues on the committee, that Sir Gerald would have considered it a serious breach of courtesy had such invitations *not* been forthcoming. She also learned that her title on the letterhead encouraged generous donations from his many acquaintances.

She'd felt foolish, and a little disappointed, especially when it was subtly made clear that apart from use of her name, plus regular contributions, no further involvement was expected of her. But with Gerald committed to the business affairs which took him regularly to London, and the house run with clockwork precision by Mrs Mudie, she *needed* something to do.

Even before their marriage, while he was still her guardian, Gerald had enjoyed her passionate curiosity, and had taken great pleasure in indulging her hunger for knowledge. She had only to express interest in a subject for him to engage someone to instruct her. Naturally these tutors had all been women. He owed her protection, he explained, from unscrupulous men for whom her youth and beauty might prove too much of a temptation.

Her early education had been sporadic, received from private tutors when her father could afford them, and at small academies run by middle-class spinsters when he could not. So, over the years, as well as absorbing the political importance of dinner-party seating plans and the grace under pressure required of a hostess, she had learned every dance from Scottish reel to military two-step. She could do fine embroidery, play the piano and flute, follow an opera sung in Italian, and ride any horse in her husband's stable. Her life was one of privilege and luxury.

But constantly reminding herself how fortunate she was didn't help. She was consumed with guilt, made worse because she didn't know what it was she wanted, only that there was an aching void within her. She had to keep busy, deny herself time to brood. Given her rank and status, charity work had been the only option. It had taken several weeks, and much polite but firm insistence. But her determination had been stronger than their reluctance, and she had achieved an active *useful* role.

But last night had been the worst yet. Even with the herbal draught Polly had prepared it had taken her a long time to fall asleep. She had heard Gerald pass her door, heard quiet murmurs and soft laughter. Then the dreams had begun: strange, fragmented, *shaming*. And for the first time she had seen a face: sun-darkened, with eyes like liquid honey. She had woken with a gasp, her throat dry, her body burning. Freeing herself from the tangled sheet she had straightened her night-gown and sipped some water. Then turning the pillow over she had lain down, her heart still thumping, and gazed wide-awake into the darkness, listening to the roaring wind and drumming rain. The sound of his voice, his changing expressions had swirled in her head like roiling water. She had tried to stop them, to shut them out by telling herself over and over again she was a married woman. *Was she going mad?*

'There we are.' Inserting the final pin, Polly ran a critical eye over her mistress's coiffeur. 'You look 'andsome, ma'am.'

Abruptly Chloe stood up. Turning away from the mirror she untied her wrapper. 'No, not that,' she said as Polly lifted the pearl-grey morning gown. I want my riding habit.'

Sir Gerald looked up, lowering his newspaper as Chloe entered. 'Good morning, my dear,' he smiled. 'You look charming. Forest green suits you. But do you think it wise to ride today? The ground will be very slippery.'

After dropping a kiss on his cheek, inhaling the fragrance of lemon verbena, Chloe slipped into her chair.

'I'm not going far: only to the shanty village.'

'You have a kind heart, my dear. I would not like to see it abused. The lower classes are not renowned for their gratitude.'

'But that is no reason to deny them help, surely? They have so little and we have so much.'

'Which is just as well.' He smiled, folding his newspaper. 'For otherwise your desire to right the world's ills would see us in the poor house.' He stood up. 'Now I must go. I am in Truro today. Is there anything you would like me to bring you?'

Chloe shook her head, wrenched by guilt. 'You are so generous,' she blurted. 'I don't deserve it.'

He laughed lightly. 'What nonsense. Of course you do. You have brought me great happiness.'

'Will you be home for dinner? Please say you will. It's lonely eating by myself.'

'Chloe, we had dinner guests on three occasions last week.'

'I know. But—'

'I'll do my best, but I can't promise. Why don't you bring a book to the table?'

She'd tried that. The butler and footmen had behaved impeccably as always while radiating such strong disapproval that she had been totally unable to concentrate.

'Yes, perhaps I will. Have a safe journey.'

He stopped behind her chair and rested his free hand on her shoulder.

'Just one thing, my dear: compliments are pleasant to receive, but men's flattery of a pretty young woman always has an ulterior motive. Be careful who you trust.'

# Chapter Five

SUNSHINE slanted across the hillside spangling lacy cobwebs that veiled the hedgerows with fragments of rainbow. The previous night's rain glittered in the grass like scattered diamonds. Gorse blossom released melted-butter fragrance into the cool morning air. Overhead, the sky was a clear pale blue, but towering white clouds formed buttresses and ramparts on the horizon.

The workings were still in deep shadow. Riding through them James was appalled. The chaos had looked bad enough from a distance: up close it was far worse. Horses limped dispiritedly through the stodgy muck. The boys leading them were hard-pressed to keep their boots on in the sucking calf-deep filth. To walk was difficult: running impossible. Navvies glanced up, surly-faced, as he passed; then spat and swung their picks in a manner that suggested they would as soon bury them in him as in the recently blasted earth and rock.

Carefully expressionless – for if they misinterpreted his anger, assumed it was directed at them, a riot could all too easily erupt – James rode on. He understood their sense of grievance. Navvies were proud of their skills. Cutting new excavations was difficult hazardous work at the best of times. Conditions like these were an invitation to disaster. Some of the labourers shovelling the heaps of loosened muck into wagons swayed and staggered as they worked, still drunk from the previous night. The wagons themselves listed dangerously on buckled rails beneath which badly laid ballast had sunk.

He had seen enough. Guiding his horse up the steep rocky incline he turned back down the line towards confrontation with the man responsible for this shambles.

Riding into the shanty village, his senses assaulted by the dilapidation and squalor, James recalled Clinton Warne's claim that the company was providing the navvies with *healthy outdoor work*, and his mouth curled in disgust. A pall of smoke and stale cooking overlay the stench of human sewage and garbage rotting where it had been thrown. The smell would linger, trapped in the hollow between the two hills until the wind rose.

The best of the dwellings were built of wood. They had glass windows and tarred felt roofs. Some, he knew, would house over a dozen people. Smaller huts – and there were far more of these – had been put together from whatever was handy. The crudest of all had walls of piled-up turf and roofs made from scraps of tarpaulin stretched over odd bits of timber.

Up ahead, a young woman carrying a huge basket of washing emerged from a lean-to attached to one of the bigger shanties. Though she had her back to him, that dark-red hair tied on the nape of her neck with a strip of cloth was unmistakable. Recalling her feisty reaction and her pride, a quality rare among navvy women, his curiosity about her was rekindled. He called out. 'Good morning.'

Starting, she glanced round, revealing a deathly pale face and shadows like bruises under her eyes.

*Damn Harold Vane.* 'You shouldn't be carrying that,' he indicated the heavy basket.

'It won't walk out by itself.' Abruptly, as if regretting her retort, she turned her head, avoiding his gaze.

He hesitated. She seemed different: changed in some way. 'I saw what happened,' he said quietly. 'The man responsible should be horsewhipped.' Her eyes widened and he saw fear. 'Is your shoulder causing you much pain?'

After a moment's blankness, realization was followed swiftly by relief. 'It's sore. But I've been told' – she hefted the washing basket – 'if I keep busy I won't have time to think about it.' Irony flickered across her mouth and he glimpsed a flash of her old spirit. 'Thank you for asking.'

'It's the least—'

'Veryan?' a voice screeched from inside the shanty. 'What're you doing? You've had time to knit that bleddy clothes line.'

She darted a panicky glance over her shoulder, whispered, 'Please excuse me,' and turned quickly away.

'Where will I find the tally shop?' he called after her. According to one of the gangers the contractor used the storeroom as his office.

Veryan jerked her head, indicating the direction. 'It's the one with the shutters.' She strode away across the muddy ground, clearly anxious not to be seen talking to him. He clicked his tongue urging his horse forward. She was a strange girl. There was so much about her that seemed wrong for this place. *And while he speculated about her he was able to avoid thinking about that other young woman whose candid blue eyes and gentle smile had haunted his dreams.*

He could hear babies wailing and the shouts of harassed mothers. Odd shrieks of laughter set his teeth on edge like fingernails scraped down a blackboard. He was aware of being watched. Young children stopped playing and women appeared in doorways as he passed.

He nodded briefly. They stared back. Some were tight-lipped and suspicious: others made lewd comments. Girls in their mid teens waggled their tongues and bared their breasts at him, giggling as they kept pace, asking if he saw anything he fancied.

Quashing both irritation and faint embarrassment he ignored them. They were what life had made them. So why was that other girl, *Veryan*, so different?

Eventually one of the older women yelled at the girls to go back to their kids or she'd tell their men and they'd get the thrashing they deserved.

James reached the tally shop. The heavy shutters were down and it looked deserted. He rode round to the back. Seeing the horse tethered to a wooden rail he smiled grimly and tied his own mount alongside. Instead of returning to the front he hammered on the back door.

'Go away,' shouted a bad-tempered voice. 'It's not time yet.'

'Mr Pascoe?' James pitched his voice loud enough to be heard through the thick wood. 'My name is James Santana. I'm the new engineer. I'd be obliged if you'd let me in.' After a few moments he heard thuds, scraping noises, a metallic clang, then the sound of bolts being drawn. The door opened.

Horace Pascoe was of average height with sloping shoulders, a belly that strained the buttons on his waistcoat, and a sunburst of fine ginger hair. His face was round with a snub nose and pouches of pale flesh beneath eyes as sharp and cunning as a weasel's.

'Sorry about that, but it's a job to get a minute's peace.' Standing back to let James enter, Pascoe closed the door behind him and shot one of the bolts across. 'You can't be too careful around here.

They'd have the fillings out of your teeth before you finished yawning.'

James made no reply. Two oil lamps supplemented the sunshine that filtered through cracks in the shutters. The small room was packed from floor to rafters with wooden crates and boxes. There was barely room for the paper-strewn table Pascoe used as a desk, or the battered captains' chair in front of it. In one corner, its door tightly closed, stood a large steel safe.

Pascoe set the chair back against a stack of crates. Gesturing for James to sit, he rested one fleshy haunch on a corner of the table, his body masking those papers he hadn't had time to turn face down. His weasel gaze slid over his guest and his mouth widened in an avuncular smile. James knew the contractor had made the usual mistake of confusing youth with inexperience. He was about to be thoroughly patronized.

'I suppose the directors sent you.' Pascoe shook his head more in sorrow than anger. 'When things are going well I never clap eyes on them. But the moment there's a problem or a delay they're looking for someone to blame. And who do they pick on? The contractor; who else? I tell you, lad, a direct line might look good *on paper*, but what with all the cuttings, embankments and bridge works, not to mention the bloody viaduct, things would have been damn sight cheaper and given us far less trouble if they had made a few more allowances for geology and the lie of the land. And how do they expect me to meet completion dates after the rain we've had?'

James said nothing. Mistaking the silence for sympathy Pascoe warmed to his theme. 'I was willing to take on more labour, but the directors wouldn't supply extra money to pay for it. And as for the men. . . .' He gave another martyred sigh. 'Call themselves navvies? They're nothing but drunken savages. Maybe not all of them,' he grudged as James raised an eyebrow. 'I've got a couple of good gangers. And p'rhaps a handful of the men are worth their pay, but as for the rest, you can't get them off the drink.' He spread his hands, helpless in the face of such incorrigible behaviour. 'And fight?' He clicked his tongue. 'I've never had so much trouble.'

Leaning back, James casually crossed one leg over the other. Pascoe was crafty. Every one of his complaints contained an element of truth. But James was familiar with contractors' tricks and excuses.

'Mr Pascoe, I've worked on a number of lines, and conditions here are some of the worst I've seen.'

The contractor nodded. 'Isn't that what I've just been telling you?'

James silenced him with a gesture. 'You and I both know that men in drink will tolerate food and lodgings a sober man would reject outright. I accept that heavy rain does indeed prevent the men from working. But when they don't work you don't pay them.'

The contractor's foot had stopped swinging and the ingratiating smile was fading fast.

'Mr Pascoe, would you agree that the purpose of being in business is to make a profit?' James waited until the contractor gave a wary nod, clearly uneasy about where the question was leading.

'I understand one of the ways contractors increase their profits is by selling beer on the works. So, as you are providing the means of the men getting drunk, it's hardly reasonable for you to complain when they do. Another profit-making venture I'm familiar with is a tally shop. Of course, as there's no competition quality doesn't matter. A man will eat anything if the alternative is starvation. And if buying from the tally shop is a condition of keeping his job then that's what he'll do. But he won't be allowed to use cash. He has to take tickets from the ganger. And with the ganger and the contractor each taking a percentage of the ticket's value, it's not unusual for a navvy to find that after paying off his tickets all he has left from his week's wages is a couple of shillings.'

'I provide a service,' Pascoe blustered. 'Penryn's miles away. There's delivery costs, and my overheads—'

'Mr Pascoe,' James interrupted, rising to his feet. 'I intend to see this line built, and built properly. My reputation is at stake and I will not permit greed or carelessness by *anyone* to endanger it, or to damage my future prospects. If you cannot fulfil your obligations I will have you replaced.'

Pascoe shot up off the table, fists clenched, head thrust forward. 'You can't sack me.'

James moved towards the door, forcing him to stand aside. 'No?'

'No! The directors would never allow it. Besides, it would cost too much.'

'There is far more at stake here than money,' James reminded him. 'The directors are also deeply concerned with power, status and future dividends. Think about it, Mr Pascoe. Having replaced the engineer, a man of considerable reputation, do you really think they'll hesitate over replacing a mere contractor?'

Pascoe swallowed, then bared his teeth in a grovelling smile. 'Look, there's no need to be hasty. It isn't easy trying to please everyone. And you can't blame me for the weather.' He rubbed his palms down the sides of his coat. 'I had to bid low to get this contract. As for the beer and the shop – how else am I supposed to make up the losses? Every contractor does it. Anyway,' – a note of truculence crept into his tone – 'the men would starve if it wasn't for me. Local tradesmen won't allow navvies to buy on tick.'

James slid back the bolt and pulled the door wide. Sunlight flooded in. 'What's your deal with the breweries? Flat rate? Or an increased percentage if you sell more than so many barrels?'

As Pascoe stood in the doorway spluttering incoherently, James untied his horse and swung himself into the saddle. He would have to watch his back from now on, but that was nothing new. It still rankled that he had been forced to leave Galicia and abandon a contract through no fault of his own. Completing this line was important.

As he joined the muddy rutted track through the village James heard approaching hooves. He looked up. And felt as if he'd been kicked in the ribs. He had hoped, but had certainly not expected to see her so soon, or so early. Accompanied by her maid and a groom, Chloe Radclyff rode sidesaddle on a toffee-coloured hunter whose coat gleamed like satin. The toes of her polished boots were just visible beneath the graceful folds of her forest-green riding habit. Their eyes met briefly.

Colouring, she dipped her head, deliberately obscuring the upper part of her face with the brim of her top hat. But the lower half, now deep rose, betrayed her.

'Lady Radclyff.' He tipped his hat, pretending mere courtesy, for all the laws of decency forbade him doing anything that might cause her embarrassment. 'Your arrival could not be more timely.'

She recovered quickly, relief in her smile. 'Good morning, Mr Santana.'

As James brought his horse alongside, the maid and groom dropped back. Women were emerging, curious but wary. Some carried children on their hips. They exchanged whispers as they watched the riders.

'You got business here, or are you just passing the time?' a fat woman shouted. Wearing several layers of filthy clothes she stood with folded arms in the doorway of one of the bigger shanties. James glimpsed Veryan behind her.

'You tell 'em, Queenie,' someone yelled, and the women peered around to see who it was.

Sensing the uncertainty Chloe was trying so hard not to show, James realized that, while there was no doubting her genuine concern for the lower classes, her experience of them was probably limited to the staff at Trewartha. 'Lady Radclyff represents a charitable organization,' he explained, raising his voice so they could all hear. 'She has come to offer help.'

'Well now, that's very kind of her,' Queenie said above the laughs and mutters. 'What kind of help would that be then?'

James glanced at Chloe, smiling encouragement. 'I think you should tell them.'

Chloe moistened her lips. 'Clothing.' She cleared her throat. 'And baby garments.' Her voice gathered strength as her confidence grew. 'Also shoes. We have adult and children's sizes. Plus linen and blankets.'

The women edged forward, listening now. 'Can you get medicine?' one asked. 'My baby got some awful chesty cough.'

'Shouldn't you see a doctor?' Chloe was cut short by the barrage of derision.

'Doctors don't want to see us.'

'D'you know how much they charge?'

'Where're we supposed to get that kind of money?'

'All right.' James raised a hand. 'You've made your point.'

'I'll do my best,' Chloe promised. 'Just give me a few days.'

'That's all right, my 'andsome,' someone shouted. 'We aren't going nowhere.'

'Now, now,' Queenie reproved. 'That's no way to talk to 'er Ladyship, not when she's being so kind an' all.'

'Is there anything else I can bring you?'

As Chloe looked round the upturned faces, James saw Veryan watching with a half-angry, half-yearning expression. She started to raise her hand but dropped it again, and turned away.

'Over there,' James murmured to Chloe. 'The big shanty.'

'You there,' Chloe called, 'the girl in the doorway. Did you want something?'

Flushing crimson as all the women craned round to stare, Veryan drew back, hugging her arms across her stomach.

'Don't be nervous,' James smiled encouragement. 'What were you going to ask for?'

'Books,' she blurted.

Several of the women raised their eyes heavenward and shook their heads.

Startled, Chloe rallied magnificently. 'Certainly. Would you like writing materials as well?'

It was like watching the sun come up, James thought as Veryan's pale face flushed with pleasure.

She nodded quickly. 'Yes please.'

As the women moved away to resume the morning's work, Chloe urged her horse forward.

'Do you run a school for the children?'

'Beg pardon, Your Ladyship,' Queenie positioned herself like a rampart between Chloe and Veryan. 'But she got too much work to do to be running a school. Anyow, who would she teach? The girls help their mothers, and look after younger brothers and sisters. And once the boys reach eight they join the line, fetching and carrying for the navvies, or working as tip boys.'

Seeing Chloe's bewilderment, James quickly explained. 'Leading the horses that pull the wagons to the tip head.'

'They don't get paid much, them being just kids,' Queenie sighed. 'But their wages means more food on the table.'

'Or more beer for their fathers,' James murmured, raising a cynical brow as he met Chloe's startled glance.

She turned back to Queenie. 'Might not the children's lives be much improved if they learned to read and write?'

'Bless you, My Lady.' Queenie's wolfish smile revealed broken and blackened teeth. 'You got a good heart, and I wish I could say you was right. But it isn't like that. See, if you go filling children's heads with such notions, well, it makes them want what they can't have.' James saw her small eyes flicker towards Veryan. 'Then they get ideas above their station. It only leads to unhappiness. So best leave well alone. But as for the clothes and suchlike, now they'll be very welcome. And to save Your Ladyship any trouble, why don't you have them brung 'ere to my place, and I'll make sure they all get given out fair and square.'

Escorting Chloe out of the village James saw her glance at him. 'That girl.' A furrow appeared between her brows and he wanted, more than he'd ever wanted anything in his life, to smooth it away with the ball of his thumb. 'Is there anything we could do for her do you think?'

'We?' he repeated gently.

She looked away, blushing deep rose. 'Th— the ladies on my committee— I'm sure we might be able—'

'Your kindness does you great credit,' he broke in. 'And I agree, she does indeed seem very different from the others. But she is no child. Perhaps she has good reason for remaining here. After all, had she wanted to leave surely she would have done so?'

She hesitated, then smiled briefly. 'Perhaps you're right.' They began to talk lightly, distantly, of other things. Only as he took his leave on the outskirts of the park did she meet his gaze. It was fleeting, but it was enough. As he rode away his heartbeat echoed the drumming of his horse's hooves.

Three days later, after another night of heavy rain, Veryan set out for the works with the men's dinner. A blustery wind chased puffs of cloud across a gauzy sky and piled them into a thick rumpled blanket. Teams of ploughing horses were followed by hordes of screaming gulls that whirled and swooped above the furrows of rich soil. Black and white cattle grazed the high hillside, picking their way between clumps of gorse and outcrops of rock. Lower down, fat sheep like blobs of cream nibbled in the patchwork of small fields divided by stone walls.

Everywhere the sepia tones of winter were being replaced by the fresh green growth of spring. She inhaled deeply. The air tasted sweet after the heat and fug of the shanty. And though the trek to the works took longer each day, it was a relief to get away from Queenie's constant needling.

Paddy's gang was working at the front of the line. To avoid running the gauntlet of the other gangs she had cut across country and angled her approach so she arrived just beyond the well-advanced cutting. Now, standing above the workings, she looked down onto the temporary track that had been laid from the cutting to the edge of the new embankment.

The end of the track had a large baulk of wood roped across it. But instead of being straight and level, the rails looked as if they were askew and sloping. Her eyes must be tired. She'd had little sleep since that dreadful night. She kept the lamp lit, partly in case Davy came, but also because the darkness was too full of memories and suffocating fear. Where *was* Davy? She had last seen him standing alongside his father, his little face a mask of terror. Had he been threatened? Or worse still, beaten again? Did he think she had killed Ned? He had looked so frightened. She wanted to seek him out, but so far she had resisted, afraid she might make things even worse.

Blinking hard, she looked down into the works. A train of wagons waited a little way back, loaded with muck excavated from the cutting. Her gaze skimmed over the men: looking for Paddy, she told herself. Spotting him quickly, she should have started down. Yet she hesitated, growing angry with herself as she sought the brawny figure of Tom Reskilly.

He had obeyed her plea to leave her alone, and had not approached her since. His capacity for work made him popular. And, easy-going, he accepted the ragging and joined in the banter. Then, a couple of evenings ago, Nipper had made a crude remark about her. Pretending it didn't hurt, that nothing they said was important enough to matter, she had caught her lower lip between her teeth, trying to stop the stupid tears that now came all too easily, and carried on dishing up the meal.

Then, aware of an unnatural silence, she had looked up to see Tom leaning across the table, one huge fist around Nipper's throat. He had spoken too softly for her to catch what he said. But Nipper had been only too eager to agree: slumping back onto the bench as he was released. Tom had not looked at her, just carried on as if nothing unusual had happened. Tempted, just for a moment, to thank him, she had resisted. She hadn't asked him to intervene, and he might get the wrong idea. Besides, she didn't want any of them thinking she couldn't look out for herself. She'd managed all right before he came. She had learned very young *never* to depend on anyone else.

There had been no more jibes or taunts. Except from Queenie, whose piggy gaze, as she teased Veryan about *her protector*, burned with curiosity and resentment.

Veryan watched one of the men detach a wagon from the train and harness a horse to it. Towing the wagon, the horse was urged into a trot then a gallop by the man running alongside. As they approached the edge of the embankment the driver unclipped the harness. Signalling the horse with a yell and a slap on the flanks, man and animal jumped clear. The wagon hurtled on, slammed into the baulk of wood, and tipped forward.

But the wet earth and rock had been jarred into a sticky mass and, instead of being flung over the edge, it clung to the inside of the wagon. Struggling to keep their footing on the steep slope below, the navvies began to shovel it out. Their curses and grunts of effort were clear in the still air.

A dark line appeared, snaking under the rails. Even as she wondered what it was, the crack spread, opening wider. With a tortured groan the rails twisted and the wagon lurched forward, tilting to one side. Horror stopped her breath. Hoarse shouts of warning turned to screams of fear as a twenty-foot chunk of the embankment subsided. With slow sickening inevitability the wagon tumbled over the edge and out of sight.

Dropping both basket and keg, Veryan plunged down the steep slope. She saw Paddy shouting for someone to go back down the line for help, and to tell Pascoe. Staggering across the mud and debris to what remained of the embankment Veryan peered over. The wagon lay halfway down the long slope, upturned and aslant, in the debris. Her heart gave a painful lurch as she saw Tom Reskilly, digging with his bare hands to free a groaning man buried up to his neck in the muck. All around him others worked just as frantically, only too aware that the unstable slope might shift again at any moment and swallow everyone on it.

Shutting her ears to the screams and groans, Veryan scrambled across to Tom. 'Have you seen Davy Thomas?'

His head flew up. Shock whitened his nostrils and darkened his violet eyes. 'What the bloody hell are you doing? You shouldn't be—'

'Was Davy working with you?' she insisted. Then, looking anxiously around she spotted a man carrying a small limp body. With a choking cry she started forward. Tom grabbed her arm.

'Get back up to the top. 'Tidn safe here.'

Wrenching free she stumbled across to intercept the man and his bloodstained burden. *Please don't let it be Davy*. It wasn't. Relief, and nausea at the child's terrible injuries, made her dizzy. She crouched for a moment, taking slow deep breaths, willing herself not to faint. Then she began picking her way across the earth and rubble, blocking out gut-churning sights and sounds as she approached the upturned wagon lying half-embedded, metal wheels in the air. She paused every few moments to shout his name.

A hand caught her arm, pulling her round, and she looked up into Tom Reskilly's glowering face.

' 'Aven't you got no sense at all? D'you know what—'

'Shush.' Veryan clapped her hand over his mouth. 'Listen. Davy?' The faint sound came again. Whirling, she fell onto her knees beside the upturned wagon. There was a small gap between the earth and the metal rim of the butt. 'Davy? Are you in there?'

'I can't move.' His voice was thin and high-pitched.

As Veryan turned anxiously, Tom's big hand briefly gripped hers in warning.

'Hold on, my 'andsome,' he called. 'We'll soon have you out of there.' But before he'd finished speaking, stones and clods of earth rolling from higher up clanged against the metal. Davy squealed with fright.

'It's all right, Davy.' Lying flat on her stomach she stuck her arm in through the gap. 'Can you see my hand? You take hold of it.' She felt small cold fingers brush hers, and hitched herself closer to the wagon. It creaked ominously. She heard Tom's sharp intake of breath, pictured the steel edge of the wagon slicing down on her outstretched arm. Fighting the image, and the urge to snatch her arm out and roll away to safety, brought her out in an icy sweat.

As Davy's fingers gripped hers she twisted her head towards Tom and whispered. 'He's lying at an angle with his head lower down the slope than his feet. 'If it subsides any more. . . .' She stopped herself.

'Come on out of the way. I'll—'

'No. You're too big.' Using her free hand she scooped away the earth and stones. 'I can wriggle in—'

'For Crissakes!' he hissed. 'If it starts shifting—'

Twisting, she looked into his eyes, her voice flat and utterly determined. 'I'm not leaving him. Now either help me, or go away.' She turned her head to call under the wagon. 'Davy? I've got to dig a hole so I can get in to you. That means I have to let go of your hand.' His grip tightened painfully. She understood. And his terror brought a lump to her throat. 'It'll only be for a moment.'

'You won't go away?'

'I promised you a story, didn't I? I've been waiting for you to come so I could read to you.' After a moment he let go and she withdrew her arm.

'We can't dig here.' Tom kept his voice low. 'All the weight's on the lower edge. If we undermine that, the wagon could either topple over, or slide further down the slope and take him with it.'

They scrambled carefully along the upper side of the wagon. With feverish haste Veryan shifted stones and lumps of rock while Tom scooped out armfuls of earth.

'Veryan!' Davy shrieked, panic-stricken. 'It's moving.'

'All right, now,' Tom panted, leaving grimy streaks on his face as he wiped away sweat with the back of an earth-caked hand. 'And don't hang about.'

Veryan wriggled between the edge of the wagon and the hollow they had dug out of the slope. There was little light and the air was close and dank. 'Right, Davy,' she spoke quietly, with deliberate cheerfulness. 'Time to go.' Crawling over to him she touched his face lightly. 'You're a very brave boy.'

'I peed myself,' he said in a small voice.

'That's nothing. Do you know, I bet most of the men did the same.' While she talked she brushed the earth away, and ran her hands over his arms and legs, felt one very swollen ankle, sticky wetness, and tried not to imagine blood. 'Can you move everything? Head? Toes and fingers?'

'My foot hurts.'

'You just crawl then, that's it.' The metal wagon seemed to be shrinking around her. She had to fight a desperate urge to hurry him. 'You're doing really well. Now, down onto your stomach.' He squirmed through. As she knelt to follow, the earth seemed to shiver.

'Veryan!' Tom shouted. '*Quick!*' As she dived out, her eyes seared by the sunshine, Tom seized her outstretched hand and, with Davy clasped in his other arm, flung himself back, lying full-length on the spoil.

Veryan shut her eyes tight, tensed every muscle, and held her breath, waiting for the slippage that would tumble her down the steep face in an avalanche of earth, mud and rock. Her heart was hammering so hard it hurt. Tom Reskilly's large hand gripped hers. And she knew with absolute certainty that no matter what happened he wouldn't let go. But the threatened earthslide didn't happen. And after a few seconds Tom's warm grip loosened and he released her.

Feeling weak and horribly shaky she began crawling up the slope. Smeared with earth and blood from numerous cuts and grazes, Davy flung his arms around her, clinging like a limpet. She held him for a moment. His right foot was already twice its normal size and turning purplish blue.

'Come on,' Tom said. 'We got to get off this.'

At the top of the embankment they saw the little boy and several men lying in the dirt. One was William Thomas. Veryan felt Davy flinch. Then he hid his face in her neck. She could feel him trembling. One of the men was badly mutilated and, as they passed, someone laid a piece of tarpaulin over him and the boy. But though his eyes were closed William had no visible injuries. Then his mouth fell open emitting a loud snore.

'Bastard's drunk,' Tom muttered. A little way away, the tip boys huddled in a shivering group. Beyond them, surrounded by navvies and labourers, Veryan could hear the contractor demanding explanations and issuing orders. He spotted Tom.

'Get rid of the woman and get back to work!' he bellowed.

Tom ignored him and turned to Veryan. 'All right are you?'

'Can you lift Davy onto my back?'

'You can't carry him all that way—'

'Well, he can't walk, and I don't see any carriage waiting for us.' She didn't want his concern. She couldn't handle it. It was too tempting.

'Dear life,' he grinned wryly. 'You got more prickles than a hedgehog.'

She felt a twinge of shame, and quickly stifled it. Not since her father had anyone cared about her wellbeing. Tom Reskilly was a decent man. But she had no choice. For a few moments back there – *No, she mustn't allow herself even to think.* He was a navvy. *His grip had been warm and strong, steadfast as a rock.* She had to focus on escape.

'You all right, Davy?' she said over her shoulder, clasping her forearms behind her back to support his weight. He was still trembling, and his wet trousers were clammy on her arms. She half-turned to Tom, careful not to meet his eyes. 'Thank you for your help.' She owed him that. 'You'd better grab your dinner before the others have it.'

'You're some rare woman,' he murmured. 'The boy's not even yours.'

'So I should have left him there?'

' 'Course not. I didn't mean—'

Already walking away, Veryan just caught his snort of frustration. Let him be angry and impatient with her. It was better that way.

# Chapter Six

STOPPING to catch her breath, Veryan hitched Davy a little higher. Her back ached fiercely, and her arms burned with the strain. Though he was small and skinny, the longer she carried him the heavier he grew. She dare not put him down, she would never find the strength to lift him up again. But nor must he realize what a struggle she was having. He had known too much guilt and blame in his short life.

'You all right back there?' she called.

'Mmm,' he mumbled, his head resting in the curve of her shoulder.

'It's not far now.' This was as much to convince herself as for his benefit. She had stayed on the hillside as long as she could, but the angle had put too great a strain on her leg muscles and she'd been forced to rejoin the path.

She plodded on, squelching through the mud and puddles, too tired to think, just taking the next step, and the next. Her breath rasped and the ache in her shoulders drilled deep into her bones.

The horse was almost upon her before the sound of hoof beats registered. She looked over her shoulder, almost losing her balance as she stumbled to the side of the path. Too weary for more than mild surprise, she watched James Santana rein in, frowning with concern.

'Is the boy badly hurt?'

She shook her head. 'No, but he can't walk.'

'He'd better ride then. You too.'

Startled, she watched him dismount. He landed in a puddle, splashing muddy water over his shiny boots and across her already soaked and filthy skirt. 'Sorry.'

'I don't think it will show.' She pulled a wry face and felt her heart lift at his swift grin and the genuine amusement in his eyes. He seemed to shed some of his formality. 'Come on.' He reached for Davy who tightened his arms around Veryan's neck and hid his face.

'It's very kind of you,' she began, 'but—'

'Don't be silly. And don't tell me he's not heavy. Look, I'm on my way to Falmouth. But first, Hetty Briggs and Flora Kessell have to be told—'

'Surely that's the ganger's job,' Veryan interrupted, hating to appear rude, but anxious to spare Davy any more reminders of the terrible sights he'd witnessed.

'It is, but every man who can hold a shovel is working to shore up the embankment, so I said I'd do it. Now, you mount first and I'll pass the boy up to you.'

'He has a name,' Veryan said sharply. 'It's Davy.'

'Well now, Davy.' James bent towards him. 'If you will allow your mother—'

'I'm not—' She stopped. *Too late.* And started again. 'I'm not Davy's mother. But if I were, I'd be really proud to have him for a son.'

'You hear that, Davy?' The engineer's gaze lingered on her for a moment, surprise evolving into curiosity. Then he moved forward, plucked the child from her back, and lifted him into the saddle. After a glance at Veryan's mud-caked boots, he turned back to the boy. 'You just hang on there a moment while I find somewhere suitable—'

'It's all right, I can manage. I've ridden before.' Placing her foot in the stirrup, Veryan swung herself up behind Davy, and put an arm around him. Isn't this comfortable?' she whispered. 'Much better than my back.'

As he led his horse along the path, James looked up. 'I heard someone call you Veryan. May I ask your full name?'

'Polmear.' Veryan cleared her throat, flustered and thrilled by his interest. 'Veryan Polmear.'

'Well, Miss Polmear, I must own that you intrigue me greatly.'

Shock zinged through her. But it wasn't unpleasant. Nor did she feel threatened or afraid. *On the contrary.*

'Oh, forgive me, I should have introduced myself properly. James Santana. I'm—'

'The new engineer. I know.'

He smiled up at her. 'News travels fast.' Perplexity drew his brows together. 'You know, I'm sure your name is familiar to me. I recall seeing or hearing it recently.'

Veryan's heart lurched into her throat. She felt sick. He couldn't know – Queenie had promised – no one wanted the magistrates involved. *She still couldn't believe*— But how could she prove her innocence when she couldn't even remember? Slamming a mental door on her terror, she moistened suddenly dry lips.

'Perhaps you heard mention of my father. He was a soldier. He died in the Crimea.'

'My condolences. I lost an uncle there. He was one of twenty-six officers killed at Alma.'

Before he could ask – as she sensed he was about to – what had brought her to the shanty village and life with a woman like Queenie, she cut in. 'Thank you for the ride. It was most kind. But I think it best if Davy and I walk now.'

'Why? It is still some distance to—'

'It's really not far. Besides,' – she looked him in the eye – 'it will not enhance your reputation to be seen with me. Nor,' she added before he could speak, 'will it do me any good among the village women. 'I am already an outsider.'

He frowned. 'Why do you stay?'

Sliding to the ground she reached up for Davy and settled him on her hip. Ruffling his hair she looked over his head at James Santana. 'I am alone, Mr Santana. Where can I go?'

She wouldn't allow herself to watch him mount up and ride on ahead. Instead she talked to Davy, telling him nursery rhymes, and reciting little poems she knew so well they rolled off her tongue, leaving her mind free to review her encounter with James Santana. *Well, Miss Polmear, I must own that you intrigue me greatly.* Clearly, he recognized that, regardless of her ragged clothing, she was different from the other navvy women. Yearning quickened her breath. Was it possible that *he* – a professional man of substance and standing in society— She hardly dared clothe the thought in words. *His interest could change everything for her.* Forgetting her aching arms and back, she mulled over the times she had seen him, dissecting each moment for evidence that might encourage the tiny bud of hope to open another petal.

Entering the village a little while later she heard wailing, and saw women bustling in and out of the shanty where the dead boy had lived. Davy's arms and her own tightened simultaneously.

Outside his shanty she told him to stand on one foot and reached for the latch. At least she wouldn't have to face his father. Pushing the door open, almost gagging at the stench, she peered into the gloom. A huddled figure lay on a makeshift bed against one rough wall.

'Stay there a moment, Davy.'

Head down, he leaned against the doorpost, his gaze fixed on the earth floor. Veryan bent over the curled figure and touched a shoulder. Bessie Thomas snorted and groaned. One hand rose a few inches then fell back onto the dirty blankets. Turning her over, Veryan recoiled at the sour stench of vomit. Bessie Thomas's eyes were blackened and swollen to mere slits, her nose and mouth crusted with blood.

'Is she dead?' A small voice pierced her boiling anger.

Veryan stood up. 'No, Davy. But she's not well enough to—'

'I tried to make him stop.'

'I'm sure you did, Davy.' Holding him close, Veryan walked out, shutting the door behind her. 'I know how brave you are.'

She managed to reach her own hut without Queenie seeing her and put Davy down on the strip of frayed canvas beside her bed. He crumpled and lay on his side, his eyes blank.

Fetching hot water from the wash-house copper, she took off his wet clothes. Then, using her preciously hoarded soap, she washed off the mud and carefully cleaned all his cuts and grazes. Some wouldn't stop bleeding. He shivered, teeth chattering.

'Nearly finished.' Patting him dry, she draped a blanket over his shaking body. She needed a bandage for his ankle, and others for an elbow and knee. With a sigh she reached for her clean chemise and began tearing it into strips. With luck she might find a replacement among the clothing Lady Radclyff had promised.

Picturing the elegant riding habit and intricately dressed blonde hair, envy twisted her insides like red-hot pincers. She'd had pretty dresses once: clothes nobody else had worn first. She would have them again. She would leave Cornwall and make a new life for herself. A vivid image of James Santana filled her mind. *You intrigue me greatly.* He was the key.

After she had buttoned the boy into an old blouse that reached to his knees, Davy turned away and, without a word, curled up in a corner of her bed like a wounded animal.

Tucking blankets around his small, shaking body she sat and stroked his head, watched his lashes flutter and close, and wondered what on earth she was going to do. She couldn't send him back to a bullying father and a mother who couldn't cope. But to keep him here with her would invite disaster on both of them.

When he reached Falmouth, James rode directly to the Royal Hotel in Market Street. A regular stop for the mail coaches until a few months ago when the post office had begun using the newly opened rail link to Truro and thence to Bristol and London, it was right in the middle of town. Handing his horse over to an ostler, he ordered food and a pint of ale and while he waited, scrawled a note to each of the directors asking them to attend as soon as possible on a matter of great urgency. He dispatched them by messenger. Within half an hour he had finished his meal and they had all arrived from their banks and offices.

'You'd better have a very good reason for this summons,' Harold Vane warned. Snapping his fingers, he ordered the servant to bring a cup of hot chocolate. 'I've had to rearrange several appointments at great inconvenience to myself and my clients.'

The other directors nodded agreement, adding their own tales of hastily cancelled meetings and schedules thrown into disarray.

'I'm sure,' Ingram Coles tried to calm the stormy waters, 'Mr Santana would not trouble us unnecessarily.'

'I should think not,' Harold Vane muttered, 'considering what we're paying him.'

'There's been an accident on the works,' James stated baldly. Having got their total attention he continued, 'Part of the new embankment collapsed causing two fatalities and several serious injuries.'

'What's the actual damage?' Clinton Warne shot his chin forward. 'Has any equipment been lost?'

'One section is badly twisted. Those rails will have to be scrapped. And one of the wagons went over. But when I left Pascoe was already organizing a recovery team.'

'Yes, but how long will it be before they can resume laying track?' Harold Vane demanded, drumming his fingers on the table. 'Time is money.'

'I understand your concern,' James said. 'But it's vital the embankment is made completely safe first. Especially,' – he raised his voice slightly above the murmuring – 'as insecure rails were the cause of the accident at Rednall back in June. Thirteen people were killed and forty injured. If something like that were to happen on this line the company's reputation would suffer incalculable damage.'

'Did you have a further reason for this meeting, Mr Santana?' Victor Tyzack, the deputy chairman, enquired. 'Other than simply informing us of the unfortunate occurrence?'

'Speaking for myself, I'm damn glad he was so quick off the mark,' Gilbert Mabey, the company secretary, announced. 'The moment the newspapers hear about it – and they will, you mark my words – they'll be baying at our doors, demanding a response. There are still a large number of people, don't forget, who have strong reservations about the spread of the railway.'

'Well, Mr Santana?' Harold Vane demanded, ignoring his colleague.

With a total absence of expression James enquired, 'Is there a contingency fund?'

The directors exchanged blank glances.

'For what purpose?' Ingram Coles enquired politely.

'Hardship payments to the families of those killed while working on the line.'

'Have you taken leave of your senses?' The solicitor glared at James. 'Charities take care of that sort of thing. We are running a business. I must say, Mr Santana, I am beginning to wonder if such liberal tendencies are conducive to the best interests of this company.'

'I was seeking information, Mr Vane,' James replied. 'Not passing judgement or making a suggestion.' His loathing of the solicitor increased each time they met, sorely testing his ability to conceal it. He turned to the deputy chairman. 'In response to your question, sir, we need more labour. Sir Gerald has allowed us a month, only because of the appalling weather. We won't get another extension. You've seen conditions on the works. The gangs at the front of the line are now three men and one boy short.'

'And the wages they would have earned will be paid to their replacements,' Clinton Warne pointed out. 'So why do you need more money?'

'Replacing those lost won't be enough. We need at least one more gang—'

A storm of protest erupted. Argument raged for a further fifteen minutes only ceasing when Ingram Coles reminded them that they all had clients and customers waiting. To be late – or worse still, to miss an appointment – might result in speculation that something was seriously wrong.

'Gentlemen, surely the last thing any of us wants is for the company's image of success to be compromised.'

'Yes, but—' Clinton Warne began, his chin jutting.

'I suggest that Mr Santana submits a written proposal stating the sum he has in mind, and details of how it would be used.'

'It will be on your desk within forty-eight hours,' James promised. 'I would stress that this is a matter of some urgency, so if—'

'You give us the figures,' Harold Vane cut in, 'we will make the decision.'

The hotel entrance was set back from the street. As he walked down the steps into the covered yard and waited for his horse to be brought from the stables, James fought growing frustration. It was becoming increasingly obvious that the directors had little understanding of, and even less interest in, the practicalities of railway construction. The more contact he had with them the clearer it became: the caution which made them good lawyers and bankers worked against them as businessmen. Immersed in detail, they had lost sight of the whole.

Riding towards Kergilliak, James was deep in thought when an open carriage containing three women emerged a few yards ahead from the drive to Bosvallon Manor. The woman facing him wore a crimson high-necked jacket. A matching hat was perched on dark, upswept hair. She said something to her companions who both looked over their shoulders.

James fought the surge of pleasure as he recognized Chloe, revealing only polite affability as he drew alongside, raising his hat. 'Good afternoon, Lady Radclyff.'

A blush crept up her throat, infusing her complexion with delicate rosy warmth.

'G-good afternoon, Mr Santana.'

The dark-haired woman's gaze was bold as it swept over him, her voice low-pitched and husky. 'Won't you introduce us, Chloe?'

'Oh, yes, of course. Mr Santana, may I introduce my friends and fellow committee members, Mrs Price-Ellis, and Mrs Hosking.'

She turned to the women. 'Diana, Loveday, this is Mr James Santana. He's a railway engineer.'

'How absolutely fascinating,' Diana Price-Ellis purred. 'Are you anything to do with the line at Trewartha?'

James inclined his head. 'I am.' He flicked a swift glance at Chloe. *And this woman is no friend of yours.*

'This is a most fortunate meeting, Lady Radclyff, for I need your help. There has been an accident at the works.' He saw her eyes darken in genuine concern.

'I'm so sorry. How many have been hurt? Do you require a doctor?'

'That is most generous, but no. One man and a boy were beyond human assistance, and those with broken limbs have been moved to the parish hospital. However, bandages would be most useful: and any kind of antiseptic lotion or ointment that will help wounds heal without infection.'

'I will send Polly to the apothecary and have supplies of both brought to the village tomorrow.'

'You are most kind.' He saluted. 'Your servant, ladies.'

'Mr Santana?' Chloe cleared her throat, asking as he turned back, 'The funerals. . . ?'

As his eyes met and locked with hers, he read the same powerful attraction he had been fighting since that first meeting. He also glimpsed bewilderment and fear. Compassion surged in him. He must take care, and not only for her sake.

'I cannot say, ma'am, for as yet I have been unable to find a clergyman willing to have the navvies in his church.' His mouth twisted. 'It seems that Christian charity is not available to those most in need of it.' His heart swelled with admiration – and something stronger, deeper – as indignation lit her eyes and heightened her colour.

'There must have been a misunderstanding, Mr Santana. I believe Tresaer is the church nearest the shanty village. I'm sure, once my husband has fully explained the circumstances to him, Reverend Carter will be happy to conduct the burial service. Meanwhile, please convey my deepest sympathy to the bereaved families.'

'Thank you, Lady Radclyff.' James bowed, fighting an almost overwhelming urge to take her hand and kiss it in appreciation of her integrity and generous spirit. But, aware of the other women's scrutiny – avid stares he found disconcerting – he remained coolly formal, and turned from Chloe to focus on them.

'Ladies, I appreciate you must have many demands on your time, but it would give great comfort to the families if you were able to attend. Your presence would most certainly generate wider public interest in the work of your charities, and in the welfare of those building the line.'

The two women exchanged a glance.

'I don't think I have any pressing engagements that day,' Loveday Hosking simpered.

'How could I refuse *you*, Mr Santana?' Diana said lightly. But Chloe detected subtle undertones, and saw James's expression harden as he turned again to her.

'And you, Lady Radclyff?'

He made it sound mere polite enquiry, but his eyes – was he trying to tell her something? *This was foolishness.* She should decline; claim a prior appointment. But how could she after her impassioned plea for his support? She had to go. She had no choice. Not trusting her voice, she gave a brief nod of assent.

Bidding them goodbye he took his leave and rode on. Not daring to watch, Chloe smoothed her gloves, still seeing him clearly.

'Well!' Loveday Hosking's brows climbed above a provocative smile.

'Chloe, my dear.' Diana Price-Ellis placed a gloved hand on her bosom and rolled her eyes. 'Where did you find him?'

'I didn't *find* him.' Chloe struggled with the turmoil rekindled by James's unexpected appearance. 'He came to the house to discuss railway business with Gerald.'

'He's very handsome,' Loveday sighed. 'I confess I do have a weakness for dark men.'

'And fair men, and those in-between,' Diana's dry remark sent Loveday into a fit of giggles. 'I must say though, he is quite the charmer. And obviously intelligent.'

'Since when,' Loveday taunted, 'have you cared about intelligence?'

'More often of late. After all,' Diana drawled with an enigmatic smile that slid like melting ice down Chloe's spine, '*some* conversation is necessary, so far better it should be interesting. And as my esteemed husband is required to remain in London for weeks at a time, I find myself in growing need of . . .' – she arched a brow – 'stimulating company.'

'Diana, you wouldn't,' Loveday gasped. But there was no disapproval in her voice, only laughter, and an undercurrent of excitement.

Diana's sloe eyes glittered. 'Oh, I would,' she said softly. 'In fact, I think I probably will.'

Having never experienced jealousy, Chloe was unprepared for its scalding, corrosive intensity.

'Why, Chloe, my dear, whatever's wrong?' Diana leaned forward. 'Have I shocked you?'

Aware both women considered her lacking in sophistication, and had for a long time regarded her with mild amusement, Chloe had made huge efforts to ensure they attributed her naïvety to shyness and a sheltered upbringing. What had begun in ignorance she had continued out of a sense of loyalty. Then, convinced the fault must somehow be hers, her self-esteem demanded she let no one discover the truth. This past year maintaining the façade had grown increasingly difficult. And now ... now suddenly her whole world was coming apart.

# Chapter Seven

TOM stood to one side of the other navvies and their women as they moved slowly through the little churchyard, and looked for Veryan. He'd glimpsed her in the church, but then she'd disappeared in the crush. The service had been short, but at least the vicar had got the names right. A couple of the other gangs who helped in the rescue had come to pay their respects. Over the press of people, Tom watched James Santana escort the three elegant ladies to a carriage with a coat of arms emblazoned on the glossy black door.

His glance passed briefly over the two strangers. He'd never seen them before but they were easy enough to recognize – all hot-eyed and hungry for a bit of excitement. A wink or a quick squeeze was often enough to send that type into a swoon. Not the dark one though. She was a hard case: courting attention in a gown of some shiny blood-red material that rustled, and a matching hat with plumes. Only the black velvet jacket that curved where she did gave a passing nod to the fact that she was attending a funeral. The other one – a silly, flighty piece, all twitches and giggles, wore a black fringed shawl over her green and lemon frills.

He looked past them to Lady Radclyff, sombre in midnight blue with a matching wool cape. Young she might be, but a true lady. There was no side to her, none of the usual arrogance he'd come to expect in women of her class. Just her coming to the church would have been enough. But not for her: she'd gone over and said a few words to the families. She hadn't stayed long. He heard her himself saying she didn't want to intrude on their grief. She didn't look down her nose at shanty people, like they were no better than dirt.

He wished he could see her face, but it was hidden behind the fine veil attached to the brim of her hat. As she climbed into the carriage her foot slipped off the step. Immediately, the engineer caught her elbow to steady her. She seemed to go totally still for a moment, like she was holding her breath. Then she got into the carriage and turned to thank him.

Why couldn't Veryan Polmear say thank you, just once? Independence was all well and good, and he admired a woman with spirit, but she was more stubborn than a dozen mules. Frustration bubbled like boiling water. A feeling new to him, it was becoming unpleasantly familiar. What the hell was the matter with her? He'd seen the day he arrived that Queenie and the men were giving her a hard time. He'd put a stop to it, but she'd given him precious little thanks – except on the embankment. They had worked well together, and he'd sensed that she trusted him. But it had all been for the boy. Once they'd got off the embankment, she'd shut him out again. He blew down his nose in frustration.

All the other women he'd known had *enjoyed* being treated like they were someone special. All right, it had got him what he wanted at the time, but so what? He'd not done any harm, and it had made them feel good. He liked women. He liked her. Well, maybe like was too soft a word for what he felt. She was different. And she stirred him like no other woman ever had; not even Annie. She also made him so mad he couldn't think straight.

Queenie wasn't the first to say he had a silver tongue, but Veryan Polmear was doing her best to pretend he didn't exist. Why? What had he done? What *hadn't* he done? He'd tried being friendly. He'd taken her at her word and left her alone. Neither had got him very far. If he had a lick of sense he'd give her up as a bad job. But, damn it, *he couldn't*. He'd never been turned down before. But it wasn't that. It was her. She was . . . *different*. And whether she liked it or not he was going to know her better.

The carriage rolled away. The engineer turned, starting along the path to the lych gate to fetch his horse. He stopped for a moment to speak to someone. The stream of people shifted, parted, and Tom saw it was Veryan. But not the thorny, self-contained girl he knew. He had never seen her smile before. He couldn't hear what they said, but, watching the way she moved, the way she lowered her eyes, the faint colour on her cheekbones, he wanted to hit the engineer. The anger died. But jealousy lingered, an ache in his gut.

Then the engineer moved on. Veryan seemed momentarily at a loss. It was, Tom decided, the best chance he'd get. She didn't have her arms full of washing, nor was she in the middle of dishing-up food: her usual excuses to avoid talking to him.

Wiping sweaty palms down the sides of his moleskin trousers, he shoved them in his pockets and sauntered over. 'All right then?' Her swift intake of breath as she glanced up told him he'd caught her off-balance. 'How's young Davy? His foot coming on all right?'

She nodded, looking anywhere but directly at him as she retreated behind the all-too-familiar mask. 'I have to go—'

Pique goaded him. 'That was some pretty smile you gave the engineer.'

She glared up at him, her colour deepening. 'He was asking after Davy. Not that it's any of your business. And a smile is merely polite. At least I didn't go all cow-eyed over Lady Radclyff.'

Tom grinned in delight. 'Well now, if I'd known you was watching me—'

'I was doing nothing of the kind. As a matter of fact, I was looking at Lady Radclyff.' The mingled sadness and yearning she couldn't quite conceal snagged his curiosity.

'She's certainly worth looking at,' he agreed. 'But handsome is as handsome does. And she's rare. There's plenty of good-looking ladies around, but few with her sweet nature.'

Veryan tossed her head. 'It's very easy to look beautiful and do good works when you have plenty of money and too little to occupy your time.'

Tom frowned, taken aback and silent for a moment. 'Why so bitter, girl?'

Startled, her face twisted and she gave a brief laugh that sounded like something tearing. 'Bitter? Me?' Suddenly her eyes filled. Whirling round she pushed her way through the milling people.

'Hey,' he shouted. 'Wait. Veryan, I didn't mean—' But she had disappeared. Exasperation seethed. Aware of curious stares he forced a grin and shrugged. But inside he was furious with himself.

'Yo, Tom.' Paddy clapped him on the shoulder, then murmured, 'Forget her, boy. You're wasting your time.'

'I need a drink,' Tom growled.

The daily tramp of feet between the untidy huddle of shacks and the new stretch of line had worn a clear track across the fields and scrubland. Walking ahead of the others who clustered in support around the bereaved women, Veryan was first to see the smoke. She took little notice, her head full of her encounter with James Santana and angry confusion inspired by Tom Reskilly. But as she drew closer to the village she realized the smoke was too thick, too dark. It wasn't a cooking fire. One of the shanties was burning.

A sudden tightness, like a clenched fist in her chest, stopped her breath. Then she was running down the hill, weaving between the squalid dwellings, dodging the washing flapping on lines held high by a notched sapling to catch the wind. Even before she rounded the far corner of Queenie's shanty, she knew with dreadful certainty that the hut on fire would be hers.

Stumbling to a halt she stared helplessly at the bright, leaping flames and the charred wood. Black smoke, acrid with the smell of burning pitch roiled skyward. It was far too late to save anything. *Davy*. She had left him inside sleeping while she went to the funeral.

'Davy!' she screamed.

'All right, all right.' Queenie waddled out of the shanty and caught her arm, pulling her away from the other women who had just arrived and were crowding round to watch the blaze and whisper. 'No need for all that. The boy's all right.'

'Who did it?' Veryan indicated the blaze.

'Who done it?' Queenie repeated, startled. 'I'll tell you who done it.' She licked her lips. 'That bleddy gypsy's brother, that's who. An' with all the men gone and me here on me own, there wasn't nothing I could do. Good job you was at the church. He'd 'ave killed anyone who tried to stop him.'

Veryan looked at her. 'But how did he know which hut was mine? And how did he know it was me who—?'

'No good asking me,' Queenie sniffed. She jerked a thumb towards the big shanty. 'I've had some job here with that boy. Little bugger wouldn't come out. W—the gypsy didn't care. Said he could burn with the hut.'

Veryan was horrified. 'No one went in for him?'

'Kid 'ad put the bolt across, didn't he?' Queenie retaliated. 'What was I s'posed to do? Shouted meself 'oarse, I did. Anyhow, when the roof caught he came out by hisself, coughing and choking with the smoke. He couldn't hardly walk, but the daft little twerp had his arms full of your books. Silly sod; if he wanted to save something why didn't he bring clothes? What good is bleddy books if you 'aven't got a rag to your back?'

'Davy?' Racing into the shanty Veryan saw him hunched on the floor by the fire, his shoulders jerking with sobs.

Kneeling, she held him close. 'Oh, Davy, I'm so glad you're safe.' She rocked him. 'Hush now. It's all right.' He shook his head. She had never seen him cry like this. 'Queenie said you saved my books.'

'Don't be angry,' he whispered.

'*Angry?* Why should I be – well maybe I am, just a little bit. But only because of the terrible risk you took. Davy, nothing – *nothing* is more important than you.' Tilting his chin the words dried in her mouth as she saw the dried blood caking his split lip and the red and purple bruising on the left side of his small tear-stained face.

'I'm s-s-sorry.' His chest heaved.

'It's all right.' She pressed his head very gently against her shoulder and rocked some more, clenching her teeth as surging fury made her tremble.

'Did the gypsy do that to you?'

He stiffened momentarily, then burrowed closer.

'What happened?' she asked softly.

'H-he tore them up. I t-tried to stop him. H-he said it was my fault. I shouldn't have stayed with you. He said you had to p-pay.'

'But how would he have known you stayed. . . ?' Suddenly she realized; it wasn't the gypsy who had hit him.

'It was your father, wasn't it?'

He sniffed and shuddered. 'I'm s-sorry.' He hid his face against her arm.

'Davy, listen to me.' Veryan smoothed his hair. 'You did your very best. Do you remember how in the stories the heroes do brave things? Like Nathaniel rescuing the colonel's daughters? Well, you're a hero.' She went on talking quietly and felt his small body growing limp and heavy as relief and exhaustion overtook him.

'Poor little mite.' Queenie stood, hands on massive hips, shaking her head. 'But it's like I told 'er Ladyship, no good comes of all this book-reading and such. You're only making it worse for him.'

Still holding Davy close, Veryan struggled to her feet, wincing at the sharp protest from her strained muscles. Carrying him to the empty bunk that had been Gypsy Ned's she laid him down gently, untied her shawl and spread it over him.

Queenie watched. 'He's not yours.'

'I know.'

'Where you going now? It'll soon be time to start their tea.'

'I won't be long.'

'Look, I don't want no more trouble—'

Veryan swung round. '*Trouble?* Everything I own has just been destroyed, and that child' – she pointed a shaking finger – 'was beaten just because he's fond of me. What am I supposed to do? Pretend it didn't happen?' Storming out, she almost collided with Tom Reskilly who nodded towards the smoking ruins of her hut.

'Accident?'

'What do you think?' She strode past him towards the Thomases' shanty. Davy's father and another man emerged, half-drunk and laughing from the shack next door.

William Thomas blinked like an owl, then sniggered. 'Whose bed will you be in tonight, then? Looks like yours will be a bit too hot. All your books gone too, shame.'

Taking a step forward, Veryan slapped his face with all her strength. The shock travelled the length of her arm, jarring her bruised shoulder. 'Never mind the books, that's for hitting Davy.' Her hand stung fiercely and she tucked it under her arm.

'Bitch!' William spat. 'Better if he'd died under the wagon. You too.' Lashing out with snake-like speed his fist caught the side of her head and sent her sprawling in the mud.

Through the ringing in her ears she heard Tom's roar of anger and realized he must have followed her. It took her several sick, shaky seconds to stagger to her feet. Upright, if unsteady, she wiped her eyes with the back of her hand and turned, ready to face the bully again. But someone else had got there first.

Fights were part of everyday life in the village. Fuelled by drink, they were usually noisy, erratic and, apart from the odd broken nose, did little lasting damage. This was different. William cringed and grunted as, with cold efficiency, Tom Reskilly beat him sense-less. It didn't take long.

Granite-faced, Tom came towards her absently rubbing his knuckles. Grateful to him for doing what she lacked the physical strength to do herself, she was about to thank him. He didn't give her the chance.

'You don't have to say anything. I didn't do it for you.' His voice was rough. 'It was for the kid, and for myself.' He licked the blood from his grazed knuckles. 'I had a child once, a boy. He—'

Abruptly he spun round and headed for the shanty.

Veryan watched him go. She couldn't afford to ask. Knowing more would only make it harder. She mustn't weaken. Not now. Reluctant, but with chores waiting and nowhere else to go, she followed him.

'Where—?' she began, looking round and seeing no sign of Davy.

'Bessie come for him,' Queenie replied. 'It's all right, she 'aven't been drinking. Well, not much. Any'ow you just leave them be. She's his mother, not you.'

Veryan didn't respond. What could she say that any of them would understand?

Standing at the table, peeling potatoes, carrots and turnips, she was very aware of Tom. He had gone directly to his bunk and seemed to be moving things around. Curiosity needled, but she refused to look.

'I s'pose you'll have to come in with me tonight,' Queenie grudged. Passing the table she waddled across to the ragged arm-chair and flopped down.

Picturing the filthy, smelly, cluttered little lean-to backing onto the wash-house and reached through a door in the corner behind the dresser, Veryan felt her stomach heave. But what choice did she have?

'A bit of gratitude wouldn' go amiss,' Queenie snapped. 'I 'ad arrangements; now they'll 'ave to be changed.'

Four years of living in the shanty had given Veryan a very clear idea of what Queenie's *arrangements* entailed. As they occurred far less frequently now; Queenie often complained about missing the extra money.

' 'Tis only out of the goodness of my heart—'

'It's all right, Queenie,' Tom said, emerging from between the bunks. 'You don't have to change nothing.'

Veryan's head flew up.

'How's that?' Queenie demanded.

'It shouldn't take me no more than a day to build her a new hut.'

'When are you going to do that then?'

'Tomorrow.'

'You'll lose a day's pay.'

'Don't you fret.' Irony edged Tom's tone. 'I got enough to pay you.'

'What you going to build it with? Nothing but cinders and charcoal left out there.'

'I've seen plenty of wood and stuff down the end. Anyhow, seeing she's only got to find somewhere for tonight she can have my bunk.' Though he was talking to Queenie, Tom's gaze was fixed on Veryan. 'I'll move on top to Nipper's and he can shift across into the gypsy's. See? No need for you to disturb yourself.' He walked out.

'Well,' Queenie huffed. 'That man do certainly take a lot on hisself.'

Speechless, her thoughts buzzing like angry wasps, Veryan turned to the fire and picked up a big pan containing meat and onions. It had been stewing slowly over the fire since the morning. Tipping in the vegetables she replaced the pan on the iron trivet. As she picked up the bowl containing the peelings, Tom returned carrying a strip of tarpaulin. Beckoning her, he went to the bunk he had just vacated. Reluctantly, still clasping the enamel basin, she followed.

'You already got a wall on two sides. Now if I tack this on here' – he held the tarpaulin against the long wooden base of the upper bunk – 'you'll be private.' He glanced over his shoulder, adding softly, 'I'll see you don't have no trouble.'

Biting her lip she nodded briefly, and hurried out. She was used to taunts and teasing, used to being ignored; kindness was something new. *Especially from a navvy.* She didn't know how to handle it.

# *Chapter Eight*

CHLOE gazed at the spoonful of creamy scrambled egg in the centre of her plate and picked up her fork. Her throat closed. *She must eat.* Compared to the alternatives: kippers, devilled kidneys, crisp bacon, and thick oatmeal porridge, eggs would lie easier on a stomach tension had made tight and painfully sore.

'Is anything wrong, my dear?'

Startled, Chloe dropped the fork, wincing as it clattered on the plate. 'No, not at all. I'm— I'm just not hungry.'

Sir Gerald folded his newspaper and set it beside his own plate on which traces of his hearty breakfast were congealing. 'This is not like you. In fact, it seems to me you have not been yourself for several days.'

Dismayed that her husband should so easily have seen through her heroic efforts to pretend – to herself as much as to him – that everything was normal, Chloe forced a smile. 'It's nothing, really.' But as he continued to study her, she looked down at her plate. Her heartbeat quickened and tears pricked her eyelids. *She must stop this foolishness. She owed Gerald so much.*

'Chloe, it's obvious something is troubling you. Come now, what is it?'

His voice was so gentle, his smile so kind. Just for an instant she was tempted – *No.* She dared not tell him the truth. Doing so might ease her guilt at feeling drawn to a man she barely knew, but such a confession could do irreparable damage to James Santana's reputation and position. And he had done nothing deserving of censure. Nor did she have the right to shift responsibility for her feelings onto him. She tried to swallow the obstruction in her throat.

'I — you're right, Gerald. I have not been quite myself, and for that I apologize.'

'If you would apologize, my dear, then let it be for not taking me into your confidence. Now, tell me what's wrong.'

'It's nothing of importance. I'm just tired, that's all.'

'Your committees do appear to have demanded a great deal of your time recently.'

Though she could not detect any nuance or hidden meaning in his remark, one could never be *entirely* sure with Gerald. 'Please don't think I'm complaining about the amount of work. It was my choice to become actively involved, and I haven't regretted it for a moment. It's just— the need is so great, and what we do seems so inadequate. I didn't know how bad— I hadn't ever seen such—' Unable to sit still she pushed back her chair and crossed to the deep window, looking out over the park towards the line.

'My dear, poverty is a fact of life. There will always be those who prefer idleness and drink to hard work and thrift. You cannot – and never will – change that.'

'Perhaps not. But when I look around – all this—' Her sweeping gaze encompassed the rich hangings, the polished furniture, the row of silver chafing dishes on the sideboard containing enough hot food to feed an entire family. 'We have so much and they have so little—'

'And were we to give everything away, do you think it would make the slightest difference in the long term?'

She faced him, clasping her elbows across her middle as if the pressure might ease an aching void that had little to do with lack of food. 'No,' she admitted reluctantly.

'Exactly. Chloe; your nature inclines you always to think the best of people. An admirable trait in many ways, but one that puts you in danger.'

'Danger?' Her voice sounded husky.

'Indeed. Of being deceived. Remember, my dear, people are not always truthful. They will say and do whatever helps them achieve their desires. You must be on your guard. And do bear in mind that charity, if it is to be effective, demands objectivity. Now come here.'

As she took his extended hand a faint chilling shiver of unease feathered over her skin.

Head at an angle, he studied her. 'You are decidedly pale, considering all the fresh air you've had lately.' His smile was warm and caring but didn't quite reach his eyes. 'I think it would be a good idea if you saw Dr Treloar.'

'I'm not ill, Gerald. Really, I don't need—'

'No arguments.' He smiled again, but it was nonetheless an order. 'Your health and wellbeing are of the utmost concern to me. How can I concentrate on important matters of business if I am worried?' He stood up. 'Go this afternoon, there's a good girl. Tell him I sent you. I want to see the bloom back in your cheeks.'

'Yes, Gerald.' *If only it were that simple.*

Despite an overcast sky, she could not face the confines of the carriage and, accompanied only by Polly, set off for Falmouth on horseback. She rode in silence. There was too much going on in her head. No longer able to discriminate between the real and imagined she longed for someone to talk to. Describing the turmoil might help her understand and make sense of it all. But whom could she tell? Who could she trust? Not just about James. *Was she being deceived? But how? He had behaved impeccably and asked nothing of her.* Undoubtedly James was the catalyst: but what about all the rest?

Pressured by gratitude into acceptance of a situation she sensed wasn't normal, she had coped by constantly reminding herself of her husband's kindness and generosity. He had insisted that, in spite of her youth, and the manner of her father's death, Cornish society accepted her, and accorded her the courtesy due a baronet's wife.

She had tried hard to match his expectations: tried also to forget the past. He had never actually shown impatience or disapproval, but she sensed he did not like her to speak of her childhood. It was pointless, he'd said, to hark back. The past could not be recalled or changed. What mattered was *now*, and the future: *their* future here at Trewartha. So when he'd asked her not to visit the house, she had given her word. It would only upset her, he'd said. And he could not bear her to be unhappy.

She had kept her promise. Yet she knew that revisiting her childhood home would not have disturbed her. Quite the contrary. For despite an upbringing that reflected her father's erratic changes of fortune, she recalled more laughter than gloom.

But during the past twelve months her pride in her role of Lady Radclyff had begun to crumble: eroded by an increasing number of sidelong glances she didn't understand and whispered conversations that stopped when she appeared. She would have shrugged this off, ascribing it to envy or something similar, except for one thing: the expression in their eyes. Man or woman, it made no difference. All observed her with the same mixture of pity, disdain, and curiosity.

She hadn't mentioned it to her husband. She wasn't sure why, only that it was in some way a test of her loyalty. And strangely, it strengthened the bond between them. He had given her his name, his protection, and status in society. In return, she took immense care, both in public and private, to maintain the façade of serenely contented wife.

But alone in the darkness with no audience but her inner self cracks had begun to appear. And now – since meeting James Santana – head and heart felt as though they might burst from the pressure of doubts and confusion.

They reached Cyrus Best's stables.

'Why don't you go and visit your mother for an hour?' Chloe suggested.

'Oh, ma'am, can I really?' Then duty clouded Polly's eagerness. 'Better not. Master said—'

'The master,' Chloe interrupted lightly, 'would not expect you to sit about idle while I am with the doctor. We will walk together to the consulting-rooms, and you can meet me there again in an hour.'

Their horses' hooves clattered over the flagstones as they walked into the yard to the rhythmic clang of hammer on anvil, and dismounted. There was a loud hiss and a cloud of steam billowed from an open doorway as red-hot iron was dipped in a barrel of water. The sweet-sharp smell of burning hoof hung on the air. Taking a shilling from her purse Chloe handed money and reins to a fair-haired boy wearing a leather apron that reached to his ankles. 'Check her off-fore will you? I think the shoe might be loose.'

'M'lady.' The boy sketched a rough salute, and led both animals away.

As they passed the rope-walk which ran alongside Arwenack Avenue, Chloe inhaled the dry, fibrous, coconut smell of manila hemp. At the bottom of Swanpool Street they turned right towards Grove Place. A cold breeze funnelled up from the Town quay. Chloe looked down the slip past the white-painted Customs House and the King's Pipe where contraband tobacco was burned, to the inner harbour. Frills of white foam streaked water the colour of beaten pewter. A row of small boats bounced unevenly on the choppy waves. Further out, between the quay and the docks, barquentines, brigs and schooners tugged restlessly against anchor chains and mooring ropes as thick as a man's forearm. Gulls rode a gusting wind that shredded their harsh cries as they soared and hovered.

'You sure it's all right, ma'am?' Polly looked anxiously from the imposing entrance back to Chloe.

'Polly, when did you last see your mother?'

'Must be almost a month now.'

'And her health?'

'Not all that good. It's her hip. She got a job to walk a lot of the time.'

'So an unexpected visit from you is sure to cheer her up. And you'll feel easier in your mind once you've seen how she is.' Chloe opened the gate. 'Off you go. And remember to give her my kind regards.'

'Thank you, ma'am,' Polly beamed. 'It's some good of you.'

Chloe waved her away with a smile then turned and walked up the path.

'Lady Radclyff, this is an unexpected pleasure.' Whitehaired, clean-shaven, and wearing a braid-edged frock coat, matching black waistcoat and dark-grey pinstriped trousers, the doctor led her into his office and bowed her to a button-back armchair, his welcome and his manners as polished as the glossy oxblood leather.

Chloe had no idea why she didn't like him. He had always treated her with perfect civility, treading the fine line between condescension and sycophancy. There was just something very slightly *reptilian* about his eyes. As she sat, folding her gloved hands in her lap, he took his own seat. She'd heard that some doctors sat behind their desk, employing it as a both physical and metaphorical barrier: Dr Treloar did not. His desk was set against the wall. He half-turned his chair so that he faced her. 'And how is Sir Gerald? Well, I hope?'

'He's very well, thank you.'

'I'm delighted to hear it. So, how may I help you?'

You can't, she thought, but of course she couldn't say so. She had once overheard him saying he had little patience with women's vapourings. It was important he be reminded that she had never been prone to such behaviour.

'I normally enjoy excellent health, and would not be here now, only my husband insisted. It's just ... Lately I've. ... I haven't been quite myself,' she finished lamely.

'Indeed? Could you perhaps be a little more specific?'

'I have no appetite. And I'm not sleeping well.'

'I see.' He nodded slowly, any irritation or impatience well hidden. 'Anything else?'

Her small dismissive gesture made light of the distress that was driving her to the edge of exhaustion. He simply waited. She began to describe the tension in her stomach, her difficulty in falling asleep, waking in the early hours, the sudden heart flutters that made her gasp for breath, and headaches that encircled her skull like an iron band. As she spoke she twisted her wedding ring round and round, trying to pluck up the courage to tell him what she had never told a living soul. But it was incredibly difficult to speak of such an intimate matter, especially to a man. Yet if she did not, how would she ever find out *why*?

When she had consulted him about her monthly problems he had been sympathetic and, anticipating what she was trying to say, he had spared her blushes.

She raised her eyes, silently begging him to help by asking the right questions. His gaze slid away.

'What you need, young lady, is to stop lingering in overheated rooms.'

Had he slapped her she could not have been more shocked.

'A wife who dwells on every minor indisposition will forfeit her husband's affection. You should get out and about more: find some worthy occupation to keep your mind busy.'

As Chloe choked down hysterical laughter he turned to his desk, and picked up a pen.

'I'm prescribing a mild tonic.' He scribbled on a sheet of headed paper. 'But the best treatment for neurasthenic conditions is plenty of fresh air and exercise.' He folded the sheet and handed it to her. 'Mr Bell will make this up for you. Might I also suggest' – his courteous choice of words did not entirely hide his impatience – 'that you take a few minutes each day to meditate upon the good fortune of your position in life?'

Indignation brought Chloe to her feet. 'You are impertinent, sir. I came to you for advice on my health, not a lecture on gratitude. No one knows better than I how much I have to be thankful for.' She felt breathless: hardly able to believe she had just spoken so to her husband's doctor. She didn't regret a single word.

He stood: his palms rasping softly as he rubbed them together. 'You misunderstand me, Lady Radclyff.' He smiled, butter-smooth. 'My intention – though perhaps I failed to make myself clear – was to indicate that, even in the best of marriages, differ-ences between the sexes mean that men and women do not always understand one another. A wife's duty is to accept this, and to fol-low her husband's lead in these matters.'

'Thank you, Dr Treloar. I assure you I have *always* fulfilled such duties as my husband required of me.'

As she walked back into the town Chloe still seethed. But her anguish came as much from conflict between her loyalty to Gerald and her disappointment at being no wiser, as from dismay at the doctor's strange behaviour.

In the apothecary's shop, surrounded by the earthy aroma of dried plants, the delicate fragrance of rosewater, and traces of something sharp and chemical, she was greeted with smiling defer-ence. Unfolding the paper, Mr Bell read it: glanced up at her over his wire-rimmed spectacles, then read it a second time.

'Is something wrong, Mr Bell?'

'No, no, Your Ladyship. I'll go and prepare it at once.' He gri-maced in apology. 'It may take some time.'

Chloe was surprised. 'You don't have any already prepared?' It was only a mild tonic. Knowing how many of her committee col-leagues depended on such aids, she would have expected him to prepare it by the gallon, and have rows of full bottles lined up on the shelf.

'I regret not, Your Ladyship.' He seemed about to say more, but didn't.

Chloe smiled. 'Never mind, I'll come back later.' At least she could be sure her tonic would be fresh. 'Would half an hour give you sufficient time?'

'Most kind, Your Ladyship. Most kind.' He continued to nod gently like a marionette as he disappeared into his dispensary.

Gathering up the heavy folds of her riding habit, she turned. As she reached for the handle, the door opened.

A soft gasp caught in her throat. James Santana stared at her, his quick smile and the sudden warmth in his eyes turning to concern.

'Are you quite well?' His voice was low, intense. He glanced over her shoulder. 'Forgive me,' he added before she could reply. 'That was hardly polite. But *are* you?'

'According to Dr Treloar,' – still smarting from the unfairness and inaccuracy of the diagnosis, she attempted a wry smile – 'I have lingered too long in overheated rooms and need more fresh air and exercise.'

'You look tired,' he said softly.

Looking up, seeing the dark circles under his eyes, the lines of tension bracketing his mouth, she blurted, 'So do you.'

'I can't sleep.'

She looked away. 'We shouldn't— This is not at all a suitable conversation—'

'I know. Believe me, I know. But I can't—' He stopped, making a visible effort to control himself. 'Will you take some refreshment with me?'

Surging pleasure was immediately swamped by guilt. 'I – I don't think—'

'Please. Something's happened at the village. You did say you wanted to help.' At that point the apothecary appeared, apologizing profusely, he hadn't heard the bell and so was unaware there was a customer waiting.

Chloe waited by the door as James collected a small package, then, sure the apothecary was watching and wondering, preceded him into the street. They didn't speak again until they were sitting at a small, pink-clothed table in Mrs Eddy's Tea Shop.

Waitresses in black dresses with white aprons and frilly white caps bustled to and from the kitchen carrying trays of pretty china, plates of dainty sandwiches, cream-filled sponges, and iced dainties. Suddenly ravenous, but fearing food would choke her, Chloe declined everything but hot chocolate. James ordered two. As the waitress hurried away Chloe glanced up.

'I really had hoped to take the clothes and other things out to the village before now, but Mrs Fox. . . .' She made a small movement with her shoulders. 'She reminded me that there are channels and procedures which must be observed.'

'Ah, yes. Of course.' His mouth quirked wryly.

His look of complicity, the shared understanding, made her shiver with delight. She was acutely aware she should not be experiencing such pleasure at being in his company. She ought to have refused his invitation. Spending time with James Santana – even in as public and innocuous a manner as this – was courting precisely the danger that Gerald had warned her about. Happiness, shame, longing and self-reproach writhed and coiled inside her. She felt as fragile as glass. The waitress arrived with a tray. When she had gone, Chloe removed her gloves to avoid looking at him.

'You said something's happened? There hasn't been another accident?'

'Do you remember the young woman who asked you for books? Her hut burned down. As it happened while most of the people from the surrounding shanties were at the funeral; no one appears to know what happened, or who might be responsible.'

Chloe stiffened. 'Are you saying it was *deliberate*?'

James shrugged. 'As nobody will talk about it – and that includes her – I don't suppose we'll ever find out. The point is, she lost everything but the clothes she was wearing.'

'The poor girl.' Chloe tried to imagine what it must feel like to own so little and then to lose even that. 'Of course I'll help. I'll sort out some of my own things as soon as I get home. It might cause difficulties for the girl if it appears she's being favoured over the others, so it would probably be best if I sent Polly.'

The way he looked at her brought heat to her face. 'You're very perceptive,' he observed softly. 'And very kind.'

She bent her head, and stirred sugar into her chocolate. She had no right to ask; it was none of her business, but she couldn't help herself. 'Is the young woman a particular friend of yours?'

'Her name is Polmear. Veryan Polmear. And no, she isn't. It's a tragic irony that her misfortune should be giving me such pleasure.' As relief turned to shock, jerking Chloe's head up, he gave a small helpless shrug. 'Would we be sitting here otherwise? Nothing since my return to Cornwall has given me as much pleasure as our conversations.'

Chloe fought terror and delight. She pushed back her chair. 'I think I should—'

'Chloe, look at me. Are you happy?'

She swallowed. 'My husband is . . . kind and generous. And constantly concerned for my well-being.'

'How did you meet him?'

'He was a close friend of my father's.'

'How long have you been married?'

'Four years.' She saw his shock.

'You must have been a child bride.'

'Indeed, I was.' Knowing her own smile lacked conviction, and was in danger of betraying things he had no right to know, she stood up. 'I really must go.'

On the narrow pavement, Chloe inhaled deeply, and saw a frantic Polly running towards her.

'Oh, ma'am, I'm some sorry. The time went so fast and—' Catching sight of James, she stumbled to a halt, her widening eyes darting from one to the other.

Appearing not to notice the maid, James turned to Chloe with a bow. 'May I thank you again, Lady Radclyff. Few could aspire to your kindness.'

Grateful for his formality, Chloe matched it with a brief inclination of her head. 'I'm pleased to be able to help. Good afternoon, Mr Santana.' Resisting the desire to watch him go, she turned to her maid. 'Come, Mr Bell should have my prescription ready by now. How is your mother? I hope you found her in good spirits?'

After dinner that evening Chloe took her first dose of the tonic. After half an hour she was aware of a slight discomfort in her stomach, but she also felt beautifully tranquil, as if all her nerves were wrapped in velvet. A little while later, finding it impossible to keep her eyes open, she begged Gerald to excuse her and went up to bed.

# Chapter Nine

CHECKING his watch, James quickened his pace. He would only just make it in time. But his thoughts, instead of being on the coming meeting, kept returning to his unexpected encounter with Chloe, and her reaction. He no longer had any doubts. Her attraction to him was as strong as his was to her. And she was clearly suffering because of it. Her loyalty to her husband was all the more remarkable for being utterly genuine. Yet he sensed something not right.

Natalia drifted briefly across his mind, confusing him. Then, clear and startling as a lightning flash, he recognized the similarity: both Natalia and Chloe were sexual innocents. *But Chloe Radclyff was a married woman.*

The implications stunned him. But there was no time to explore further, he had reached Harold Vane's offices in Church Street. Halfway up the staircase, hearing the murmur of voices, he deliberately stopped and took a slow, deep breath. Then, mentally checking his ammunition in preparation for the battle ahead, he opened the panelled door to the boardroom.

'Ah, Mr Santana has deigned to grace us with his presence at last.' Harold Vane's soft wet mouth puckered like a sea anemone.

James ignored the comment. He took the seat left for him at the far end of the polished mahogany table, and the chairman opened the meeting. Forty minutes later, after various discussions, none of which involved James, Ingram Coles beamed down the table.

'Mr Santana, I hope you are going to tell us that progress is being made at last?'

'Not enough, unfortunately.' As Clinton Warne sniffed, James

95

rested his forearms on the gleaming wood. He didn't need notes. His impressions of the line were etched deep on his memory. 'There are three major problems.'

'Only three?' Harold Vane enquired sarcastically.

'The first,' James continued, 'is the contractor. I recommend that you replace Pascoe as soon as possible.'

'With whom?'

'We can't do that.'

'On what grounds?'

'The man's doing his best.'

'The weather's been against him right from the start.'

James had expected resistance. His criticism of Pascoe was indirectly a criticism of them for having hired him. So, knowing they would demand reasons and examples, he had rehearsed both. But from the vehemence and immediacy of their objections, it was obvious that convincing them was going to be far harder than he'd anticipated.

He pressed on. But his detailed instances of Pascoe's carelessness and greed were greeted with shaking heads, and impatient gestures.

'Every line has its share of fatalities.'

'It's a hazardous job, injuries are inevitable.'

'Navvies are always taking chances. It's a hard job, but they are hard men. And they certainly get paid enough.'

It began to dawn on James that nothing he said was going to make any difference. For reasons he could not fathom, the directors had no intention of dismissing Horace Pascoe.

Not so long ago, he too would have responded with similar irritation. But now, after meeting Chloe, after inspecting conditions on the line and in the shanty village, and having seen the way men, women, and children were forced to live, the directors' attitude repelled him.

'And the other problems, Mr Santana?' Ingram Coles raised his voice above the mutters of opposition.

'I see that my predecessor specified Barlow rail?'

'That is correct,' Ingram Coles nodded. 'I believe he was influenced by the fact that Mr Brunel chose it in preference to other rails for the Truro to Penzance line. In Mr Brunel's opinion, it compared most favourably in terms both of initial cost and subsequent maintenance. And as that line has been operating with great success since 1852 the choice would appear justified.'

Despite Ingram Coles's genial smile, James sensed growing reserve.

'Not any longer,' he said carefully.

'Are you questioning the judgement of one of the great railway engineers of the age?' Harold Vane demanded.

'Not at all. Mr Brunel made his choice based on what was known at the time. It's only in the past few years we've discovered that, under certain conditions, the Barlow rail can become unstable. On a few occasions this has resulted in derailment.'

'Well, I've never heard about it,' Harold Vane snorted, 'so it can't have occurred that often.'

'It hasn't,' James admitted. 'But my concern is—'

'Besides,' Harold Vane cut him short, 'companies wouldn't have continued using it if there were serious doubts about its safety.'

'Actually, the South West Railway began replacing all their Barlow rail five years ago,' James said. 'But I take your point. And the problem can be overcome with careful attention to ballast work and regular maintenance. However, I have an obligation to bring the matter to your attention. And I'd ask you to consider whether it might not be wiser in the long term to replace the Barlow with steel rails?'

'With six miles of track already laid?' Clinton Warne's voice climbed.

'I really don't think the company can afford that,' Victor Tyzack, the deputy chairman, stated quietly.

'How do you suggest we explain the cost to our shareholders?' Gilbert Mabey arched a laconic eyebrow.

'In any case, such a move is totally unnecessary,' Harold Vane added. 'Maintenance is the obvious answer. Labour is far cheaper than steel rails. Let's move on, for goodness' sake.'

'And the third problem, Mr Santana?' The chairman's smile was considerably cooler.

'The locomotives.'

'What about them?' Clinton Warne's chin jutted belligerently. 'The agreement I negotiated with Evans and Company obtained us a most favourable price.' He glanced around the table for confirmation.

James spoke over the murmurs and nods of approval. 'Indeed, the terms are excellent,' James agreed. 'The problem is, this particular locomotive is too heavy for the line.'

In the tense silence, street sounds seemed suddenly loud: clopping hooves, the rumble of carriage and cart wheels, their drivers bellowing at street urchins to get out of the road; dogs barking, gulls screaming, and the raucous laughter of women working on the fish quay below.

'You're quite wrong.' Stretching his neck like a turkey, Warne glanced round his colleagues. 'He's wrong. Do you think I didn't check? Of course I did. And the company assured me that the weight of the engine is within the capability of the rails.'

*But were their calculations based on steel or Barlow rails? And did they include the weight of carriages in addition to that of the locomotive?*

'Gentlemen.' Ingram Coles raised his hand for silence. But he gave James no chance to raise these points. 'We are indebted to Mr Santana for his diligent investigation. He has not suggested how we are supposed to finance his proposals, however I imagine he considers that to be our responsibility. Which indeed it is. Now, before moving on to other business, we should perhaps applaud his thoroughness and concern for safety?'

As the other directors gazed at the table and made vague noises in their throats, Harold Vane clapped his hands, twice, in slow calculated insult.

Masking angry frustration with a bland smile, James inclined his head and addressed the fat, fair-haired company secretary. 'Mr Mabey, I'd be obliged if you would record my recommendation that, in the event of these locomotives being used, all curving viaducts should have extra shoring on their outer sides? Without this additional support the outward pressure of the trains could push them over sideways.' He heard a soft intake of breath, but continued without pause. 'Will you also note my concern that every point I raised was overruled? I'm sure you understand.'

'I do, Mr Santana.' Gilbert Mabey's heavy-lidded eyes gleamed with ironic amusement. 'Perfectly.'

The meeting continued, but James's opinions were neither sought nor offered. When it ended he excused himself and left quickly. He had just reached the street door when someone called his name. He turned to see Gilbert Mabey giving the lie to the assertion that fat people were light on their feet.

'Are you expected somewhere?' he panted, thumping, flat-footed and clumsy, down the stairs.

'No.'

'Care for a drink?'

In spite of his still-simmering anger, James suddenly grinned. 'Does it show?'

'You do realize,' Gilbert puffed, following him out onto the street, now crowded as shops and businesses closed and people made their way home or into the ale-houses and taverns, 'that you are ruffling a lot of feathers.'

James raised an eyebrow. 'What did they expect?'

'I'm supposed to tell you to ease off.'

'Why you?'

'Ingram doesn't like confrontations: Victor has another appointment: and you've already crossed swords with Clinton and Harold.' He shrugged. 'There's only me left.'

'My reputation is on this line.'

'Ah, but it's their company.'

'Is that what this is all about?' James stared at him. 'Wounded pride?' He shook his head. 'I can't believe it.'

'No one likes being made to look foolish.'

'It's not me who's done that; they managed it all by themselves. Can't they see what risks they're taking?'

'Maybe when they've calmed down, had time to think—'

'They don't *have* time. If things don't improve pretty damn quickly—'

'My dear chap, you mustn't take it all so personally. You said your piece – which came as something of a shock to my esteemed colleagues. I don't imagine for one moment they were expecting quite such a drubbing.'

'Is that how it sounded?'

Gilbert nodded. 'You're young, you see.'

'I'm right.'

'Probably.' Gilbert sighed, leading the way up the steps into the Royal Hotel.

Over a glass of Madeira they began to talk about their respective backgrounds. James found Gilbert amusing and irreverent. One glass was followed by a second. Gilbert suggested dinner and James accepted. He had nothing to go back to, and knew he would only brood about Chloe. After a meal of spring lamb, followed by apple tart with clotted cream, and a bottle of St Emilion, Gilbert grew even more expansive.

Seeing his chance, James refilled Gilbert's glass. 'Do you know Sir Gerald well?'

'I don't think anyone knows him *well*. He's a strange cove. Certainly not one to cross.'

'Oh.' James raised his glass to his lips, feigning mild interest while every nerve tensed with a compelling desire to know more.

Gilbert leaned forward. 'One hears rumours,' he confided. 'Not that I believe them, it's all just gossip, I'm sure.' He bent to the water biscuits and Stilton on his plate.

'What kind of rumours?'

Glancing round to make sure they couldn't be overheard, Gilbert whispered, 'About his *private* life. Mind you, the man has known his share of tragedy.'

'Oh?' James prompted, forcing himself to relax.

'Mmm,' Gilbert nodded, chewing. 'His first wife died, you know. Only been married a couple of years. Took her own life. No children.' Knifing a crumbly lump of cheese onto a piece of biscuit, Gilbert crammed it into his mouth, spraying crumbs as he continued. 'Of course, women love a tragic figure. Within months he was the target of every widow and match-making mother in the district. But he told everyone that after the shock of his bereavement he would not remarry. No one believed him. They thought it was just the grief talking. But the years went by. Eventually everyone assumed he would remain single. He had an excellent housekeeper and staff. He took care always to attend important social occasions with a different partner. Of course, by that time, we'd all heard the odd whisper. But there was never any proof. So we simply assumed they were just malicious stories put about by people he'd bested in business deals.'

'What *is* his business?' James asked, pouring a tiny amount of wine into his own glass before generously topping up Gilbert's. 'What does he do?'

Gilbert shrugged. 'He has a finger in any number of pies. And he's a serious gambler. He rarely loses. The man has nerves of iron.' He wiped his mouth. 'You see, it wasn't just the *fact* of his remarriage that raised eyebrows, it was how he got his wife.' He leaned forward, his eyes bright with alcohol and enjoyment of the story. 'Would you believe, on the turn of a card?'

'*What?*' It would have been impossible to hide his shock. Fortunately, his reaction delighted Gilbert.

'You never heard this from me.'

'No, no, of course not. Go on.'

'Well, apparently Richard Polglase, Chloe's father – he was a widower too: lost his wife to pneumonia when the girl was very young – anyway, Polglase was a close pal of Sir Gerald's. He was a gambler too. But he didn't have Radclyff's luck, or his self discipline. Over the years he gambled away large chunks of his estate. One night, in a high-stakes game, he lost the rest. After scribbling a note entrusting care of his daughter – she was only fourteen – to Sir Gerald, he shot himself.'

'But—' James had to clear his throat. 'Why him? Why Radclyff?'

Gilbert shrugged. 'Polglase's gambling had caused a lot of bad feeling on both sides of the family. And with no money for a dowry none of his – or his late wife's – relatives were willing to take her on.'

*Chloe.* Incandescent with fury at her feckless father, James stared blindly at the inch of blood-red wine in his glass, twisting the stem round and round. He had never been closer to losing his self-control.

'Everyone expected him to hire a companion for her. But damn me if, as soon as she was sixteen, he didn't up and marry the girl. Caused quite a stir, I can tell you. Still, it did put a stop to the rumours.'

*What rumours?* But James didn't dare interrupt Gilbert's wine-induced confidences to ask.

'Of course, there were plenty ready to say he was asking for trouble: what with the age difference and her being such a pretty little thing. But there's not been so much as a whisper. Not about *her*, at any rate.' He shook his head. Amazement? Disbelief? Envy? James couldn't tell.

'Mind you, he's extremely protective. She's a superb horse-woman, but he won't let her ride to hounds. Though when you hear what goes on during a hunt, who's to blame him? And she seems to think the world of him. It would be a foolhardy man who entertained any ideas in that direction. I certainly wouldn't like to cross him. In fact, if you want the truth, I think he could be dangerous.'

Back at his lodgings, James paced the floor, replaying Gilbert's words over and over again, comparing them with his own impressions gleaned from conversations with Chloe. In the early hours, exhausted and still sleepless, he slumped into an armchair. There were only two positive aspects to the entire problem: his growing regard for Chloe was reciprocated, and as yet no one else was aware.

This couldn't last. The only sure way he could protect her would be to leave. But how could he abandon her? Especially when it was obvious to him – and possibly suspected by others – that the celebrated marital harmony was just a façade. He needed an acknowledgement her loyalty would not allow.

Desperate for respite from a problem that appeared, for now at least, to have no solution, he picked up that day's edition of the *West Briton and Royal Cornwall Gazette*. He scanned the pages, skimming over news stories that, a few weeks ago, would have had his undivided attention. He turned another page. After a few minutes, not having taken in a single word, he gave a grunt of disgust and started to close the paper.

Something caught his eye. Angling the page to the lamplight he read the legal notice once more. His arms fell, crumpling the paper in his lap. So *that* was why the name had seemed familiar. He had glimpsed the same notice in the previous week's paper.

Veryan held the wooden plank in place as Tom hammered it onto the partly repaired panel. The vibration jarred up through her arms to her teeth. It was mid-afternoon. They had both risen at first light.

She hadn't slept much. The men's snoring, and other, coarser, noises had kept her awake. At least, that was what she told herself. In her heart of hearts she knew the real reason sleep eluded her was the man lying in the bunk above. She had wanted to think about the engineer: the way he'd turned back on the path to ask if she was all right. And how, after the accident, he'd insisted she and Davy ride. She wanted to ponder possibilities, test her hopes. But *he* kept pushing into her thoughts.

As she'd stared into the darkness her confusion had grown. Helping her build a new hut would cost him a day's pay. Why would he do that? What would he expect in return? But she hadn't asked for his help. He'd offered: insisted. So she didn't owe him anything. And she would make sure she did her share. Then she wouldn't be beholden, and he wouldn't get any ideas.

So, as soon as she heard the slats creak as he swung himself quietly to the floor, she had wriggled into her old skirt and blouse. As she'd slept in her chemise and petticoats it hadn't taken more than a few minutes. He had stoked up the fire while she went outside. When she returned, face and hands washed, hair combed and tied back, she quickly dismissed her reaction to his admiration as hunger and lack of sleep. While she prepared breakfast he went to the wood dump for the first load of planks.

Queenie had been more than usually waspish. 'What about the men's dinner? Who's going to get that ready and take it down the line? No good looking at me. It's your job; I got more'n enough to do.'

'Here, girl,' Paddy had grunted. 'You get it ready. I'll take it.' That had put Queenie in even more of a snit, and she had waddled between the fire, the dresser and the table, deliberately getting in the way. Biting her tongue, Veryan had got on as best she could. She had no idea why Queenie was being so difficult. But asking would only invite more trouble.

Breakfast over, the men left. Tom had gone too, to fetch more wood. Working around Queenie, Veryan had cleared away the breakfast dishes, got the washing done as fast as possible, and hung it out. The veil of thin high cloud hazing the pale-blue sky promised a few days of warm, dry weather.

'That should give'n some strength,' Tom said, straightening up and flexing his shoulders. 'I'll try and bring back a drop of creosote tomorrow. He'll stink for a day or two, but he'll keep out the wet and slow the rot.' He shot her a sidelong glance. 'Queenie give you any trouble this morning?'

'No more than—' Veryan began automatically, then stopped. 'Well, as a matter of fact—' She glanced up, suspicious. 'Why do you ask?'

'How come you and she don't share a room?'

Veryan wiped her forearm across her sweating forehead. 'Have you *seen* Queenie's room?'

'Nope. Mind you, she did ask me.' Bending, he picked up another plank. Veryan knew how heavy they were. She'd helped carry them. But in his big hands the wood looked weightless.

'Asked you what?'

He raised his eyes to hers. 'If I wanted to go with her.'

As she held the plank in place, Veryan felt an odd twist beneath her ribs.

'But you didn't.'

' 'Course I bleddy didn't. What d'you take me for?'

The flash of temper startled her, and she realized that though she'd seen him angry, it had never been directed at her.

'I know you didn't, or you'd have known what her room was like,' she responded tartly. 'So that was what had upset her. I wondered.' She'd assumed it was Lady Radclyff's maid arriving with a bundle of clothes.

'I ain't never been *that* desperate,' Tom growled. 'Ugghh.' He shuddered.

'Yes, all right. You've made your point. Anyway, *that's* why I don't share with her. At least, it's one of the reasons. I did, for a little while, after—' She saw her mother, a human torch, and swiftly blocked the image. 'But whenever Queenie . . . had company. . . .' Veryan looked away, furious with herself for blushing. Working in the shanty where such matters were talked of openly, and in much cruder terms, she couldn't help knowing what went on behind the closed door. And when the men baited her she had schooled herself not to react, taking refuge in silence. Now, speaking of it to Tom Reskilly made her feel ridiculously shy.

'The men would . . . they made jokes. It was— I couldn't—' She shook her head. 'So I hid a candle in the wash house, and I'd go in there and read. That was something else; she said my reading kept her awake. It didn't. But her snoring stopped *me* from sleeping.'

'Dear life, girl,' Tom grinned. 'Had some time of it, haven't you?' As she raised one shoulder, he said, 'You don't have to put up with it, you know. I heard her this morning, going on to you.'

Veryan turned her head as guilt, pushed aside but ever present, dried her throat. Queenie's taunting had been venomous, muttered behind her while she dished up the porridge.

*'Do you reckon 'Er Ladyship would be so generous if she knew the truth about you? Don't you go getting too much above yourself, miss, else someone might have to put 'er wise.'*

'All that stuff about you owing her for the roof over your head?' Tom reminded. 'And the clothes on your back, the food in your mouth? That's boll— that's rubbish, that is,' he corrected quickly with a delicacy as touching as it was unexpected. 'You think a minute. The only clothes you got now is what Lady Radclyff sent. The roof' – he gestured from the pile of charred remains to the new panels ready to be erected – 'is what we've built between us. And as for food . . . seeing as how you do all the cooking, 'tis only right you eat your share. She got no hold over you.'

Veryan gazed at him, hope battling with despair, and losing. 'It's not that simple.'

Hauling one of the panels upright, Tom gestured for her to support it while he raised a second, fitting it against the corner post. 'Hold 'er steady while I get a couple of nails in.'

Within minutes three and a half panels were in place and Tom was fitting the door, using the old hinges salvaged from the ashes.

Holding the door while he tightened the screws, Veryan found herself looking at his arms, fascinated by the play of muscle. She could feel the warmth emanating from him, smell the sweet muskiness of his sweat. As he forced the screws in tight, grunting softly with the effort, her gaze flicked, shy and curious, to his thick neck and strong jaw, black with a heavy growth of stubble. The navvies only shaved at the weekend, some didn't even bother then. She had never been this close to a man, *except* – she shuddered, mentally recoiling.

He glanced down.

Quickly she turned her head away. 'Can I let go now?'

A slight frown deepened the twin creases between his heavy brows. 'What're you doing here, my 'andsome?' he asked softly. 'You don't belong on the line.'

'How would you know?'

'Father worked on the lines. I was born in a shanty and started as a tip-boy with him when I was seven.'

'Where are they now?' Against her will, Veryan was curious. She's never met a navvy like Tom Reskilly.

'Mother died when I was twelve, and father was killed six year ago when a tunnel collapsed on him. Here, pass me they screws.'

She did as he asked. 'You said – you said you had a son.'

He eyed her. 'I know what you're doing, my 'andsome. It's all right though, I don't mind telling you,' he said, as she opened her mouth. 'But it works both ways. That's fair, isn't it? Yes, I had son. I was working just outside London, a branch of the Great Northern Line. Doreen – that was 'er name – was in service in one of the big houses on the edge of the village. She didn't have no family, and said she wanted to travel. So when I moved on she went with me. The boy came along about a year later. Dear little soul he was, fat as a dumpling, and always smiling.' Tom's expression softened as he murmured, 'Thomas Henry.' Grief shadowed his broad strong face, dimming his smile. 'Just toddling, he was.' He fell silent, caught up in his memories.

'What happened?' Veryan asked softly.

Inhaling deeply, Tom wedged the door open against his foot to check the latch. 'The croup. She didn't stay long after that. I b'lieve she went back into service.' He stood back, surveying his handi-work. 'So, what brought you here?'

'The men haven't told you?' Disbelief frosted her voice.

'They've told me all sorts. But half of 'em don't know which way is up. Any'ow, I'd sooner hear it from you.'

'Why?' she demanded: wary, unsettled by the sudden urge to tell him. He would listen and not judge her. She could trust him. *Was she mad? How did she know that?* 'What difference does it make?'

'None,' he said simply.

So, helping him fashion a roof for the hut out of more planks and scraps of heavy tarpaulin, she recounted, briefly and without emotion, her childhood and the events which had led to her working for Queenie.

'You know what?' He looked sideways at her. 'You and me, we're two of a kind.'

'No, we're not,' she refuted immediately. 'I wasn't born to this life, nor did I choose it: I was forced here by circumstance. But one day I'll get out. I want a better life.' Her look dared him to mock. Instead he eyed her thoughtfully.

'You go for it, girl,' he urged. 'You got spirit.'

Having expected, and prepared herself for mockery, this encouragement threw her. Doubts seeped in. Where could she go? How would she support herself? And, most frightening of all, if Queenie carried out her threats, would she spend the rest of her life living in fear of discovery, always looking over her shoulder? What kind of life would that be? *Surely better than this.*

# Chapter Ten

SINCE the moment Veryan had entered the shanty to light the fire and start breakfast Queenie had followed her about, her curiosity spiked with malice.

'He didn't do all that for free. I was watching. I seen the way he looked at you. You wait. Before the week's out he'll want paying, one way or another.'

Refusing to be drawn, Veryan said nothing.

Queenie peered into Veryan's face. 'I bet you won't fight neither. I seen plenty like you. All touch-me-not one minute and skirts over your head the next. And he've got the charm of the devil. We wondered where he'd gone last night. He wasn't in here with us. He was with you, wasn't he?' Losing patience, Queenie grabbed her arm. 'I'm talking to you, girl. I asked you a question.'

Veryan jerked free. 'I'm not obliged to answer.'

'Well!' Queenie gasped. 'Some gratitude that is. After all I done for you—'

'Oh, please,' Veryan muttered in weary disgust. Turning back to the table and the waiting men with downcast eyes, she ladled porridge into each bowl. She was all too aware of their speculation, and of Queenie watching her every move.

Already hot, she felt perspiration dew her skin as she recognized his broad, scarred hand. Keeping her head bent, she scooped out the thick oatmeal, willing him not to say anything. She owed him thanks. But not here, not now. He didn't speak; she couldn't. As he moved away to the table to join the others, her relief was tempered by a strange sense of anti-climax. Against her will, she found herself wondering. Where *had* he been? She hadn't seen him since last night's evening meal.

After clearing up, she had gone to the bunk to collect her bundle

107

of clothes. They'd gone. *Surely Queenie hadn't*— Then she realized the thin mattress and blankets were missing as well. She raced
out to the hut. Opening the door she stood quite still. Mattress,
blankets, and clothes were all there: laid neatly on a *bed*. Made of
six-foot planks nailed crosswise onto sleepers with an extra one at
the head to stop her pillow failing off, it stood clear of the earth
floor, which was now covered by a strip of canvas.

Her eyes pricked. Was it just kindness? Anguish and anger tore
at her. She hadn't asked – certainly hadn't expected – not since her
father had anyone— *What did he want?* Why *him?*

When he left with the rest of the men for the works he still made
no attempt to speak, or even to catch her eye. It was as if the unexpected intimacy of the previous day had never existed. Her confusion increased. Wasn't that what she wanted? At least it proved
Queenie wrong. *So why, instead of relief did she feel so . . . at a loss?*
She hauled a bucketful of hot water from the copper for the dishes.

'Well.' Queenie folded her hands under her sagging bosom.
'Looks like your fancy man 'ave had second thoughts. I bet I know
why.' She cackled with spiteful laughter. 'He's afraid if he cross you
he'll end up like Gypsy Ned. What's wrong? What you looking
like that for? Can't you take a joke?'

And so it continued, a deliberate goading that dripped on and
on, poisoning the sunny morning. Biting her tongue, Veryan willed
herself not to react. There was a short respite when she returned,
empty-handed from the tally shop.

'What you been doing?' Queenie demanded. 'You was supposed
to be going to the shop.'

'I did. It's closed.'

'What d'you mean, closed? It can't be, not this time of the morning.'

'The shutters are still up. Pascoe isn't there. People are banging
on the door. There's a whole crowd of them waiting.'

At the clop and squelch of approaching hooves they both looked
towards the window.

'Maybe that's him now,' Queenie said. 'He don't normally come
in from this end. But I s'pose he could've been up the line first.'

Veryan heard the jingle of harness and a soft thud as someone
dismounted.

Queenie threw a malicious smirk over her shoulder. 'I know, it's
Her Ladyship come to invite you to—'

Veryan started violently as James Santana's head appeared round the open door.

'Miss Polmear? I wonder if I might have a word?'

'Well, now.' Queenie's bright sharp smile revealed a mouthful of decay. 'Seeing as this young lady is in my care, p'rhaps you'd better tell me what you want with her?'

He ignored her. 'Miss Polmear?'

Nervously smoothing her hands over the pale-grey dress, one of two in the parcel from Lady Radclyff, Veryan hurried to join him, heart hammering. *Miss Polmear?*

Knuckles on her massive hips, Queenie squared up to him. 'Now 'ang on a minute—'

James placed himself between her and Veryan. 'This is a private matter. We won't be long.' He shut the door, cutting off Queenie's roar of protest. She promptly yanked it open again but remained, narrow-eyed and muttering furiously, on the threshold.

Veryan stood beside his horse's head. She stroked the soft muzzle and felt the animal's hot breath against her work-roughened palm.

James Santana glanced round. Following his gaze she saw the women watching curiously, some from their own doorways, others in a group outside the tally shop.

'Is there somewhere we might speak privately?'

After a moment's hesitation she nodded, and, with her heart fluttering somewhere near her throat, led him towards her hut.

'Good Lord!' His astonished realization sent a thrill of pride and pleasure through her. 'I didn't realize. . . . But how – when—?'

'Yesterday.' She saw the frown form, drawing his brows together as he scrutinized the panels and planking, and guessed what was coming. *She couldn't have built this by herself.*

'How many of the navvies—'

She lifted her chin proudly. 'Only one. With the ganger's permission,' she added quickly. 'We did it between us.'

'Only one? He must think very highly of you.'

'No.' She shook her head. 'He isn't— I mean, we're not—' She felt herself flush. She wanted him to understand that, though she appreciated Tom's help, there was nothing between them. Well, there wasn't. She still didn't understand why he hadn't spoken to her this morning. Or where he'd gone last night. Not that she cared; it wasn't any of her business what he did.

James Santana wasn't listening. He reached into his pocket. 'I saw this in the paper yesterday.' Unfolding the clipping he passed it to her.

It wasn't very long. She read it twice and the tremor in her hands increased. But at least now there was a reason she could admit to. She looked up at him. Guilt and terror dried her mouth. She had to run her tongue over her lips before she could speak. 'Wh-why would a solicitor want to see me?' *Had the body been found?* No, it couldn't be that. The police would have come.

'Don't look so worried.' He smiled reassuringly as he stroked his horse's glossy neck. 'When someone is asked to contact a firm of solicitors, it is often related to a family matter.'

Veryan was bewildered. What family? Her parents were dead. She had no brothers or sisters. She had faint memories of older people she'd been told were her grandparents. But she had been very young and couldn't remember their faces.

'Yes, but why a solicitor?' She was still apprehensive.

James shrugged. 'To show that it's important the person is found. Especially if,' he added carefully, 'no one knows where to look or who to ask.' He gathered up his horse's reins. 'Anyway, I thought you should see it.'

'Thank you. I'm – it's very kind of you.'

He placed one polished boot in the stirrup and swung himself into the saddle. 'I'd go and see them if I were you. It might be good news.'

After all these years? Anyway, why would they want to see her now? Her mother had always blamed the family for the loss of her home. As the two of them had moved around the country she had become frighteningly unpredictable, her tears of self-pity changing within seconds to rage, bitterness, and wild-eyed vows of revenge. Veryan had quickly learned to think of her grandparents as the enemy: cold-hearted and cruel.

'I think that's very unlikely. Anyway, even if I did—' She stopped, staring blindly at the now-crumpled paper.

'What?'

She looked up, narrowing her eyes against the sun and against sudden despair. 'How do I prove who I am?'

'Don't you have anything—?' He frowned. 'No, of course, the fire.'

Veryan screwed up her courage. 'I don't suppose—'

'Would it help if—'

'Please.' She gestured for him to speak first, hoping.

'I have no wish to intrude on your personal business, but it *was* I who brought this matter to your attention, so I feel a certain responsibility. Perhaps if I were to escort you. . . ?'

'Would you? Would you really?'

'Shall we say the end of next week? Meanwhile, I will inform them that you have seen the notice and will be coming in.'

'You're very kind.'

'It's no trouble. Until next week, then. Now I have to see Mr Pascoe.' Clicking his tongue, he turned his mount.

'He's not there.'

'What?' His horse, gleaming like a polished chestnut, danced restlessly. Shortening the reins, he glanced from her to the group of women who milled impatiently outside the shuttered shop. The horse tossed and shook its head, mouthing the bit.

'He hasn't arrived yet. That's why they are all waiting.'

'I see.' His face was suddenly wiped clean of all expression. With his heels in its sides, the horse leapt forward.

Veryan watched him canter past the women, ignoring their demands to know. what was going on, why wasn't the shop open, where was Pascoe, and how were they supposed to feed their families, as he headed up the hill, taking the shortest route to the line.

'So, what was that all about then?' Queenie's eyes were hawk-sharp, her expression avid, as Veryan passed her.

'I just told him Pascoe's not here.' Veryan scooped up the dirty clothes that had been thrown at – and missed – the washing basket.

Queenie tutted impatiently. 'I didn't mean that. As you perfectly well know. What did he want with you?'

'Perhaps you should ask him.' Veryan picked up the loaded basket, resting it on her hip.

'Don't you get uppity with me, miss,' Queenie snapped. 'I dunno what's got into you lately. Lord knows I always done my best for you—'

'Your *best*?' Veryan stared at her. 'How can you even— You would have let them—' Veryan caught her lower lip hard between her teeth.

'Listen, girl, it's time you—' A commotion outside cut her short. 'Dear life! What's going on now? Like a bleddy fairground out there this morning, it is.'

Bessie Thomas stuck her grimy, tousled head around the door. 'Queen, it's that Lady Wassname come with two of 'er friends. Looks like she've brung the clothes and stuff.'

'Out the way, Bess. Let the dog see the rabbit.' Tugging her filthy shawl around her shoulders, Queenie pushed past Veryan and swiftly waddled out.

Veryan followed more slowly. Skirting round the back of the throng to the wash house, she glanced briefly at the gleaming open carriage in which the three elegantly dressed women had arrived. Behind it was a four-wheeled cart. Loaded with huge wicker baskets, all piled high with clothes and linen, it was in the charge of a second, much younger coachman who, judging by his crimson face, was being mercilessly teased and propositioned by the waiting women.

Veryan had rubbed four soaped shirts against the ribbed washboard then, after a quick twist to wring out most of the water, tossed them into a tin bath to be rinsed later. Reaching into the basket she picked up the fifth. Turned inside out, it was rolled up. As she shook it out, recognizing it as the one Tom had been wearing the previous night, the foul smell made her recoil. There were dark stains across one shoulder and down the front. *Where had he been? What had he been doing?* She plunged it into the hot sudsy water. It was none of her business.

Deliberately she turned her thoughts to the newspaper clipping. Who wanted to find her? And why? And what was she to make of Mr Santana seeking her out? Going to such trouble must surely signify more than just a passing interest on his part?

A shadow crossed the doorway. She took no notice. Then a soft, beautifully spoken female voice enquired, 'Miss Polmear?' And she started violently.

'L-Lady Radclyff.'

'I just wanted to say how sorry I was, about the fire. To lose treasured possessions – it must have been devastating.'

'Thank you for the clothes.' Veryan knew she sounded stiff and cool, knew also that her visitor's kindness deserved better. But just looking at the maroon ankle-length walking dress, the matching jacket, smart little hat, and polished shoes, made her ache with envy. It wasn't just the clothes – though God knew she was sick to her soul of ill-fitting, worn-out cast-offs – it was the world they represented: a world of privilege, of freedom to choose: what to eat, what to wear, who to see, and the most interesting and entertaining ways to fill one's days. Best of all, it was a world free from fear. She had belonged to that world: once: long, wretched years ago.

'I'm glad they have proved useful.'

It seemed to Veryan that, although the stilted thanks were accepted with more grace than they deserved, Lady Radclyff's thoughts were elsewhere.

'Actually, I've sought you out because – well, for two reasons really. The first concerns the books and writing materials you asked for. Do you want them put in the big—'

'No!'

'I thought perhaps not.' Her quick smile held understanding. 'So where should Robbins take them?'

'Oh, er—' Veryan hastily dried red, dripping hands on the torn shirt she had tied around her waist by the sleeves in place of an apron. 'I'll show you.' Aware of watching eyes and whispers amid the clamour, she straightened her back.

Queenie had managed to haul herself up onto the cart. Amid shouting and edgy banter she was sorting and distributing the garments as if they were her own property. Yet no one had the courage to join her or take her place.

'Who is that person?'

'Queenie Spargo? She runs lodgings in the big shanty for one of the gangs.'

'She appears to speak on behalf of everyone here.'

'Self-elected,' Veryan said wearily. 'She has a louder voice than anyone else.'

'Ah.' Chloe Radclyff's quiet acknowledgement held recognition. 'The ideal committee chairwoman.' She signalled the coachman, who reached into the cart. 'The books are in a wooden box. I thought – if you have nothing better – it is somewhere safe to keep them. And turned on its side, the box offers a flat surface on which to write.'

'Nothing *better*?' Veryan faced her benefactor. 'Where would I be likely to find—?' She looked away, resentful, embarrassed, ashamed, and tucked an escaped curl behind her ear. 'Sorry. Look, I don't mean to sound rude, but why are you doing this? You don't know me.'

'No.' Chloe Radclyff's skin bloomed a delicate pink and a shy smile lifted the corners of her mouth. 'But I'm acquainted with someone who does. Mr Santana told me about the fire, and asked if—'

'Oh,' Veryan gasped. *James Santana* had requested Lady Radclyff's help for her? She pressed one hand to her midriff, and felt her heart thumping unevenly. A gloved hand rested for a moment on her arm.

'Are you unwell? Forgive me, a foolish question. The shock of the fire—'

'No. No, I'm all right. It's – I—' Reaching into the pocket of her dress, Veryan drew out the clipping. 'Your mention of Mr Santana – he came this morning to bring me this.' She unfolded it. 'In fact, he'd only just gone when you arrived. Apparently he saw it last night when he was reading the newspaper.' She handed the clipping to Chloe, surprised to see that the narrow hands encased in fine kid gloves were trembling almost as much as her own had earlier. But this observation was swept aside by a rush of excitement. 'He has promised to go with me to the solicitor's office next week.' She hugged herself. 'He is the kindest man I have ever met.'

As the words left her lips, she suddenly thought of Tom Reskilly. For an instant she could feel the warmth of his strong rough-skinned hand gripping hers, just as it had when they sprawled on the side of the collapsed embankment. She remembered the cold fury with which he had beaten William Thomas into unconsciousness, and pictured with startling clarity the bunching and flexing of muscle in his arms and shoulders as he raised panels and hammered nails. Were it not for him she would still be sleeping in the shanty, with no privacy and no escape from Queenie's spiteful tongue. *He had even built her a proper bed. He had done it in secret, and had not spoken to her since – let alone looked for thanks.*

Thrown off balance by the vivid images, and the confusion they evoked, she wiped her hand down her dress as if to rub away the sensation, relieved at the length of time the golden head remained bent over the short legal notice.

Eventually Lady Radclyff looked up. 'It would seem so.' Her smile was muted, less certain. 'I hope you receive good news.'

'Mr Santana expressed the same wishes.' As she slipped into the vocabulary and speech patterns of her youth, Veryan was startled to find she felt awkward and gauche, like a child mimicking its betters. But pride kept her going. 'I think it unlikely. But, as he pointed out, what do I have to lose? And having his support will make the experience far easier for me.'

'Indeed.' Handing back the clipping, Lady Radclyff beckoned the young coachman whose green and gold livery was almost hidden by the large wooden crate.

As he approached, leaning back to counter the weight, Veryan couldn't help noticing how Lady Radclyff's thumb rubbed ceaselessly against the gloved back of her other hand. Yet, though the mannerism suggested stress, her expression – as far as Veryan could tell from a quick sideways glance – was perfectly tranquil.

The coachman set the box down inside the door. With a brief bow and a murmured, 'Ma'am,' he returned to the cart.

'I hope the books give you pleasure. Good day to you, Miss Polmear.' With a quick smile, Lady Radclyff turned towards the carriage where her companions waited, clearly impatient to leave.

'Lady Radclyff?'

She looked back. 'Yes?'

'You mentioned two reasons? For wanting to see me?'

'Ah, yes. We, that is—' She gestured, as if momentarily lost for words. 'When I heard about the fire. . . . But I see my worries were unfounded.' She indicated the hut. It would appear you have other kind friends besides Mr Santana.' Her lips twitched in what seemed to Veryan a small, rather sad smile.

As she walked to the carriage, Chloe fought to maintain her composure. She had come because James had asked her. While she had been indulging in foolish reverie, imagining his request indicated an increasing interest in her concerns: *in her*: his real interest and concern were for Miss Polmear. And why not? He was unattached. So, presumably, was the young woman. She, on the other hand, was not. She should remember that, and be grateful for all the benefits of her comfortable lifestyle.

Her head felt strangely light. Blackness hovered at the edge of her vision. She raised a hand to her throat. There wasn't enough air.

'Begging your pardon, ma'am.' The senior coachman took her arm. She watched his lips moving and wondered why his voice sounded so far away. 'Are you all right? Gone white, you have.'

She touched her gloved fingertips lightly to her lips, swallowed the nausea, and nodded. On no account could she make an exhibition of herself. Gerald would be furious. In his opinion such behaviour, regardless of the circumstances, was a betrayal of one's class, and the height of bad manners. Her breath reversed sharply on a sob of laughter. Control was all. *And she was losing it.* Shock sobered her. She felt as fragile as an eggshell. She had thought, had really believed—

'My dear Chloe! You're as pale as a ghost.'

'Really, Loveday,' Diana Price-Ellis drawled. 'What do you expect? All this filth and poverty. And Chloe is far too soft hearted for her own good. Anyway, go on, what about Sarah Tremelling?'

Immeasurably relieved at being offered a ready-made excuse, and from the least likely source, Chloe sank back against the padded cream leather.

'My dear, I have it on the best authority. She's—' Suddenly remembering the coachman whose solid back was less than a yard away, Loveday leaned forward, her china-blue eyes alight with scandalized pleasure, and hissed, 'in an interesting condition.'

'Such carelessness will cost her dear.' With an irritated sigh, Diana adjusted deep folds of emerald satin trimmed with black velvet.

Chloe was startled, even though she had sensed in Loveday's manner connotations beyond those normally associated with such news.

'I don't understand. Why—'

Absently, as if Chloe were slow-witted, Diana patted her hand. 'The child is not her husband's.'

'How do you know?' She shouldn't have asked. No doubt it only confirmed her ignorance of matters that appeared to be common knowledge among their circle. But it was out now. And in truth, she was curious.

Diana rolled her eyes in amused impatience. 'George and Sarah haven't lived as husband and wife for years. His passion is food. Which probably accounts for his gout and all that weight. So once she'd done her duty and provided him with an heir and spare, it was understood that he would turn a blind eye, provided she was discreet.'

Loveday sucked in her breath, her eyes widening as a thought struck her. 'You don't think – surely she wouldn't have *wanted* – I mean, I know she's besotted with him, but—'

'No.' Diana was firm. 'Sarah always considered maternity tiresome, necessary to secure the title, but not an experience to be willingly repeated. I remember her saying she could not have borne being one of those middle-class wives.'

'What did she mean?' Chloe asked.

'They are nothing more than brood mares, my dear,' Loveday confided. 'Producing child after child, and quite likely dying in the process. All because they are too stupid and their husbands too selfish.'

Bewildered, Chloe stared at her. 'I'm sorry, I don't. . . .' She saw them exchange a look. 'Never mind.'

'A romantic liaison,' Loveday whispered, a gloved hand to her bosom, 'is about passion and excitement.'

'In such circumstances,' Diana took over, 'pregnancy would be at best a severe embarrassment, and at worst a disaster. So one is careful to avoid it.'

Curious to know more about an aspect of life of which she was totally ignorant, Chloe swallowed.

'How?'

Diana waved a languid hand. 'Vinegar.'

'What?' Not sure if she was being teased, Chloe looked from one to the other.

'Truly,' Loveday nodded. 'On a piece of soft sponge.' As Chloe tried desperately not to let them see her bafflement, Loveday glanced round and lowered her voice still further. 'Cut into the shape of a small ball with a narrow ribbon attached, it's very effective. If more women employed such a simple remedy, there would be fewer children deprived of a mother's loving care and fewer men left to bring up their large families by themselves.'

Diana's gaze was speculative. 'You didn't know?'

Realizing instantly that to lie was not only pointless, it might even be dangerous – one could never be quite sure about Diana – Chloe shook her head. But some instinct of self-preservation made her add, 'Not about that particular method.' She thought of the navvy women in the shanty village, sullen-faced and old before their time; and of the crying babies and whining toddlers. 'Why aren't women being told?'

'And given power over their own bodies?' Diana's throaty laugh made her jump. 'You are preaching sedition, my dear. Sexual pleasure is a *man*'s prerogative. Both the Church and the medical profession are appalled by the idea of women deriving similar enjoyment. Still,' – her smile left her eyes quite cold – 'it appears that you, like us, are among the fortunate.'

Loveday's gaze sharpened. And Chloe sensed, with an intuition honed over four years, the direction the conversation was about to take.

Calmly, Chloe returned her smile. 'I am blessed with a most considerate husband.'

'Oh yes,' Diana drawled. 'Married four years and still childless: that is consideration indeed.'

Loveday's intake of breath was almost silent, but Chloe heard it and lifted one shoulder in an elaborately casual shrug.

'I am only twenty.' She forced out words she prayed were true. 'There will be plenty of time for children.'

# Chapter Eleven

J AMES cantered past the ballast tip. He expected to see vast undulating mounds of crushed granite and men shovelling more from the long train of wagons hauled up that morning from the quarry at Penryn. But there were no wagons. Instead the men were scraping together what remained of the depleted heap. It contained barely enough ballast for two more days' work. *Where were the wagons?*

He passed carts returning to the tip for fresh loads of ballast, and gangs of men fixing rails to newly laid sleepers. Further on, a team of two horses dragged a wide metal and wood scraper heavily weighted with boulders to flatten the stone bed on which the rails would lie. Ordinarily, more rails and sleepers were delivered to the railhead each morning along track laid the previous day. A gang should be unloading and stacking them now. Where were they? James's irritation increased. This was Pascoe's responsibility, not his. Where *was* the contractor?

Up ahead he could see Paddy Maginn's gang working on the embankment. Reining in his sweat-darkened horse, he hailed the ganger in charge of the ballast crew.

'Has Mr Pascoe been by this morning?'

'Haven't seen him. Wagons coming, are they?'

After an instant's hesitation James called, 'They're probably on their way.'

'They better be,' the ganger bellowed, and the men leaned on their long iron bars and shovels, grunting agreement. 'Bleddy ridic'lous, it is. First bit o' dry weather we've 'ad fer weeks, and if they wagons don't come soon we're going to be sat 'ere with bugger-all to do.'

'Keep going as long as you can. I'll find out what's happening.' Wheeling his horse, James headed back the way he'd come, irritation darkening into anxiety and suspicion.

119

Back at the shanty village the tally shop was still closed and shuttered. The number of women waiting had increased, and they were
angry. Ignoring their shouts and demands to know what was happening, and why Pascoe hadn't come to open up, James examined
the door then turned to the watching women.

'Has anyone got a crowbar?'

Awe and excitement rippled through the crowd. One woman
offered a small chopper obviously used for cutting firewood.
Another, mocking that as a toy fit only for a child, dragged over an
axe with a handle three feet long and as thick as a man's wrist.
Warning them all to stand back, James took a swing, smashing the
lock and splintering the wood. Leaning the axe against the wall, he
pushed the door wide.

Light spilled in, illuminating the safe. For a moment James
hoped, but as he took a step forward, he realized it wasn't locked.
It wasn't even shut, opening easily as he grasped the handle. The
cash tins lay upside down on the top shelf: empty. His stomach
roiled queasily. Then, like a terrier shaking a rat, cold rage gripped
him. He had warned them, but they'd refused to listen. Now they
would expect, no *demand* he sort out the mess.

Taking a deep breath he deliberately set aside his seething anger.
If the contractor had absconded, and it certainly looked that way,
he would need a clear head and iron nerves, not to mention the
devil's own luck, if he was to prevent a riot and keep the men working. When he reappeared in the doorway, the women besieged him
with questions.

'Where's Pascoe?'

'How long have we got to wait here?'

'When's he coming to open the shop?'

James raised his arms to silence the clamour. Lies might be pointless, but the unvarnished truth would only cause panic. 'I can't tell
you.' He didn't add, *because I don't know*.

'Why not?'

'Some bleddy help you are.'

'We got no food.'

'What do we give our kids?'

'And the men?'

Uproar broke out again, and once more James raised his arms.
Waiting for the shouting to diminish to resentful mutters, he
looked for the woman who'd given him the axe. About forty, and

strongly built, she stood at the front with folded arms. He had a feeling she'd already guessed what had happened, but was waiting to see what he intended to do about it before reacting. She looked cleaner than many. But it was the frayed apron she wore over her faded blouse and dark skirt that decided him. Like Veryan Polmear, she had standards. He beckoned her forward.

'What's your name?'

'Mary Tallack. Why? What's it to you?'

'You'll see. Stand beside me.' As she did so, James addressed the restless crowd, 'As Mr Pascoe hasn't turned up yet, and you need food, I'm authorizing Mary Tallack to take his place. She will distribute whatever is in the shop according to need. Women with young children take priority.'

'Not here, they don't,' one woman yelled. 'Men can't work on empty bellies, and they're the ones earning the money.'

'You shut yer yap, Liza Mitchell,' another voice screeched back. 'Just 'cos you 'aven't got no kids.' A buzz of argument broke out.

James turned to Mary. 'You'll probably need some help. Just be wary—'

'Don't you fret, my 'andsome.' She smiled grimly. 'I've raised four sons. I don't put up with no nonsense.'

Unexpectedly, James felt himself grin. 'No. Right; as soon as you've chosen your assistants come round to the front.'

The women hooted and clapped as he knocked the padlocks off the shutters and the shop door.

'Here, mister,' a voice shouted, 'what about tickets?'

'No tickets today. To compensate for the inconvenience caused by Mr Pascoe's absence, your provisions will be free.' He paused, waiting for the whoops of approval and relief to die down. Then he added, 'Just remember, if there's any trouble I'll close the shop. It's a long walk to Penryn.'

His final glance at Mary answered by a reassuring nod, he swung himself into the saddle, masking a smile as he glimpsed Queenie, furious that she might be missing something, hurrying as fast as her bulk would allow towards the shuffling queue.

Handing his panting, sweat-lathered mount over to the ostler at the Royal Hotel, James walked quickly along Church Street to the Cornish Bank building.

'I trust this is important, Mr Santana.' Gilbert Mabey's normally good-natured face betrayed irritation as he took out his watch. 'I am expecting a very important client—'

James caught his elbow, drawing him aside. 'Have you seen Pascoe in the past few days?'

'Yes, as a matter of fact he was in here yesterday.'

'In here?' The sudden heaviness in James's stomach was reflect- ed in his voice.

'Yes. He came in to draw the wages. Why?'

'The end of the month is *next* week.'

'I didn't see him myself, I had someone with me, but all the paperwork was in order so I really don't see what—'

'I think Pascoe's done a bunk,' James said flatly.

'*What?*' Gilbert stared at him. 'No, he can't have. He wouldn't.' He glanced round, drew closer, his voice low, full of doubt, want- ing not to believe. 'How do you know?'

'No one has seen him this morning. The safe in his office is open and the cash tins are empty. But what's even more worrying, the ballast train hasn't arrived, nor have the rails and sleepers. Have any of you been checking the monthly accounts?'

Gilbert was ashen. 'What are you suggesting?'

'Isn't it obvious?' James controlled himself with an effort. 'Pascoe hasn't been paying the suppliers.'

Gilbert stared at him in horror. Then swallowed audibly. 'We–ah, we must—'

'An emergency meeting?' James suggested.

'Yes, yes. Good idea.' The bank manager's face was the colour of wet clay. 'I'll send a message to the others. At once.' He patted his pockets vaguely. 'I can't believe—'

*Why not? The signs were clear enough.* James bit back his frus- tration. 'Can I have Pascoe's address?'

Gilbert blinked. 'Yes. Yes, of course.' He snapped his fingers at a clerk. 'Maybe he's ill, maybe—?' At James's look he seemed to deflate. 'No. You warned us, but we didn't listen. And now. . . .'

Hiring a fresh horse, James wove through carriages, carts, and pedestrians, riding as fast as conditions permitted to Pascoe's lodg- ings in Penwerris Terrace.

'He went out last night and didn't come back,' James reported to the directors. After returning to the bank, a clerk had directed him to Harold Vane's offices. Once again he was sitting at the long table in the panelled conference room. Only this time, instead of bland dismissal or mild irritation, the directors' faces were etched with stunned disbelief.

'Does his landlady have any idea where he might have gone?' Ingram Coles pressed a spotless white handkerchief to his forehead and upper lip.

James shrugged. 'She said he mentioned Plymouth. But had no idea if he was going by train, or boat. He could be in London by now, or on his way abroad. He's gone, gentlemen.'

'I do hope you're not going to gloat, Mr Santana,' Victor Tyzack said quietly. Catching the deputy chairman's eye James glimpsed the man's realization that he would be perfectly entitled.

'No, no, I'm sure Mr Santana is far too much of a gentleman—' Ingram Coles waved his handkerchief.

'No one could have foreseen—' Gilbert Mabey began.

'Well, *we* certainly can't be held responsible.' Harold Vane's statement dared anyone to contradict.

'Spoken like a true solicitor,' James murmured, winning himself a murderous glare.

'Yes, but what are we going to *do*?' Clinton Warne's white collar was so stiff and high he appeared in real danger of cutting his own throat.

'Sir Gerald . . . the penalty clauses. . . .' Ingram Coles mopped his face again, shaking his head.

'Gentlemen, the steel company, the quarry, and the lumber mill *have* to be paid,' James stated quietly. 'Without rails, sleepers, and ballast the line cannot be completed. And men are owed a month's wages.'

'Fortunately they aren't due to be paid until next week.' Relief softened the lines of worry furrowing the chairman's face.

James glanced across the table and felt a twist of sympathy as Gilbert caught his eye.

Taking a deep breath, Gilbert announced, 'I'm afraid Pascoe drew that money out yesterday.' There was an instant's shocked silence, then pandemonium as accusations and counter-charges flew back and forth.

'Please, gentlemen, please.' Ingram Coles flapped ineffectually. 'This is getting us nowhere.' As the noise gradually subsided, he turned in mute appeal to his deputy.

'The suppliers' accounts must be settled with all possible speed,' Victor Tyzack was firm. 'I suggest we accompany payment with an explanatory letter and an apology on behalf of the company.'

'It wasn't *our* fault,' Clinton Warne grumbled.

'No,' Victor agreed. 'But we need their goodwill.'

'And a resumption of deliveries to the line by tomorrow,' James added.

'Well, all right, if we must, we'll pay the suppliers.' Harold Vane slapped one hand on the polished table. 'But that's all.'

'What do you mean, *that's all*?' Gilbert demanded. 'What about the men?'

'Legally, wages are the *contractor's* responsibility.'

'Yes, but Pascoe has—'

'I know what he's done, dammit.' Vane was testy. 'But if we stand fast, what can they do? Nothing.'

'You'll have a mutiny on your hands,' James warned.

'No, we won't. Oh, they'll complain, but they do that anyway. The difference is that this time they have something to complain about. But they won't leave. There's nowhere for them to go and no other work available. They'll get paid *next* month.'

James's nails dug deep into his palm, but he forced himself to appear calm. 'They might work without pay, but they certainly won't work without food.'

After an exchange of glances, there was general, if reluctant, agreement that extra funds should be allocated.

'Who will arrange purchase and distribution?' Clinton Warne asked. 'I can't possibly take on any more—'

'Who better than Mr Santana?' Harold Vane suggested with a bland smile. 'He will be on the line every day. He deals directly with the men. He's the obvious choice.'

About to protest that the contractor's flight would double his already heavy workload, and that in any case it wasn't his job, James bit his tongue as he remembered what Chloe said at their first meeting about people's attitudes to the navvies. She had been proved right on every point.

Not trusting himself to speak, he simply nodded to indicate his acquiescence. But Harold Vane hadn't finished.

'Someone will have to tell Sir Gerald. We must get the penalty clauses set aside. And as Mr Santana was so successful last time, I can't think of anyone more suited to the task.'

'Plead extenuating circumstances,' Gilbert advised.

'Acute shortage of available money,' the traffic manager

stretched his chin, revealing a red line where his collar rubbed.

'Completing the line must take priority where funding is concerned.' The deputy chairman held James's gaze. 'Otherwise *no one*, and that includes Sir Gerald, will retrieve a penny of their investment.'

'Indeed,' Ingram Coles nodded quickly. 'Like us, he took part of his fee in Railway Company shares.'

Leaving the meeting, James returned to the Royal Hotel, his muscles aching from the morning's hard ride. He was sweaty, grubby, and ravenous. While a bath was prepared he ate two helpings of beef stew. Then, clean and replete, his travel-stained clothes brushed and pressed, boots buffed to a mirror shine, he set off for Trewartha.

The interview would not be pleasant, but at least it gave him an above-board reason to visit the house and maybe see Chloe again – if she was there. Perhaps it would be better if she were not. For seeing her and Sir Gerald together, a couple. . . . James's mind sheered away from an image that tortured him with jealousy even though he knew the image to be false, a distortion of the truth.

Despite the amount on his mind, it would have been impossible not to notice the changes wrought by the few days of warm sunshine. Deep puddles had evaporated and water had drained from the cartwheel ruts. The hedgerows had suddenly burgeoned with lush greenery brightened by random patches of celandines and violets, cushions of primroses, and swathes of red campion. Tall stands of cow parsley reached for the sun with flower heads like white lace doilies, and hawthorn bushes scattered tiny petals like snowflakes.

He rode in the dappled shade of beeches and sycamores, past clumps of rhododendron bushes whose deep pink trumpet-like flowers were just starting to open. Entering Trewartha land, he rode through a carpet of bluebells that stretched across the park from the edge of the drive, surrounding elms, oaks and copper beeches like a fragrant rippling sea. Above the sighing wind he could hear blackbirds and robins, and the raucous squabbling of crows.

As he approached the front door, conscious of his boots crunching on the gravel, he was aware of an unusual tension beneath his ribs, and knew a moment's bitter amusement as he thought of all the reasons he might claim as its cause.

While he waited in the hall for the butler to return, he mentally rehearsed the points he hoped would persuade the baronet against pressing for compensation.

'This way, sir, if you please.' Opening the drawing-room door, the butler stood aside to let him pass.

Taking a breath, James walked into the sunlit room. As the door closed quietly behind him, formal words of greeting died unuttered, on his lips. Chloe sat alone, straight-backed, her hands clasped tight, at one side of the blazing fire. Despite the room's comfortable warmth, her face was devoid of colour except for plum shadows like bruises beneath each eye.

He hurried forward, his carefully prepared speech forgotten. 'What's wrong? Have you received bad news? Are you unwell?' He saw her throat work.

'Good afternoon, Mr Santana.' Her voice sounded husky and nasal, as if she were suffering from a cold. *Or had been crying.* 'I'm quite well, thank you.' Her cheek muscles twitched and her lips parted briefly, baring her teeth in what he realized with terrible compassion was an attempted smile. 'I'm afraid my husband isn't available right now. But as Hawkins said the matter was urgent, if you would care to leave a message with me—'

'Chloe, in God's name—' The words burst out, then he stopped. To press her would be tantamount to bullying. She was so tense she was practically vibrating, and her superficial calm was more unnerving than a scream. 'Forgive me. Concern is no excuse for bad manners.' He indicated a chair, facing hers but not too close. 'May I?'

Her brief nod was almost imperceptible. But, as he sat, her shoulders lost a little of their rigidity.

So, at least she was not anxious for him to leave. Nor did he intend doing so until he found out what was troubling her. But it would need extreme care.

'I only wish my visit was for a happier purpose. Though seeing you—'

'Please, Mr Santana, I have never sought compliments. And false ones demean both of us.'

'I swear to you' – he deliberately held her gaze – 'that I have never been more sincere.' He saw her eyes widen, saw confusion in their depths, and sensed he was a step closer. 'Seeing you makes the most difficult day easier to bear. And these are difficult days indeed.' As she searched his face warily, he forced his thoughts away from kissing her soft mouth, and tried to concentrate. 'I'm afraid the Railway Company is now without a contractor.' He watched it register.

'Why? What's happened?'

'Horace Pascoe has absconded with a large sum of money. Obviously this will have serious consequences for the line. The directors held an emergency meeting this morning, and I'm here to ask . . . Sir Gerald,' he could not bring himself to say *your husband*, 'not to press for compensation.'

'I'm so sorry.'

As he told her about the problems Pascoe had left behind, and the directors' refusal to pay the men, her hand crept to her mouth. 'But they can't *not* pay them.'

'Wages are the contractor's responsibility. So the directors are not legally bound—'

'You cannot support that argument.' Her passionate cry mingled horror with a plea for reassurance.

'I don't. But I have no voting rights, and mine was the only dissenting voice.'

'But what about the children?'

'Exactly. Look, I hesitate to ask as you've done so much already—'

'There's no question we will help. This is clearly an emergency. I will send messages to the committee this very afternoon.'

'Until I met you,' he said, 'navvies were simply the means by which my surveys and plans were transformed from figures and lines on paper into the reality of a railway track. But your generosity and your compassion have forced me to rethink my attitudes. My whole life has changed because of you.'

She stared at him, digging with unconscious savagery at the broken skin around her thumbnail. Then her tongue snaked out to moisten her lips.

'M–Miss Polmear told me of your great kindness to her. She is very appreciative of all you have done. The credit for that is yours alone.'

He shook his head. 'It's you who provided her with clothes and books.'

'At your request,' she reminded him. Looking down, she fingered the material of her skirts. 'She is looking forward with particular pleasure to your company when she visits the solicitor's office.'

'Oh Lord, I forgot.'

'*Forgot?*' she echoed.

'To tell them she'd been found. She has no proof of identity, you see. So I offered to vouch for her. It seemed the least I could do, as it was I who had brought the notice to her attention. But this business with Pascoe put it right out of my head.'

The bewilderment on her pale face evolved slowly into realization, and he sensed she was replaying certain scenes and conversations in the light of what he'd just said. Just as he glimpsed a dawning hope, she looked quickly away. Suddenly he understood. *She had thought he and Veryan Polmear....* The urge to take her in his arms was overpowering. He restrained himself, but the effort was considerable. He chose his words with great care.

'You have spoken to the young woman almost as often as I have. I'm sure you would agree she has many fine qualities. Let us both hope that someday soon she will be fortunate enough to meet a man worthy of her, someone with whom she can be truly happy.'

Chloe's eyes widened. 'You mean . . . it's *not*—?' The first faint touches of colour appeared along her cheekbones.

'No.' He was quietly firm. 'It never was. Never could be.'

Nibbling her lower lip, she averted her head.

An ormolu clock on the marble mantle struck the hour, reminding James of the responsibility now resting on him. Yet something had changed. It did not weigh quite as heavily as it had an hour ago. He leaned towards her.

'There is so much I want to discuss with you. But as soon as I've spoken to Sir Gerald I must—'

'He isn't here.' Her colour deepened. 'He's in Truro attending a business meeting. He wasn't sure if he would be back tonight. But the moment he returns I will tell him about Mr Pascoe. Though regarding the penalty clauses and so on, I think you, or one of the other directors, will need to speak to him personally.'

James rose to his feet, his mouth twisting. 'It will be me.' After a pause he said, 'I am staying at the Royal Hotel in Falmouth until I find permanent lodgings. Perhaps Sir Gerald could send word there when it's convenient for him to see me?'

She nodded. 'I should have offered you some refreshment.'

He smiled. 'Next time?'

They both moved towards the door. He reached it first and turned to face her. Her lashes fluttered down.

'Thank you for coming.' Her manner was formal, correct, but in her tone he detected relief and gratitude.

He waited, knowing courtesy demanded she offer her hand, understanding – probably better than she did – her reluctance. When she did, he held her fingers lightly for a moment, then lifted them to his lips.

He saw her breath catch; saw the warm wash of colour rise from her throat to her hairline as she turned her head away. Her mouth quivered and she began to tremble.

Moved beyond words, James covered her hand with his own.

'No,' she whispered, rigid.

He stood perfectly still, neither tightening nor loosening his hold. It had to be her choice. Watching her inner battle he suffered for her, biting his tongue so hard he tasted blood.

She looked up at him, shaking, agonized.

'This is wrong. I am married. I made my vows before God.'

'You live in his house. You bear his name. But you do not share his bed.'

He watched the colour drain from her face. She swayed, and reached blindly for a chair. He helped her sit then crouched beside her, still holding her hand. Her response spoke for itself.

'Is it so – have I – does it *show* in some way? I've been so careful—' Her fingers tightened convulsively. She looked up, her face gaunt with dread. 'Do other people know?'

He was tempted to deny it, purely to comfort her. But she had lived with lies for too long. Only the truth could free her. But the truth would hurt. He had to be gentle.

'No one can *know*, unless you've told them—'

'I haven't, I haven't.' She shook her head violently.

'But Chloe, there's more than a little *suspicion*—'

'Diana and Loveday,' she murmured.

He remained silent. The perplexing rumours Gilbert Mabey had mentioned could wait.

'How – how did *you* know?'

'Your eyes. Certain experiences change a woman. It's a change that shows in her eyes. You don't have that look. Your eyes, my sweet Chloe, are innocent. I see in them not cynicism or dissembling, but sadness, and a longing to be loved. And I do love you, Chloe, just as you love me.'

'Stop it. Please. It's impossible. I can't—' Pressing her fist to her mouth she shook her head.

'You love me, Chloe,' he stated quietly. He had never expected, hadn't imagined ever feeling like this. And as she raised exhausted, tear-bright eyes, he saw how the battle she'd been fighting with herself had taken her to the limits of her strength.

A deep sigh shuddered through her. 'Yes. But it makes no difference.' She stood up, porcelain pale but erect. 'I gave my word.'

He rose, facing her. 'Chloe, it's not a marriage, it's a sham.'

'I cannot leave him.' She tugged the bell-pull.

'I won't accept that.' His voice roughened and he tried to swallow the stiffness in his throat. 'You cannot continue with this charade. It is destroying your health.'

Her fragile composure cracked. 'I was managing until you came.'

'Were you? Was that why you were at the apothecary's? Because you are managing so well?'

'A tonic – the doctor suggested— I *was* managing. I knew no different. But now. ... Do you know what you've done?' Her voice was a strangled whisper. 'The cruelty? Showing me something I can never have?'

'Chloe, my dearest—'

'Shh.' She tensed, then drew a deep breath and folded her hands. The door opened. 'Hawkins, will you ask Nathan to bring Mr Santana's horse, please?'

The butler bowed and retreated, leaving the door open. Chloe walked out into the hall. James's hat and gloves lay on a side table. She stopped beside them, avoiding his eye, and spoke for anyone who might be listening.

'Food will be delivered to the shanty village as soon as arrangements can be made: certainly no later than the day after tomorrow.'

'You'll come yourself?' He wanted to lift her in his arms, put her on his horse, and carry her away forever from this elegant, soulless house of lies. 'I'm sure the men and their families would welcome the opportunity to show their appreciation.'

'I – ah—' She turned her head, and he realized she was trying to blink away tears before they spilled over and betrayed her.

He couldn't leave her. *He couldn't stay.* 'Please?' Sensing the butler's flicker of surprise he forced jovial concern into his voice. 'You really should. Your committee will want confirmation that their gifts are going where they are most needed.'

'I'm sure Lady Diana and Mrs Hosking will come if their other engagements permit. Apparently they were much impressed by their last visit.' Her wry tone almost disguised the tremor in her voice. 'On the journey home they talked of little else.' She walked to the open front door and stood waiting, leaving him no alternative but to leave.

'I'm sorry you had a wasted journey, Mr Santana. But rest assured, even if I am not here, my husband will be told of your visit the moment he returns.'

Those words, and their implication, echoed in his mind long after he had left Trewartha land.

# Chapter Twelve

'WHAT the 'ell d'you call this?' Nipper stared at the contents of his bowl. 'Where's the veg? Where the meat? There's nothing 'ere but potatoes and gristle.'

'And dumplings,' Veryan pointed out. 'You've got the same as everyone else.'

'This isn't *food*, it's just slop. I seen dishwater wi' more meat in it.'

'I can only cook what's available.'

'How's a man s'posed to work without proper food in his belly?'

'Stop your moaning,' Queenie snapped from her chair by the beer barrels. 'If I hadn't stood in that bleddy queue for hours, all you'd have is bleddy nettle soup. So just shut up, all right? Bleddy Pascoe. If I got my hands on him, he'd know what for.'

'What about our money?' Mac fretted. 'If they're not going to pay us—'

'It's all that engineer's fault,' Yorky growled. 'Ever since he came–'

'How can it be his fault?' Tom showed rare impatience. 'It wasn't him who ran off with the money. Would you have had the nerve to come on the line like he did this afternoon, and tell us what had happened? No, you wouldn't. If it wasn't for him, we'd still be in the dark. You can't say the man 'aven't got guts.'

'Listen, you lot,' Queenie interrupted, 'I been thinking.'

'Dear life,' someone groaned. 'What now?'

She could not have missed the sighs and mutters but chose to ignore them. 'Seeing you aren't going to get paid this month, I'll give you tickets for your board and beer.'

'Oh aye?' Mac's dour face was even more gloomy than usual. 'And how much extra will that cost us?'

'Nothing *extra*. I aren't greedy. No, I won't ask no more than the ten per cent Pascoe charged. That's fair, isn't it? After all, it's my money, and my risk. And I still got to pay the brewery. So I reckon you're doing all right. But I'm warning you now: all tickets are to be paid off the day you get your wages. Anybody don't like it, they know what they can do.'

'Some choice,' Paddy grumbled, and the queue shuffled forward.

During their meal the men continued to discuss Pascoe's disappearance and the likely repercussions. Even after they finished eating, they were still so absorbed they virtually ignored Veryan when she began collecting the dirty dishes. As Queenie levered herself out of her chair and disappeared out to the latrine before the evening's drinking started, Veryan carried half the bowls to the small table to be washed up. Picking up the rest, Tom followed her.

'Can I see you later?' He kept his voice low and his back to the men. 'There's something—'

'No.' She felt aggrieved that he so obviously wanted to hide the fact he was speaking to her. She knew it was irrational, and the knowledge increased her confusion and her anger. She wasn't even sure who she was angry with: herself or him. 'I promised Davy a story.' Head bent she plunged the bowls into hot water. First he deliberately ignored her; now all of a sudden he wanted— What exactly did he want? *Don't let Queenie be right.*

'Ah. Tell you what, how don't I come and listen? I wouldn't mind—'

'No, that's Davy's special time. He gets little enough attention. I don't—'

'Oh yes, what's going on here, then?' Queenie demanded, loud and sickeningly coy, as she collapsed with a grunt into her chair. Immediately the men looked round.

Veryan flushed. 'Nothing.' She glared at Tom who shrugged and returned to his seat amid muttered warnings.

'Wasting your time there, boy.'

'Mad, are 'e? What do 'e want with a bitch like she?'

'I wouldn't touch it with yours.'

'Better not turn your back on 'er.'

Flame-faced, Veryan kept her head down. As soon as she had finished, she headed for the door.

'Told you, didn't I?' Queenie hissed with malevolent delight.

'You don't get nothing for free. When a man do you a favour, he want twice as much back.'

'What a nasty suspicious mind you have.'

'Think so? We'll see.' Smug and gloating, Queenie settled herself.

Veryan left the shanty without a backward glance.

An hour later, as Davy's head drooped and she felt him slump against her, she closed the book.

'Come on, time you were in bed.'

He struggled up, bleary-eyed and blinking in the lamplight. 'Can I have another one? I'm not tired, honest.'

Setting the heavy book beside her on the blanket, she cupped his small face between her hands and shook her head. 'Davy Thomas, you need twigs to prop your eyes open.'

'Go on, just a short one? You read lovely.'

Laughing, she shook her head. 'And you—' *have the charm of the devil*. A knock on the door made them both jump. And she realized that she had been half dreading, half expecting it.

'Who's that?' Davy whispered, his eyes huge.

'I can't see through the door.'

Rolling his eyes, Davy pushed her arm. 'Ask, then.'

'Who is it?' she called, knowing already.

'Tom.'

She was about to say *Tom who*, just to make a point, but Davy had scrambled off the bed and was already pulling back the bolt. 'You should've come sooner.' He grabbed the big hand and pulled the man inside. Previously cosy, the hut now felt much too small. 'Veryan been reading me a story—'

'She has? Like stories, do you?' Tom ruffled the boy's hair.

Davy nodded. 'Ask her to read us another one. Go on. Please?'

She glanced from the child's face, where eagerness battled with exhaustion – and lost – to the man's. Tom's brows lifted a fraction. He grinned wryly, and waited.

Reluctantly she shook her head. She would have liked to keep Davy with her, at least until Tom went. But her own selfishness disgusted her. How could she even contemplate using the child as a barrier? 'Not tonight, Davy. You're out on your feet. Shall I take you back—?'

'No!' The boy hitched up his too-large trousers, glowering. 'I aren't a babby. Any case, you know what'd happen if me da catch me with you.'

She nodded. 'I'll leave the door open so you can see your way across. I don't want you tripping over and hurting that ankle again.'

With a shrug intended to show he wasn't scared of the dark, Davy snatched up his torn jacket and shoved his bare feet into the broken-down boots. 'See you tomorrow, Tom.'

'Mind you go straight to sleep now.'

Veryan watched him scamper across the open ground to his own shanty. Standing in the open doorway, she listened intently. But there was no roar of anger, no drunken demand to know where he'd been. Either William was already in a drunken stupor, or he hadn't returned home yet.

With a sound like a sigh, rain began to fall, pattering onto the muddy ground. Aware of Tom close behind her she felt edgy and darted a sidelong glance at him.

''Tis only a shower.' Hands in his pockets, shoulders hunched, he peered past her. 'There was another one earlier. Didn't you hear it? Quite heavy it was.'

Just for an instant she wondered. Nervous? Tom Reskilly? A man who, the first time she'd met him on the path, had given the impression he didn't just think – he *knew* – himself God's gift to women? Her hand on the bolt, she turned to face him. But he didn't give her the chance to speak.

'Look, I know you said I shouldn't come.' He stood, strong and solid as a granite slab.

'So why did you?'

He shrugged. 'I thought, if you didn't mind, like, I could have a look at the books you got from Lady Radclyff. I like a good story.' His gaze wavered, then dropped to the wrinkled canvas. 'I'll see if I can find a bit better piece. This don't fit proper. But I wanted to get something down quick.'

Veryan looked at his bent head. His hair was wet and dishevelled. He must have been outside during the earlier shower. Near the crown a small tuft stuck up at an angle. It reminded her of Davy. She caught herself. This was no vulnerable child: Tom Reskilly was a grown man: *a silver-tongued charmer*. He knew what he was doing. Suspicion snaked through her.

'Is this supposed to be a joke?'

He seemed thrown. 'What?'

'Was it your idea? Or did the men put you up to it? What was the bet? I suppose they're drinking themselves silly while they wait for you to go back and—'

'No!' His anger shocked her. 'It's not – I wouldn't—' He snatched the book from the blanket and brandished it at her. She recoiled. 'I want to learn to read, all right?'

Flushed, he dropped the book and turned away, rubbing one hand over his unshaven jaw with a dry rasping sound. She had never seen him lost for words. He swung round on her. 'You think I'm just like the rest of them. All right, so I like a drink and a laugh. But that's not all I am, no more than you're just a slave for that old besom, Queenie Spargo.'

Closing the door on the blowing rain, Veryan leaned back against her hands. 'So why did you—?'

'Lie?' He snorted impatiently. 'Bleddy obvious, isn't it? Because I thought you'd laugh at me.' He gestured, shamefaced. 'Sorry, I shouldn't've swore. . . .'

Still wary, she was also curious. 'Why?'

'Why what?'

'Why do you want to learn to read? I mean, why now?'

'Last line I was on I didn't get paid. Now, that bastard Pascoe 'ave run off with my money. I tell 'e straight, maid, I'm pi— I'm fed up tramping round the country for jobs like these. I know I can do better.' He paused. 'It's like the engineer. . . .' He looked down, picking at a scab on one of his knuckles.

She tensed. 'What about him?'

'People respect a man like that. You do. I seen the way you look at him.'

She didn't believe it. 'You want to learn to read because of *me*?'

'Isn't that a good enough reason, then?' He grinned. 'You're right though; it isn't the only one. Like I told you, my 'andsome, I want to better myself. But I got to be able to read, and sign my name proper.'

Bemused, Veryan spread her hands. 'Look—'

'Still, if you don't want to teach me, I'll find someone else.'

'Not on the works, you won't.'

He shrugged. 'I could ask Lady Radclyff. She's bound know someone.'

'Fine. Ask her then.'

'I would, only she isn't here and I want to start now. Look, I see you every day. So don't it make better sense for you to do it? Go on, maid,' he urged.

She knew she owed him, not just for rebuilding the hut, but for all the extras like the bed and the canvas on the floor. *And stopping the men's insults? Saving her on the embankment? Beating William Thomas?*

'Come on, girl. I'm a quick learner, and I got a good memory. Tell you what' – he pointed upward – 'that tarpaulin isn't going to last long. An easterly gale will rip 'n right off the timbers. Tar and felt is what you need. See if I can get some, shall I?'

How could she say no? And if she accepted, how could she refuse to teach him? 'All right. Thank you.'

'You don't 'ave to thank me. 'Tis a fair swap.' Wiping his hand on his trousers, he held it out. Though scarred and calloused, it was clean. She could smell soap. 'This is 'ow the gentry do deals, isn't it? On a 'andshake?'

'Yes, but it's not necessary,' she blurted. He had gone to the trouble of washing before coming to see her. 'I trust you to keep your word.'

'And so I shall. But I want to be certain you'll keep yours.'

'How dare you! Of course I will.'

He turned his palm and cocked an eyebrow.

It was only a handshake. *Why did he stir up such confusion?* Irritated, she took his hand intending the contact to be a fleeting formality, but as they touched, something leapt inside her. Her shock must have shown for his grin faded. Pulling free she brushed off the front of her dress. He wasn't the only one with ambitions. She had plans too: plans that could not include him. He might be – *was* – different from the other navvies, but for all his grand ideas he would be on the line forever. And that was a future she refused even to contemplate.

'So—' She cleared her throat. 'When would you want to start?'

He shifted from one foot to the other, then grinned. 'Now?'

She glanced round the hut in dismay. About eight feet square, the blissful privacy made it seem almost spacious when she was alone. His presence made it feel like a cupboard. 'You mean – here?'

'You got a better idea?'

She chewed her lip. He was right. The shanty offered only noise, taunts and ridicule for both of them. 'You'd better sit down. That end.' She pointed to the foot of the bed.

As he lowered himself, legs akimbo, she crouched in front of the wooden box and took out paper, pen and a bottle of ink.

'We'll start with the alphabet. You have to be able to recognize letters before you can read words.'

Eighteen hours later Tom swung his pick, felt it bite into the stony soil, twisted it loose, and swung again. Between white-painted posts that marked the intended line, Nipper, Mac and himself were excavating a gullet for the wagons that would carry the earth away. Behind them the rest of the gang shovelled the loose muck into carts.

The sun was high and hot. There was a breeze, but the steep sides of the little cutting prevented it from reaching them. Tom blinked as sweat stung his eyes. His shirt hung open at the front, and clung to his back. Wiping his forehead with the back of a grimy hand, he resettled his cap then swung the pick once more. Beside him, Nipper leaned on the haft and groaned.

'I need a drink. 'Tidn right, expecting a man to work in this heat *and* pay for his own beer. So where was you last night then?'

'Out.' Tom resumed the easy efficient rhythm that kept the men behind him busy. Sweat trickled down his chest and soaked into the waistband of his trousers.

'I know that, don't I,' Nipper scoffed. 'You wad'n in, so you had to be out. But *where*? Bleddy 'ell, what's on 'ere, then? Think they might be looking for a bit o' rough?'

Alerted by Nipper's lascivious tone, Tom glanced round. The rest of the gang had stopped work to stare at the two women who had appeared at the top of the cutting. One, in a gown of garnet red and a jaunty hat of feathers and ribbons, had walked right to the edge and was gazing boldly down.

'Get back.' Tom waved. 'It's not safe.'

'Shut up,' Yorky hissed. 'If she fall, I want to be underneath.'

Tom turned to Nipper, letting his pick drop. 'Where's Paddy?'

'Dunno. Here, where you going?'

Clambering past the leering men, Tom caught Davy by the shoulder. 'Unhitch one of the horses and find Mr Santana. He's somewhere on the line.' He turned back to the grinning men. 'Hey, watch your mouths. Show a bit of respect.'

'That's no' what they want tae see,' Mac muttered. 'Look at that tall one, If that's no' brazen. . . .

'Dear life, she's coming down!' Excitement rippled through the gang.

Behind the woman in red, now picking her way down the slope on the rough but shallow path used by the carts, Tom saw another approach the one watching. Tom recognized the fair hair and slim figure of Lady Radclyff. She laid her hand on the other's forearm, apparently pleading. But the restraint was shaken off and, clutching an open parasol in one hand, and a handful of buttercup satin skirt in the other, her giggling companion teetered down the slope.

Looking both ways as if for help, Lady Radclyff clearly didn't know what to do.

Taking the shortest route and avoiding the other two women, Tom hauled himself up the side of the cutting.

As he appeared over the lip she gasped, her hand flying to her mouth.

'Sorry, ma'am,' he panted, touching his cap. 'Didn't mean to frighten you.'

Pale-faced and anxious, she tried to smile. 'Do you know where Mr Santana might be? We. . . .' She indicated an open carriage and a flat bed cart piled with bulging sacks and wooden crates. 'We've brought food.'

'That's some good of you, ma'am. I sent a boy—' Hearing drumming hooves Tom looked past her. 'That's him now.' Leaning forward in the saddle, the engineer came up the grassy incline at a gallop.

'Thank you, Mr—'

'Reskilly. Tom Reskilly, ma'am.' He could tell she wasn't listening. She seemed even more nervous: twisting her fingers. She wasn't pale now. From the lace at her throat right up to her hat her skin was rosy. *So that's the way of it.*

James jumped down, breathless, and whipped off his hat. It left a red mark on his forehead. 'Lady Radclyff, this is a most pleasant surprise.'

'I do hope we have not inconvenienced you. We've brought food for the shop.'

'So I see. How very kind.'

'But before delivering it to the village my companions wanted to see the line. They' – she swallowed – 'they were most insistent. I fear I was unable to dissuade them.'

Perplexed, James glanced round. 'Where—'

As Chloe indicated the lip of the cutting, Tom snatched off his cap and, crushing it in his big hands, he stepped forward.

'Fetch, 'em back up, shall I?'

'That's very kind of you, Mr Reskilly,' Chloe answered with palpable relief.

'No trouble, ma'am.' He ducked his head. 'I 'spec' they seen everything they want to by now.' *And maybe more than they had bargained for.* He received a nod of approval from James Santana who then turned to Lady Radclyff. The look they exchanged confirmed Tom's guess that there was more going on between them than charity. He felt a pang of envy. Not for *her*. He liked and admired her, but that was all. His envy was for the engineer: for the way she looked at him, even though she pretended she wasn't.

Sliding down into the excavation he compared Lady Radclyff's sweetness and vulnerability with Veryan's prickly independence. A man *needed* to feel protective. It was part of who he was; what he was for. But defending Veryan was like trying to look after a wild cat: you had to watch out for the claws. He grinned to himself. He'd tame her yet.

The woman in red stood at the bottom of the slope and gazed around with disdainful amusement. Below her in the earth and rubble of the excavation, the gang rested their picks and leaned on their shovels, watching. Though she appeared totally oblivious to the crude comments and guffaws of laughter, her companion clearly was not. Standing some way behind, she looked hot and flustered. And though she was still giggling, Tom could see it was from unease. Serve her right. These were working men, not freaks like those on show at the travelling fair. He skidded to a halt a few feet away. Both women looked round.

He touched his cap. 'Mr Santana says—'

'Does he indeed?' As the men whooped and crowed, Diana Price-Ellis's bold gaze swept over him. 'And you are . . .'

*Time someone taught you a lesson, my 'andsome.* Tom never turned down a challenge. Studying her with equal boldness, he caught the flash of excitement in her eyes. *A bitch in heat.* He strolled towards her, hooking his thumbs in his waistband. 'Name's Tom, what's yours?'

'My name is none of your business.'

'What? You come all the way out here to see me, and you won't even tell me your name?' He shrugged heavily muscled shoulders and winked at her. 'Still, who needs names?'

'What do you do, Tom?'

He grinned. 'Tell me what you like and I'll do it.'

There was a chorus of crudity from the watching men.

'Diana,' her companion called with a nervous giggle, 'I really think we should—'

'It's all right, Loveday.' She waved languidly. 'He's just trying to shock me, aren't you, Tom?'

'That would be a waste of time, wouldn't it: a *lady* like you.' His roguish grin drew a small collusive smile. Then she met his eye and read the contempt there. He glimpsed the flicker of uncertainty, instantly covered. He heard the men's intake of breath as she took a step closer, touched her gloved index finger to his bare chest then passed it under her nose, inhaling as if she were testing an expensive perfume. He'd heard about women like her: women who went, masked, to bare-knuckle prize-fights and offered themselves as reward to the winner.

'Careful, lady,' he warned softly.

'Am I in danger then, Tom?' She was goading him, daring him, knowing full well – as he did – that if he laid so much as a finger on her it would cost him his job.

'Not from me, lady. But this lot' – he jerked his thumb towards the men who had inched closer, their rank odour thick and oppressive in the still air of the cutting – 'they'll take anything.'

'Are you threatening me?'

'Why would I do that?'

'Diana—'

Tom turned. 'Shall I see you back up to the top, ma'am?'

'Yes. Please,' Loveday said gratefully. 'It's so hot down here.' She dabbed her face with a lace handkerchief. 'How do you stand it?'

'We're used to it, ma'am. 'Sides, it do make a nice change from weeks of rain.' Behind him one of the men deliberately hawked and spat while others mimicked him in mincing tones. He ignored them. Five years from now they would still be eating pig swill and sweating their guts out for pennies. He'd be long gone by then. He offered his arm and, handing him her parasol – which provoked an explosion of mirth from the avidly watching gang – she took it, gathering her skirts with her free hand. She glanced over her shoulder.

'Diana—'

'Oh, go along, Loveday.'

'I'm sure one of the other men would—'

'Don't be absurd.' Her retort frosted the humid air.

As they reached the top, Loveday thanked Tom prettily. Then, retrieving her parasol, she hurried towards Lady Radclyff.

'Chloe, you would not believe—'

Tom found himself facing James Santana.

'Where—?'

He indicated the slope.

'No trouble, I hope?'

Tom shrugged. 'There might be.'

'Oh? Why? I told her I wasn't interested.'

The engineer's sharp look was followed by a brief nod. He understood. Navvies, with their powerful muscular bodies and unconventional lifestyle, had always attracted bored society women who liked to embroider the encounters and relate them as amusing dinner conversation. As the plumed and ribboned garnet hat appeared, Tom and James exchanged an expressionless glance, then the engineer walked forward to offer assistance.

Glancing back at Lady Radclyff and her friend Loveday, Tom touched his cap then slithered back down to the stinking humidity and Nipper's lascivious questions.

# Chapter Thirteen

'I KNOW who I am, Mr Lumby.' Agitation made Veryan's heart thump and she could feel her cheeks burning. James Santana had warned her to expect scepticism, but the attorney's arrogant disbelief was little short of insult. 'Why else would I have come?'

Elbows on his massive desk, the tall attorney placed his fingertips together and looked down his great beak of a nose. 'And why *did* you come?'

She glanced at James Santana for reassurance then back again. 'Because the notice in the paper asked me to.'

'Young woman, you would be astonished at the number of people claiming to be someone they're not.'

'But I'm not doing that.'

'How can I be sure?' The attorney radiated disapproval. 'How do I know you are the person you say you are? Your appearance is not what one would expect of the person you claim to be.'

Veryan's flush deepened and her chin rose. 'I am aware of that. My circumstances—'

'The law requires proof.'

'And I've already explained: all my possessions were lost in the fire. Mr Santana will confirm—'

The attorney turned to James. 'Mr Santana, did you have personal knowledge of these possessions?'

'No.' Veryan answered before he could answer. 'He did not. What I meant was that he could confirm there was a fire, and that my hut was destroyed, along with everything in it.'

'Leaving aside the question of how – having no prior knowledge of the contents he could offer such confirmation – the fact that a fire occurred is not sufficient reason for me to waive the need for evidence.' The attorney shook his head, his smile cold and humourless. 'That is not the way the law works.'

She swept him with a gaze. Superbly tailored in black morning coat, striped trousers and stiff white collar, he was immaculately groomed. His chin was closely shaved, his white hair parted on the side and curling in front of his ears, and he smelled faintly of cologne. Judging by his thick gold cuff links, his ornate fob watch and heavy signet ring with its single diamond he was a wealthy man. And his professional standing was the result of a first-class education.

She had been trembling with nerves when James escorted her into the lavishly appointed office. And the attorney's intimidating manner had threatened to overwhelm her. But her awe and uncertainty had been edged aside by indignation. He was just another bully. But she was used to men like him. How dare he assume she was an impostor?

'So how does it work in a case like this, Mr Lumby? I have no documents to show you, and I've explained why. What do I do now?'

The attorney stiffened. His lips thinned, and the area around his aquiline nostrils turned white. Clearly unused to challenge, especially from a woman, and particularly one as young as she, he was speechless.

'We thought,' James suggested quietly, 'perhaps a sworn statement?' He had discussed with her the difficulty of proving her identity before they entered the building housing the attorney's office.

After walking from the shanty village to the line she had hitched a ride to Penryn on one of the flat-bed wagons, then walked to Falmouth. Her route had taken her past Turnpike creek to Penwerris, along Greenbank, down High Street to the noisy junction and quay at Market Strand.

The sight of James waiting on the wide steps of the Royal Hotel had banished the discomfort of her rubbed, aching feet. Acutely aware of the mud and stains around the hem of her dress, of ill fitting underwear that clung, damp with perspiration, and of her untidy hair, she had blushed as she self-consciously tucked back loose tendrils from her neck and temples.

The attorney blew down his nose. 'Without corroborating evidence I cannot see—'

'If Miss Polmear gives information about her parents which could only be known by close family,' James suggested, 'surely that would establish her identity beyond question?'

Edward Lumby drummed his fingertips on the leather-framed blotter. 'It might help,' he conceded ungraciously. He picked up a small silver bell from one corner of his desk and gave it a brief imperious shake. The door opened to reveal a short, round, balding clerk. So quick was the response Veryan wondered if the clerk had been standing waiting for the summons.

But in that case, it meant the attorney had intended, *even before they arrived*, that she should make a sworn statement. So why had he been so obstructive?

The clerk peered over pince-nez that sat slightly askew on his pug nose. Anxiety had scored deep grooves between his sparse brows and around a mouth that wanted to smile but wasn't sure if it should. Knowing what that was like, she felt a twinge of sympathy.

'Bellis, this young woman wishes to swear an affidavit in support of a claim on the Hatfield estate.' He eyed Veryan sternly. 'Mr Bellis is a notary. He will take a statement from you, which you will then sign under oath. This will be passed on to the family for examination.'

*The family.* 'Would it not be simpler for me to meet them myself?' Veryan suggested. 'Then all this—'

'Certainly not! The very idea.'

'But—'

'Don't argue with me, young woman.'

Chagrin made Veryan's skin prickle as she flushed.

'As executors charged with administering the estate of the late Mrs Hatfield, all matters pertaining thereto are the responsibility of this firm. The family made it quite clear that they have no wish for any contact with legatees of whom they have no personal knowledge. Veryan Polmear is one such legatee. Now kindly go with Mr Bellis. Your statement will be passed on to the family. *If –*' he weighted the word with doubt – 'they consider it worthy of further investigation you will receive a letter to that effect. As Mr Santana has taken it upon himself to support your claim, no doubt he will find time to read it to you.'

'Miss Polmear,' James stated firmly, 'is quite capable of reading any correspondence for herself.'

'Indeed.' It sounded noncommittal but Veryan knew he believed James was bluffing. 'And where should it be sent?'

She tensed. There was no mail delivery to the shanty village.

'To the Royal Hotel,' James said smoothly. 'Care of myself. With your permission, Miss Polmear?'

Relief and gratitude brought quick tears to her eyes. She swallowed. 'Thank you, Mr Santana. You are very kind.'

'If you'll excuse me.' Edward Lumby stood up. 'I have pressing matters to attend to.' From his tone and manner it was plain he considered their visit an irritating waste of time.

Taking her cue from James, Veryan rose and started towards the door and the waiting clerk. Then she turned back.

'May I ask one question, Mr Lumby?'

'Well?' He frowned impatiently.

'What exactly has my grandmother left me?' She was more curious than expectant. A small piece of jewellery perhaps? Some token of her mother's childhood? She watched his mouth purse and feared he was going to refuse to tell her. Then the words fell, terse and disapproving, into the silence.

'Veryan Polmear, if she is found, is to receive the sum of five hundred pounds.'

Veryan felt James take her arm and, head swimming, she was led out to another much smaller office.

An hour later, her statement duly signed and witnessed, she walked out, still dazed, into the brightness and noise of Church Street. Standing on the wide pavement as carts and carriages clopped past, and people hurried by intent on their own business, she was still struggling to believe it. *Five hundred pounds.*

'Let me be the first to congratulate you on your good fortune.' The warmth in James Santana's voice made her heart swell. She swung round to face him.

'All thanks to you. If you hadn't seen the notice, and then gone to the trouble of telling me. . . . Many would not have bothered. And then arranging the appointment.' She knew she was babbling but couldn't stop. Too much had happened too quickly. 'That awful man! You'd have thought it was *his* money. How *dare* he try to browbeat me.'

'He didn't succeed though.' James grinned.

Pressing one hand hard against her ribs as if to still the upheaval beneath, she rubbed it with the other. 'How can I thank you? Ever since that day on the path, d'you remember? You've shown me such . . . warmth.'

He lifted one shoulder, seeming slightly uncomfortable. 'I just happened to be— Really, such thanks are unnecessary.'

'No, don't,' she begged. 'Don't say it was nothing. There isn't much kindness around a navvy village, especially for someone who doesn't fit in.' Tom Reskilly's face appeared in her mind. *No.* She felt perspiration break out on her skin. Her heart began to race. 'I am so grateful. I can hardly believe all the trouble you've gone to on my behalf.'

Frowning, visibly disconcerted, he seemed about to speak then stopped and looked away. He was too modest, Veryan decided, too self-effacing. She felt a rush of . . . what? She was so jumpy, her emotions so tangled, she didn't *know* what she felt.

His mouth widened in a hearty smile. 'And why not? It was obvious to me, and to Lady Radclyff, that you were – are – different from the other women. If the little I have done has been helpful to you, that is reward enough.' She would have spoken, but he gave her no chance. 'I have no doubt within a very short time your good fortune will be confirmed. Then you will be free to leave the line and go where you will. I only wish—' He shook his head and turned aside, gazing first at the pavement, then down the street. He seemed, indeed she sensed, he was waiting, *wanting* her to ask.

'What?' She could hardly breathe, and every nerve was tight with anticipation. 'What do you wish?'

He looked at her now. But instead of the warm intimacy she had so hoped for, his gaze held diffidence and compassion. Apprehension clutched at her with icy fingers.

'I wish my own future held as much promise. Still, as the demands of my job appear to be increasing each day, I shall have little time to feel sorry for myself.'

Staring at him she felt hope drain away like melting snow. 'I don't understand.' She forced the words out. 'What do you mean?'

'I have lost my heart,' he confided, 'to someone not free to return my affection.'

Despite the churning shock and disappointment, and the drenching scarlet heat of embarrassment, she found his small, helpless shrug unexpectedly moving. Her painful laugh never reached her lips. She touched his arm. 'I—' *I know how you feel.* 'I'm so sorry.'

'Now it's you who are kind.' He inhaled deeply then smiled, and his relief provoked a tiny stab of hurt. 'And now I hope you'll forgive me, but I have to get back to work.'

'Of course,' she said quickly. 'I really am grateful—'

He raised a hand, softening the gesture with a smile. 'You've thanked me enough.' He paused. 'Will you treat what I told you as a confidence? For myself it does not matter, but—'

'Of course.' Who did he think she would tell? In any case it was a bitter-sweet secret she didn't want to share with anyone.

'I'm sorry. I didn't mean to suggest—'

'I know. It's all right. Really.'

'As soon as I receive the letter—'

'Yes. Thank you. 'Bye.' A final bright smile and she turned away.

'Wait! How are you getting back?'

She shrugged. 'The same way I came. Walking.'

He took a coin from his pocket and pressed it into her palm. 'Take a cab to Penryn station. You might be in time to get a lift on one of the extra ballast wagons.'

'Th—' She stopped as he wagged a finger.

'Go on.'

She went, clutching the coin. So, James Santana loved a lady who wasn't free. No prizes for guessing who. The stab of jealousy was sharp. Then she realized; though she admired and liked the engineer, it wasn't *him* she had yearned for, it was what he represented – *escape*. But now she would be independent. That money was her ticket out of the village and into a new life.

Back at the shanty Queenie's incessant questions rasped her nerves until they were raw and quivering. Queenie was determined to find out where she had been and why. But Veryan was equally determined not to tell her.

The interrogation shifted between cajolery, demand, and threat, a battle of wills suspended only when the men arrived back from the line. Veryan knew it wasn't over. The coercion and browbeating would resume at the first opportunity. But this time, no matter what the cost, she had to remain silent.

She wanted to be far away before news of her legacy finally leaked out. It wasn't just that Queenie would immediately demand a share of the money: what really terrified her was Queenie's threat, if she ever tried to leave, to make public her part in the gypsy's death. There would be plenty of people willing to listen, willing to believe she had killed him deliberately. And how could she prove otherwise?

With so much on her mind she prepared the meal and did her chores like an automaton, hardly aware of the men except for a brief moment of gratitude when she realized that whatever they were talking about had caught Queenie's interest and diverted attention away from herself. Tom spoke to her and she started, trying to focus. He wasn't exactly frowning, but seemed slightly anxious. He seemed to be the butt of envious taunts, but before she had gathered her scattered wits he bellowed at the men to shut up. In the uproar of laughter and jeering that followed she thought he asked if she was all right. So she nodded, and continued dishing up the meal.

She had done without so many things and worked so hard to save up the few pounds she had in the Savings Bank. While she waited for the family to confirm the legitimacy of her claim, she could use that money to buy herself a new dress or some underclothes: things no one else had worn.

*And wear them here in the village?* It didn't require a lot of imagination to picture the response of the other women. But where else was there? She could go into Falmouth, and browse in the shops like a lady of leisure. She could visit a tea-shop and sit at a table by herself: a table covered by a glistening damask cloth. There would be fine china with a delicate pattern and maybe a tiny vase of fresh flowers. There would be dainty sandwiches, rich crumbly scones, and a choice of feather-light cakes and pastries. And a waitress would ask her what she would like, then bring it to her on a tray.

She didn't expect to be idle. Five hundred pounds sounded like a fortune, but she would have to find somewhere to live as well as feed and clothe herself while she looked for work. What she would really like to do was teach. But without references what chance did she have? Her background was far too complicated to explain. And anyway, who would entrust their children to an ex-navvy woman?

Despair lapped about her like a rising tide. She had craved escape from the line. But now it was within her grasp, she was afraid. Despite wanting desperately to get away from the shanty, and Queenie, and the men's drinking and fighting, and the sheer drudgery, the prospect of going out into the world alone was far more daunting than she had anticipated.

A little while later, exhausted and footsore, she lay under the blankets and stared into the darkness, her thoughts roiling and churning.

She had got what she had wanted for so long. At last she could leave the line. *And go where?* It didn't matter. She could even leave Cornwall if she wished. *The family didn't want to know her.* Well, what of it? She couldn't remember them either. She had been alone for a long time. She was used to it. She liked it that way. She didn't have to consult anybody else about where to go or what she should do.

She was in a fast-flowing river. Her fears were jagged rocks jutting out of the water lying in wait to catch her, trap her, drown her. The current had her in its grip, sweeping her closer and closer to a black stump of rock, sharp as a broken tooth. Suddenly she saw the gypsy's face. It grew huge, filling her vision. The leering, laughing mouth became a black tunnel and the river was carrying her into it. She was screaming and screaming but not making any sound. She flailed desperately with arms and legs but the current was too strong and swept her onward into the darkness. And the black rocks became people. She shrieked for help, but they turned away and the river plunged over a precipice and she was falling. . . .

She jerked upright, her flying hand jarring painfully against the wooden panel. Gasping, she covered her face with shaking hands. As she waited for the frantic hammering in her chest to subside she kept telling herself it was just a bad dream. It didn't mean anything.

She pushed back sweat-damp hair, her head hot against her palms. The money would buy her freedom from Queenie and the shanty village. She would have the means to begin a new life wherever she chose.

But no matter how far she travelled she could not escape from herself. *She had killed a man.* And that terrible truth would cast its long shadow wherever she went and whatever she did.

# *Chapter Fourteen*

CHLOE lay in the darkness and stared upward. The feather mattress was soft, the sheets crisp and smelling faintly of lavender. Was it minutes or hours that she had been lying here? Sleep taunted her: beckoning yet ever elusive. She had no idea what time it was, but dared not relight the lamp. If Gerald had not yet retired and saw light beneath her door when he passed by, he would want to know why. She didn't want him to ask, for what could she say? Lying was difficult: but to tell him the truth was impossible.

On their wedding day he had promised always to protect and take care of her. When they reached the hotel in Paris where they were to begin their honeymoon tour he had told her she should not be afraid, he would make no demands except to enjoy her company and friendship. Exhausted after the rough sea crossing, the cumulative effects of wedding preparations and the lingering shock of her father's death, she had been grateful for his kindness and restraint.

Looking back now, she realized how naïve she had been, though it had taken several months for her perception of his forbearance to evolve into a sense of rejection. And guilt had added its own weight to her strain. For somehow she was made to feel selfish. Yet how could she harbour negative thoughts about someone so indulgent and generous: someone to whom she owed so much?

While causing her considerable anguish, this inner conflict had remained manageable until James Santana's arrival. But the tiny spark of recognition, struck the first day they met, had flared into a holocaust that now threatened everything she had believed important to her. And the pitiless flames illuminated her own part in the conspiracy that had shrouded her marriage with shadows of deception. For so long – *too long* – she had avoided looking too

153

closely, fearing what she might see: that her husband preferred intimacy with others rather than with her: that she had failed him in some way she didn't understand. But it was too late now to close her eyes. *Your marriage is a sham.*

The heat had reached into her soul, melting the confident façade behind which she had hidden her feelings of inadequacy, igniting a hunger, a yearning too strong to fight and too destructive to acknowledge. Her eyes pricked and burned, then scalding tears slid, slow and silent, down her temples into her hair. *What am I to do?*

She thought of the little bottle on the night table beside the large four-poster bed. Briefly tempted, she made no effort to reach for it. It certainly soothed her nerves. But she didn't like the other effects: the feeling of detachment, the way she seemed to be looking out at the world from somewhere far back in her head. And it made her see.... She could never quite grasp what they were, for they were right at the edge of her vision. But they frightened her, these unnamed *things*. And though the pungent brown liquid made her feel sleepy, it also provoked strange, vivid dreams and a deep sense of unease that lingered for several hours after she woke.

Not wanting to appear complaining or ungrateful, or to worry him, she hadn't said anything to Gerald. As she hadn't misread the directions, clearly written on the label, the only other explanation she could think of was sensitivity to one of the ingredients. So she simply stopped taking it. But that caused another problem. Expecting the tonic to have improved her appetite, at every mealtime Gerald checked the amount on her plate. Thus, despite the constant lump in her throat and a stomach made painfully tender by stress, she had to force down food she didn't want and convince him she was enjoying every mouthful. Had it not been for his smile of pleasure and obvious relief that she seemed so much better, she would not have had the courage or the strength to continue.

She turned over, seeking a cool place on the pillow. How much longer could she go on like this? *What was the alternative?*

Exhausted, she closed her eyes. And to escape the clamour in her mind she pictured once more the elegant airy house that had been her childhood home. South-facing, with tall windows, it had always seemed full of sunlight. After a visit from the bailiffs there hadn't been much furniture left in the reception rooms. But her father had laughed and shrugged, declaring the absence of clutter an advantage. For was it not now easier to appreciate the excellent proportions and architectural features? His light-hearted manner had reassured, enabling her to view their erratic finances as an inconvenience rather than a tragedy.

Older now, and wiser, she recognized her father's fecklessness, yet it did not diminish her love for him. For with painful insight gained during the past few weeks, she saw now that his mercurial temperament and his gambling had been a façade to mask a loneliness he had been unable to share with anyone, even her.

Though she had promised not to visit the house, there was nothing to stop her thinking of it, and remembering. Strange that it should be so comforting.

She thought she heard something. But, wanting to remain cocooned in memory, protected from the grinding stress of her daily existence, she refused to acknowledge it, and drifted off again.

Suddenly her eyes were open. She lay perfectly still. Then she heard a low cry and a muffled strangled sound abruptly cut off. Properly awake now she sat up and reached for the lucifer matches. The flare made her blink and the acrid smell caught sharply at the back of her nose as she lit the wick and replaced the glass funnel.

A robe of frilled white cotton lawn threaded with sky blue ribbon lay on the linen chest at the foot of the bed. Pulling it on over her night-gown, she quickly tied the sash, pushed her feet into slippers, and picked up the lamp. Her long golden braid fell over one shoulder to her breast.

Opening the door she peered out, listening intently. A new sound, harsh and guttural, like an animal in pain, made her jump. Shivering, she started down the passage. Now she could hear frantic pleading whispers and realized both sounds were coming from her husband's room.

She hesitated, inexplicably nervous, her hand poised to knock. Geraid had made it clear when he first brought her to the house that respect for each other's privacy was paramount in their relationship. In the four years of their marriage she had seen his room only once, when he had taken her on a tour of the house.

She knocked. 'Gerald?' There was a thump and scuffling, but no reply. 'Gerald?' She opened the door. 'Forgive the intrusion but I—' She stopped, as startled as the valet who stumbled backwards from the bed. 'Henry?'

'Oh, ma'am, I was just coming to get you.' Pale, dishevelled, and sweating profusely, he was clearly terrified.

Looking past him, she saw her husband sprawled on his back, his face greyish-purple and contorted as he strained for breath, grunting and gargling as if he were about to choke. The sheet and blankets lay, as if hastily piled there, in a tangled heap across his lower body and legs. His discarded night-shirt lay on the floor.

She found the disarray deeply shocking, for she had rarely seen her husband other than fully dressed. And even on those infrequent occasions he had been wearing an ankle-length robe of maroon brocaded silk with a cravat at his throat, his hair neatly brushed, emanating the lemony fragrance of cologne.

With a hollow dread in the pit of her stomach, she rushed forward. 'What happened? What's wrong?'

'It wasn't my fault, ma'am. Honest to God, it wasn't.' He wiped his hands down the sides of his trousers as Chloe looked at him in astonishment.

'It's all right, Henry, no one is blaming you.' Setting her lamp beside the one already lit on her husband's night table, Chloe touched his limp hand. 'Gerald? Can you hear me?' There was no reaction and the sound of his laboured breathing filled the room. She turned to the trembling valet who was shifting from one foot to the other and looked as if he might be sick at any moment. 'Go and wake Nathan. Tell him to ride for Dr Treloar at once.'

'Yes, ma'am.' Snatching up one of the lamps, the young man ran out, his bare feet making no sound on the carpet.

Feeling like a trespasser in this intensely masculine room of dark oak furniture, glass-fronted bookcases, and bold patterns in kingfisher and crimson, Chloe straightened the bedcovers. Below her husband's throat the skin was startlingly white. A few dark hairs sprouted from the centre of his heaving chest. Uncomfortable without understanding why, she drew the sheet up so it rested lightly across his shoulders. Appearance was important to Gerald. He would hate to be seen in a state of untidiness even by the doctor.

Racked with guilt about her unease, her attraction to James, her unhappiness, she poured water from the large jug on the nightstand into the blue and white patterned china basin. Dipping a corner of the clean towel, she tentatively wiped his glistening forehead.

'The doctor will be here soon.' Her voice sounded unnaturally loud, even though she had to compete with the wheezing rattle in his throat. Then there were footsteps in the passage, and hushed voices, followed by a soft tapping on the door.

'Come in.'

Hawkins entered, followed by Mrs Mudie; both were wearing night-clothes covered by sober woollen dressing-gowns. Henry must have alerted them when he went to wake Nathan.

Within moments Chloe found herself gently ushered out of the room into the care of a bleary-eyed Polly. As she passed, the butler promised that, while Mrs Mudie took care of the bedding, in the absence of Henry who was too upset to be of use to anyone at present, he would ensure Sir Gerald was properly attired and made comfortable for the doctor's visit. No doubt Madam would welcome the opportunity to do likewise?

Dressed in white-spotted violet silk, Chloe sat at the dressing-table while Polly put up her hair. Gazing blankly at her reflection, almost too tired to think, she suddenly frowned. What had the valet been doing in Gerald's bedroom at that time of night? And why, instead of his uniform, had he been wearing only trousers and a crumpled shirt that wasn't even properly buttoned?

'What are 'e doing?' Nipper demanded curiously, as Tom emerged from the wash house stripped to the waist and carrying a bucket half-full of soapy water.

'What do it look like?' Tom hurled the water over some bushes and turned back, rubbing his wet hair with the frayed and thread-bare towel hanging round his neck.

'Well, it isn't pay day, and it isn't Saturday, so what's going on?'

With no intention of telling him, Tom side-stepped the question. 'If that's the only time you wash, 'tis no wonder your bunk do smell like a midden.'

Nipper shrugged. 'Don't see no point if you aren't going nowhere.' He hopped from one foot to the other. 'I'm breaking me neck for a pee.'

'Go on, then. I aren't stopping you.' Tom returned to the wash house. He pulled on the clean shirt he had brought out with him, and raked a broken comb through his shaggy curls. The coarse bristles on his jaw rasped against his palm and he hesitated. No, if he shaved mid-week he'd never hear the end of it.

After a quick look out, he took a deep breath, hooked his

thumbs in his belt and sauntered across to the little hut. He'd still have come even if the whole gang had been lined up watching. But he wasn't sorry they weren't.

Some women you could joke about. Like those two this afternoon. Some *ladies* they were. But not her, not Veryan, she didn't deserve that. He tapped his scarred knuckles against the door.

'All right, then?' he said by way of greeting, and was filled with irritation at himself. He was supposed to have a way with words. So how was it the more he saw of her, the dumber he sounded?

'Come in. No, leave the door,' she said, as he started to close it. 'We may as well use the last of the daylight.'

'What about. . . ?' He indicated the shanty.

Her mouth twisted wearily. 'At this time of the evening all they'll be looking at is the bottom of a beer mug. Sit down.'

He lowered himself onto the bottom end of the bed, feeling big and clumsy in the confined space. When he was settled she passed him paper, pen, and a piece of smooth wood to rest on. Then, drawing her legs up under her skirt she huddled in the top corner. 'Show me what you remember from last time.'

With fierce concentration he inscribed the letters, silently saying them to himself as he wrote. After several sweating minutes he glanced up, ready to mock his slowness before she did. But the words remained unspoken. Her head rested against the wall and she was staring into space.

'Something wrong?' he asked quietly.

She started. 'No.' It was so quick, so sharp, he knew she was lying.

'Come on, girl. I aren't blind.'

She glared, about to challenge him, then sighed and gave a small shrug that tried to be off-hand, and failed.

'The engineer?' He hadn't meant it to come out blunt like that. But now he'd said it he wasn't sorry.

She stiffened defensively. 'Why should you think that?'

'No secrets in a shanty village, my bird. Everyone knows he come looking for you and wanted to speak to you in private. And I seen the way you smiled at him. So what's wrong?' His fingers tightened on the pen and he felt tension creep up his forearms. 'Didn't try anything, did he?'

'Certainly not! Mr Santana has always treated me with respect.'

'So I should hope.' The tension drained out of Tom, replaced by relief. He liked the engineer who seemed a straight, decent man. But he'd seen the way James Santana and Lady Radclyff had looked at each other. And when a man couldn't get what he wanted, he would sometimes take what he could get.

'So what's wrong then?'

'Wrong?' She gave the peculiar twisted smile again. 'Nothing. Honestly,' she said as he opened his mouth to contradict her. 'In fact, you could say my dearest wish has come true.'

'Is that right?' He set the pen down carefully. 'So, are you going to tell me, or what?'

Her brief laugh sounded like a sob and she looked away, hunching her shoulders. 'I might as well. There's no one else. The funny thing is, you are probably the one person who will understand.'

He felt a thrill of pride and gratification. But listening as she told him about the legacy, he found himself torn between pleasure at her good fortune and deep dismay.

'Well, that's 'andsome, that is.' He forced a smile. 'I s'pose as soon as the money comes, you'll be gone. Just what you wanted, isn't it? To get off the line?'

'Yes,' she agreed sombrely. 'That's what I've always wanted.'

'Well, I'd better get on while you're still here. If you don't mind?' He had hoped that if he showed her he would treat her right, showed her he was serious about bettering himself, maybe, given a bit of time, she would ... but the money changed everything. What could he offer compared to that? Bending his head he picked up the pen once more. He'd had his share of knocks: over the years he'd lost all his family, and more than one job. But that was life and you got on with it. This time was different. She had a chance to go back where she belonged. And he had no right to try and stop her. He cursed long and hard, in silence.

As he waited for Hawkins to open the door, James mentally ran through all the points Sir Gerald was likely to make, and his own responses. Had he missed anything? He'd know soon enough.

'Good afternoon, Hawkins.'

'Sir?' The butler displayed his usual imperturbability, but James sensed a tiny crack in the polished façade.

'I'm here to see Sir Gerald. We have an appointment.'

'I regret, sir, that Sir Gerald is indisposed and unable to see anyone.'

'It's all right, Hawkins.' The butler looked round as Chloe hurried towards the front door. 'I will see Mr Santana.'

'With respect, ma'am,' the butler lowered his voice. 'You've been under great strain. I'm sure the gentleman will understand—'

'Thank you, Hawkins. I appreciate your concern, but as my husband is unable to keep his appointment, the least I can do is offer Mr Santana some refreshment.' Though obviously distracted, her new – if slightly nervous – determination piqued James's curiosity. 'Mr Santana, do come in. Hawkins, please have tea brought to the drawing-room.'

'Ma'am.'

The butler's bow was as respectful as always. But as James stepped into the hall, he happened to catch the man's eye. The contact lasted only an instant. But that was long enough. Dropping his gaze, the butler withdrew.

As he followed Chloe, James's thoughts raced. Had Sir Gerald somehow become suspicious of Chloe and himself? He dismissed the thought as it occurred. It wasn't accusation he had glimpsed; it was anxiety.

As he entered the drawing-room, Chloe whirled, closing the door behind them, shedding her composure like a too-heavy burden.

'Oh, James, so much has happened. You've come all this way, and I know how busy you are, and it's a wasted journey. I should have sent a message—'

'Sshhh.' Cupping her elbow he led her to a chair. 'How could any journey with you at the end of it be wasted?' As she sat, he took the chair opposite, leaning forward slightly. 'I gather Sir Gerald is unwell?'

She clasped and unclasped her hands. The violet shadows beneath her eyes emphasized her pallor now that the brief bloom of colour had faded from her face. Slanting sunshine highlighted cheekbones more pronounced than he remembered, as were the hollows beneath them. His heart twisted at her fragility. *He had done this.*

'Three nights ago he – he had a seizure. Henry was with him. Henry's his valet. Gerald hasn't had him long. He must have been there when it happened.'

'How serious is it?'

'I'm not sure.' She made a gesture of helplessness. 'Dr Treloar says he's as well as can be expected. But what does that mean? They treat me as if I were a half-wit.'

James felt anger stir like a slumbering beast. 'Who does?'

'All of them. The doctor, Hawkins, Mrs Mudie. I may be naïve, but I'm not stupid. I know there's something they're not telling me.' She shook her head. 'I'm sorry. I'm probably being ridiculous. It's just ... I haven't slept properly for weeks. And the last few nights—'

'I do understand,' he reminded her gently.

She held his gaze for a moment. 'Yes. You do, don't you.' She glanced towards the door. 'James, there's something—' She sat straighter as a rattle of china was followed immediately by the door opening to reveal Polly with a tray.

'Thank you, Polly,' Chloe said as she set it down on the low table.

The maid bobbed a curtsey and started for the door. Just before she reached it she turned. James saw her glance flit from Chloe to himself and back.

'Beg pardon, ma'am, but will you be wanting fresh tea for the doctor when he comes down?'

Chloe shook her head wearily. 'No, thank you, Polly. He prefers a glass of sherry or Madeira.'

With another bob the maid went out, closing the door behind her.

James spoke quietly. 'Do you have a confidante? A close friend? Your maid perhaps?' Before he had finished she was shaking her head.

'I do not have close friends.' Though it was a simple statement, not a plea for sympathy, it still wrenched him.

*But Polly knew just the same.* He fiddled with his cuff links, fighting an overwhelming urge to touch her. 'For pity's sake, Chloe, pour the tea.'

She blinked, caught her breath, and quickly lowered her eyes as a tide of colour surged from her throat to her hairline. Leaning forward she picked up a bone-china milk jug decorated in crimson and gold. It rattled against the edge of the cup.

'Chloe, what did you mean? About the valet?'

'I don't understand why he was there. Gerald had retired for the night. He was in bed.' She replaced the jug and lifted the teapot. 'And Henry wasn't dressed. Well, not properly. And it was the

middle of the night.' She shook her head again. 'The way he looked
. . . it frightened me.'

'The valet?'

'No, Gerald. He was almost blue, and making this dreadful noise
as he tried to breathe. Henry looked ghastly too. He had the most
awful shakes. He kept saying it wasn't his fault.' She shook her
head in bewilderment. 'Why would he think we'd blame him?
When the noises woke me—' She broke off, and James saw her
forehead wrinkle.

'What is it?'

'I'd forgotten. . . .'

'Forgotten what?'

'The smell. I noticed it when I first went in. There was a peculiar
smell, like yeast . . . or sour milk.'

As realization stabbed, for the first time James's iron self-control
threatened to desert him. *He had to be wrong. There must be
another explanation.* But he knew there wasn't. How did he tell her
the appalling truth? For she had to be told.

'Anyway.' She drew a shaky breath. 'Henry said he'd been about
to come and fetch me. I told him to wake Nathan – the groom –
and send him for the doctor straight away. Then Hawkins and Mrs
Mudie arrived and took over. Doctor Treloar has visited every day.
He is most attentive.'

As she looked up he saw the strain and exhaustion in her face
echoed in the line of her shoulders. 'James? What's wrong?' Her
eyes widened, filling with alarm.

'Chloe,' he hesitated, trying to phrase the question as tactfully as
possible while fighting a cold bitter rage against the baronet. 'Why
do *you* think your husband did not . . . behave towards you as a
husband should?'

'Oh but he—' she began, and stopped just quickly, flinching as
she realized what he meant.

'I don't know.' She gave a helpless shrug. 'I can only assume he
did not find me' – her voice dropped to a whisper – 'desirable. I've
thought so hard, tried to understand. . . .'

He saw how doubt had insidiously undermined her self-esteem.
Yet she had bravely hidden her anguish and, with heart-breaking
stoicism, played to perfection the role Sir Gerald had assigned her.

'It wasn't that I was particularly *anxious* to experience . . . I had
never thought of him in that way. He was kind and generous and

'... but naturally one hears ... and I know that to have children it is necessary to....' Unable to sit still any longer, she rose and turned away, her wide skirts swaying as she crossed to the window and gazed out. 'He never actually said I'd done anything to displease him.'

James watched as she clasped her elbows, holding her arms tightly across her stomach as if in pain.

'But there must be something about me ... I didn't realize at first ... the business trips to Truro and to London....' She glanced at James. 'He was always *different* when he returned. I suppose I must be stupid, but it didn't occur to me at first.'

'What didn't?' he prompted.

'That Gerald was seeing other women.' She turned back to the window, lifting her chin. 'After all, he's so much older and more sophisticated than I am, I suppose it would be perfectly natural for him to—'

'Chloe, there's nothing *natural*—' He stopped himself. 'Please, come and sit down.' He waited, furious that he, who loved her, was about to cause her more suffering. Yet he had no choice. Until she knew the truth she could not begin to heal. 'My dear,' he leaned forward, reaching for her hand, 'it is not other *women* your husband prefers; his desire is for men.'

He watched her face reflect shock, disbelief and horror as she absorbed what he'd said. Her hand clenched and her entire body grew rigid as she rejected it.

'No! No, you're wrong. He wouldn't. He couldn't – the risk – his position— No.' But it was a plea, not a denial.

Suffering for her, he sweated. 'Long before he married you there were rumours. Believe me, Chloe, I'm not wrong.' *And, God help him, how could he wish he were, when the truth so helped his own cause?* 'Do you remember what you told me? That you may be naïve, but you're not stupid? Think back, not just to the night he was taken ill, but before that, all the years you've been married—'

She stood up. 'You have to go.'

He shot to his feet, his knee catching the edge of the table. The china clattered and the untouched tea, now cold and filmed with scum, spilled into the saucers. 'Chloe, I'm so sorry, but there was no easy way to—'

'No, no.' Agitated, she shook her head. 'It's not – you weren't—

Oh, God in Heaven.' Turning away she covered her face and he could only watch, agonized and powerless. She swung round. 'I never even imagined – how could I? What would I know of—' Her voice broke, and she steepled her fingers against her lips to hide their quivering. 'I must . . . I need time to—' She clasped her arms across her stomach again. 'The doctor will be down soon. Please, James, you must go.'

He started towards the door, reluctant to leave her, but not wanting to add to her distress. Then he stopped. 'I'll come back later.'

'No—'

'We have to talk.' He was determined.

'But what about—'

'The servants?' His mouth twisted in grim irony. 'Chloe, you are the mistress of this house. Besides, under the circumstances, they are hardly likely to gossip about *us*, are they?'

Her eyes darkened. 'You mean . . . all the time . . . they've *known*?'

James knew he would never forget the look on her face, the depth of hurt and betrayal.

She bit her lip and heaved a shuddering sigh. 'All right. But it's such a long way, and you've already—'

He brushed her cheek with his fingertips. 'I'd ride to Hell and back for you. Stop worrying about me and start thinking about yourself for a change.' He felt a tightening in his chest as she tried to smile.

'I've been told I do too much of that.'

'Not by anyone who matters,' he said softly.

# Chapter Fifteen

A FTER James had gone Chloe was unable to keep still. She paced the drawing-room, gnawing at the torn skin around her nails as she re-examined events, conversations, and her husband's manner towards her, in the light of James's shocking revelation. She didn't want to believe it. Gerald and *Henry*? She had not the knowledge or experience even to imagine. . . . Yet she knew James would not have lied.

Horrified, she was also suffused with anguish. What did it say about her that he could be that way? Was it worse to be rejected by one's husband for a *man* rather than another woman? Such activity was against all Christian teaching, yet every Sunday that he wasn't in London Gerald had escorted her to church and taken his place in the family pew. And all the time. . . .

Had she been the only person of his close acquaintance not to know? How could she have been so blind? Yet how could she have known, given her ignorance and the fact that he had been protected by a conspiracy of silence?

Her awareness of such matters had been limited to vehement but coded thunderings from the pulpit by a visiting preacher. Occasionally at a dinner party she would overhear some luckless public figure being discussed in the shocked undertones reserved for serious scandal. But as the subject was instantly changed as soon as her presence was noticed, etiquette demanded she did not enquire further.

On the rare occasions she had accompanied Gerald to London she had glimpsed flamboyantly dressed gentlemen with extravagantly foppish manners. Steering her away, Gerald had declined to explain, declaring such people of no interest to a young woman.

And now she had to accept that he was one of them? And that, knowing he was, and professing fondness and admiration for her, he had still married her. How could he have done that? *Why* had he done it? *Because her father had asked him to.*

All her life she had been conditioned to accept without question that men were superior to women, simply because they were men. Now, for the first time, she recognized the breathtaking arrogance of this claim.

Her father had abandoned her, preferring to die rather than face the consequences of his own recklessness, and bequeathing her as if she were a piece of furniture to his friend. Had her father known of Gerald's inclinations? She recoiled inwardly, the thought too painful to pursue.

Still recovering from the shock of his death, she had found herself, at sixteen, married to a man more than thirty years her senior: a man who went to great lengths to win her admiration and affection, and her trust. It hadn't been difficult.

He had installed her in luxury and treated her with kindly indulgence while exercising total control over every aspect of her life, even to the selection of her personal maid. And he had become her mentor. Under his tutelage she had immersed herself in the study of art, antiques, architecture and history; and through it – through *him* – had discovered a wondrous world of beauty.

This increased her desire to repay his kindness and to please him – for was he not her husband? His delight at her progress gave her a sense of pride and achievement. This was further enhanced by the satisfaction she derived from her charity work.

At one level her life had been deeply satisfying. Yet as time passed she found it ever more difficult to ignore the suspicion that all was not as it should be. But she had always believed – and she realized now, had been subtly encouraged in this belief – that if she was not entirely content then, in some way she didn't understand, the fault lay with her. That was the cruellest cut of all.

Hearing footsteps and voices in the hall, she quickly wiped her eyes, took a deep breath to steady herself, and slipped into the role to which she had been so well trained: Lady Radclyff, mistress of Trewartha.

'Come in,' she called, resuming her seat and arranging the folds of her gown. 'Ah, Dr Treloar. No doubt you are ready for your glass. Which is it to be? Sherry or Madeira?'

The doctor came forward, his hands making a dry, papery sound as he rubbed them briskly. 'Most kind. A glass of Madeira would go down very well, thank you.'

'See to it will you, Hawkins? And remove the tea tray, please?' Neither man appeared to notice the slight edge to her voice. Perhaps they had, but were attributing it to concern about her husband.

Taking the crystal glass proffered by the butler on a small silver salver, the doctor came towards the fireplace and lowered himself into the chair Chloe indicated as Hawkins picked up the tea tray.

'Will there be anything else, madam?'

'No, thank you, Hawkins.'

Chloe waited until the door closed behind him before she spoke. 'How do you find Sir Gerald today?'

'One hesitates to be too bold, Lady Radclyff, but I think I can safely say that steady progress is being made. Each day I see small signs of improvement. I have left some more pills on his night-table. They will ease any pain and help him to sleep.'

Chloe looked at the self-satisfied, patronizing smile, and nodded. Her hands were neatly folded on her lap, concealing the raw, torn skin. Her back was ramrod straight.

'Tell me, Dr Treloar,' she enquired with a calm that astonished her and boosted her courage, 'how long have you known of my husband's sexual preference for men? Oh dear. Never mind, I'm sure the stain will come out.'

Whipping a pristine handkerchief from his pocket, the doctor dabbed with clumsy haste at the dark patch on the padded brocade chair arm made by the spilt wine. 'Really, madam,' he blustered, crimson-faced, and avoiding her gaze. 'That is not the sort of language one expects to hear from the lips of a lady such as yourself.'

'It is not a question any wife should be called upon to ask,' Chloe responded. 'But of necessity I *have* asked it, and I should be obliged to receive an answer.'

'I cannot possibly discuss such matters with you,' the doctor huffed, shifting to make further ineffectual swipes at his trousers. 'Quite apart from the impropriety of such a conversation, I must remind you that the doctor-patient relationship is built on utter confidentiality—'

'What about *me*?' Chloe's tight control slipped, pierced by hurt and anger. 'I was your patient too. When I consulted you about my nervous troubles and being unable to sleep, you acted as though the fault was *mine*. Yet all the time you knew that my marriage was – that my husband could not, or would not— What made you think that prescribing fresh air and tonics for me would change anything? Was I not entitled to know that my husband had no interest in' – her face flamed but she held his gaze – 'in married love?'

'That was not my responsibility.'

'Whose was it then?' she cried. 'I trusted you. You knew I had no mother to tell me what a young woman is supposed to know about married life. And that the governesses my father employed were all single women.'

Tossing the wine down his throat with no regard for its flavour or pedigree, he placed the glass over-firmly on the low table. 'I know women who would be grateful to be in your position. Many find their husband's attentions a burden from which they would willingly be freed were it not for their sense of duty. In fact' – his voice grew stronger, more censorious – 'there is something less than wholesome about your attitude. Instead of wallowing in emotions which, I have to say I find unhealthy and quite improper, you should be counting your blessings. You have a beautiful home, servants to attend your every wish, and a life many would envy.'

'But no babies,' she reminded him. 'Are children not the purpose for which marriage was ordained? Are they not the cornerstone of the family? A woman's reason for being?' His eyes slid away as his face reddened. 'Sir, you have betrayed your calling.'

The doctor stiffened and his mouth grew thin and tight. 'I did what I believed was best. In marrying you, Sir Gerald was clearly trying to overcome his ... weakness ... and lead a normal life.'

Chloe gazed at him in disbelief. 'How can you say that? You, of all people, *know* our life together wasn't normal.'

'As his wife,' the doctor persisted with lofty arrogance, 'you owe him loyalty and understanding.'

Rising to her feet, unable to take any more, Chloe tugged sharply at the braided silk bell pull. 'Dr Treloar, you are the very last person to lecture me on duty, or anything else. Hawkins will show you out.'

Nauseated by the very thought of food, but knowing the pains in her stomach would grow worse if she didn't eat, Chloe forced down some dinner. Then she sat quietly with her husband, watching him as he slept.

*

'What are you going to do?' James asked when he returned later that evening. He had brought a leather case of papers with him as camouflage.

She gestured helplessly. 'I don't know.'

'I love you, Chloe. You do believe that?'

She nodded. 'I—' Her mouth was dry, and she had to wet her lips. 'I – I'm—' She turned away, unable to speak.

'Sit down,' he said gently. 'Talk to me. Tell me what you've been thinking about.'

Smiling gratefully, she shook her head to dash away tears. 'My father. He was a very handsome man, warm and witty and impulsively generous when fortune smiled on him, laughing to cover his despair when it didn't.'

'What about your mother?'

'I don't remember her. All I can remember is that from the time she died until my wedding, life for me was a constant swoop of highs and lows. I remember my father coming home in the early hours, waking me with his singing. I'd come downstairs and see a pouch full of gold coins poured out onto the table. On other days we would have to hide and pretend to be out when the bailiffs came hammering on the door. He made it a game, an adventure. But it was exhausting, James. When I married Gerald, for the first time in my life I felt safe. No one was going to burst in and take away the furniture.'

'But it's not a real marriage.' James's frustration showed in his frown. 'Chloe, it's just a pretence, a charade for his benefit.'

'I know. But despite his deception I still owe Gerald a debt of gratitude. After my father . . . after he . . . died and the lawyers took over, I was left with nothing. I had no money and no home. And no one to turn to for help. What would have become of me if Gerald had not honoured my father's dying wish? He has always been kind to me, and I have lacked for nothing.'

James managed to hold his tongue, but he couldn't stop the ironic lift of his brows.

'I know. I know.' Chloe was despairing. 'But I cannot simply walk out on him. Though he's recovering, the doctor isn't sure yet what the long-term effects will be. Can you imagine public reaction if I were to leave the husband who has treated me so well just when his need of me is greatest? I would be an outcast, shunned by all society.'

'A society that connived at your ignorance,' James lashed out in anger. 'Whispering the rumours to each other behind your back, mocking you even as they accepted your hospitality.'

'Diana Price-Ellis and Loveday Hosking certainly suspected all was not well,' Chloe said wearily. 'But I never said a word, so they couldn't have known why.'

'You think not?' James's tone left no doubt as to his opinion of the two women. 'Chloe, of course they knew. Women like them thrive on gossip and intrigue. They would want to know what *you* knew, but would be very careful not to reveal how much *they* had heard. Sir Gerald is a very powerful man. That is what has protected him all these years. Chloe, you cannot stay.'

'I cannot leave. Where would I go?'

'I will take care of you.'

'Oh James.' She rested her hand on his sleeve, quickly bending her head but not before he had seen the glitter of tears. 'Don't you realize what would happen to your reputation? You would find it almost impossible to obtain the commissions you deserve.'

'Chloe—'

'No, please listen. Believe me, it is as difficult for me to say as it is for you to hear. But I have thought very hard about this. You told me yourself the circumstances surrounding your departure from Spain. And I know how conscientiously you have applied yourself since joining the Railway Company. James, do you think I would willingly destroy all you have worked for?'

'No, of course not, but—'

'If I leave Gerald and come to you, you will lose everything. My dearest James,' her voice quivered, 'you mean too much . . . I cannot—'

He gathered her in his arms with infinite care, wary of frightening her, and pressed his lips to her temple. He could feel her trembling, hear her quickened breath.

'Oh, Chloe,' he whispered against her hot cheek. She turned her head and he saw her eyes were brimming. He could not stop himself, and cupped her face gently in one hand as he bent to her mouth. Her lashes closed and he heard a soft jerky catch in her throat.

Her lips were soft and sweet and innocent, and when, reluctantly, he eased back, tears had left silver tracks down her flushed face, but her eyes shone bright as stars.

Her quiet inhalation was barely audible. 'James, I was so frightened.'

'Of what?' He frowned. 'You must know I would never do anything to hurt you.'

'No, I didn't mean ... not frightened of *you*. What scared me was what I felt – feel – when I'm near you.' She pressed her palm to the centre of her ribcage beneath the swell of her bodice. 'I thought it meant I was wicked or depraved.'

Trying to contain his fury as he speculated on the source of those lies, he shook his head and smiled.

'Chloe, I never have, nor am I likely to, meet anyone less wicked or depraved than you. Those feelings are right and natural. That is the way a man and woman *should* feel about each other.'

Her eyes widened. 'You mean *you—*?'

He nodded, his smile self-mocking. 'Oh yes. Me too. So much so that – well, never mind.' He watched her blush deepen and she eased away. He let her go. They dared not risk discovery by the servants. Besides which, so great was his hunger for her, his self-control was perilously close to breaking. Physical distance was necessary if he was not to frighten her with the strength of his passion.

Yet, as she moved slowly about the room, straightening ornaments already perfectly positioned, he could feel himself connected to her as if by some invisible cord. He knew that, despite all she had said, the kiss had taken them another step down a path from which there was no retreat. But she would need time to recognize this.

Reaching the fireplace she turned and faced him, still flushed with shy radiance. Yet beneath it the strain of recent weeks was all too visible. They needed to talk. But now was not the time. And this was certainly not the place.

She cleared her throat. 'How is everything on the line?'

He knew she had chosen the topic as much to justify her decision, by reminding him of his responsibility to the men and their families who depended on him to fight on their behalf, as to show her interest in his work. He longed to tell her what was happening, about the battles he was having with the directors. But to add his worries to the terrible burden she already carried would be selfish and cruel.

'Very busy, as I'm sure you can imagine. Especially as I am now doing Pascoe's work as well as my own.' One corner of his mouth lifted in a wry grin. 'Sleep was difficult before he left; now,' he shrugged, 'it has become something of a luxury.' As her face clouded with anxiety he continued, meaning every word, 'But nothing could have restored my spirits as much as seeing you. Even so, I must go now. You need to rest.'

She twisted her hands. 'I am not free to leave the house—'

Hearing a sound in the hall, he touched his lips with his index finger in silent warning, indicating the door with a slight sideways nod. 'I understand perfectly, Lady Radclyff. As you'll appreciate, the directors are most anxious about Sir Gerald's health. They are keen to receive news of his progress as often as possible. So, with your permission, I will call again soon?'

He could see new tension in her shoulders. And her face, now the rosy blush was fading, looked small and pale and tired.

'Of course. I shall be happy to receive you, Mr Santana.'

'Meanwhile, if there is anything you need, or any way in which I might be of service, just send word to the Royal Hotel in Falmouth, and I will come at once.'

'Thank you. You are very kind.'

Turning away was one of the hardest things he had ever done. He hated to leave her but he had no choice. *For the moment.*

Tom sat with the rest of the gang on the flat-bed wagon as it clattered along the line, pushed by the little engine. The morning sun was still low in a pale-blue sky. Crows and jackdaws flapped and squabbled; seagulls wheeled overhead before dropping to a newly ploughed field. High overhead, a buzzard soared in a lazy spiral. The air was cool and dew-fresh, a breeze just beginning to stir. It caught the plume of steam and smoke that rose in puffing bursts from the funnel, stretching and shredding it until it dissolved.

'Well, if you want to know what I think—' Nipper began.

'We all know what you think,' Paddy interrupted. 'You've talked of little else since the engineer told us. You think they're mad.'

'And so they are,' Nipper defended himself. 'Bleddy line isn't half finished, and they want to run a train on it?' He spat over the side. 'What's the point of it? That's what I'd like to know.'

'Aye, well, they're no' likely tae tell ye,' Mac grunted. 'So gi' us all a rest.'

'It's about money,' Yorky declared. 'They're doing it to prove that Pascoe sloping off hasn't dropped them in the you-know-what.'

'They told you that, did they?' Paddy enquired drily.

'Obvious, isn't it? Put on a big show so people can see everything is fine and dandy.'

'Here, Paddy,' Fen shouted from the far end of the wagon. 'How long are we off the cutting?'

'Engineer said just today. Arf's gang is up there blasting this morning. If they can shift that rock we'll be back tomorrow.'

Tom looked out across the patchwork of fields and woods. He didn't understand how people could talk about trees being *green*, like it was just one colour. From where he was sitting he could see beech leaves as pale as seawater, aspens that were silver-grey, young oak leaves with an orange tint, sycamores as bright as new grass, and holly so rich and glossy the leaves seemed almost black.

Beyond the dark-brown earth and outcrops of rock through which the permanent way had been cut, the hedgerows were laced with cow parsley and hawthorn blossom. Foxgloves were beginning to unfurl tall, pink spears. Pools of bluebells lingered in the shadows beneath stands of trees, and buttercups dotted grazing pastures with brilliant yellow.

He wished . . . he wished she was here with him, just the two of them. He wanted to share it with her, to make her understand that though he couldn't read or write *yet*, it didn't mean he was ignorant, or stupid. He recognized beauty. It wasn't just something you *saw*: it was something you *felt*.

She hadn't said a word this morning. Dropping his head forward he lifted his cap, shoved a hand through his hair and settled the cap once more as the wagon trundled towards the viaduct. She'd dished-up the porridge like she always did. But she hadn't even looked up. Probably planning what she was going to do with the money. And who could blame her?

He'd only been on the line a few weeks, but it was plain as day she'd had a hell of a life. She deserved better. And he'd have worked night and day to give it to her. She certainly had no reason to trust men, but he'd have won her over. He'd have done anything. But what chance did he have now? A good navvy was a skilled man. But in her eyes he was *just a navvy*. Before the money that hadn't mattered, because he had ambition, he had plans. But those were no longer enough.

The engine slowed as it rounded the bend and approached the viaduct.

'What will you do, Tom?' Fen nudged him.

Tom glanced round. 'What about?'

'When we finish here. Mac says he's going to try for canal work.'

'I've heard there's plans for more drainage on the Somerset Levels,' Fen chipped in. 'That might be worth a look.'

'Prob'ly all be finished by the time we get off of this line,' Nipper grumbled.

'Dear life,' Tom snorted, 'you're some happy soul.'

'All right,' Nipper challenged, 'so where're you going then? There's no more main-line work. Even branch lines like this is hard to come by.'

'In this country, maybe,' Tom said. 'But what about France, and Germany? Or America? They're building railways thousands of miles long in America.'

'That's *abroad*.' Nipper shuddered. 'I've heard about *abroad*. They eat frogs and stuff like that. Yeugh!'

'You eat cockles and eels,' Fen said. 'What's the difference?'

With squealing brakes and a hissing cloud of steam, the little engine jerked to a halt. The men reached for picks, shovels, iron bars and wheelbarrows, and clambered off the wagon. As they gathered at the side of the track, Paddy signalled the driver. Releasing another cloud of steam and an explosion of snorts and belches, the engine trundled across the viaduct and, picking up speed, headed back to Penryn to collect wagonloads of stone and rails.

'What are we doing here anyway?' Nipper demanded plaintively, as the men split into their usual pairs and headed towards the pile of stone chippings to load the barrows.

'Engineer said to check the ballast and the levels.'

'That's the inspection crew's job,' Mac objected.

'What inspection crew?' Paddy pulled a face. 'They've been laying sleepers and rail with the other gangs to try and make up for time lost to the rain.'

As the morning passed and the sun climbed higher, the temperature rose with it. The breeze died, and the men sweated and cursed. Tom and Mac were working on the right-hand side of the track, the outer curve of the viaduct. Nipper and Fen were a few feet behind them on the left.

Tom poked his iron bar into a zig-zagging gap in the stone chippings. 'What d'you think?' He glanced at the Scot who had more experience of ballast work.

Mac shoved his own bar in and hammered it down hard, testing the resistance. 'Och, dinnae fash yersel'. It's just settlement after all yon rain.'

'That four in the last ten yards,' Tom reminded him.

'Aye, and given this heat we'll likely see another four in the next. It's only surface, lad. The base is solid and the rails have nae shifted. We'll fill in and level off and it'll be fine.'

A dull *crump* as the rock blocking the cutting was dynamited made them both look up. Then Paddy whistled, signalling the dinner break. Dropping their tools, they sat down with their backs against the parapet and waited for the rest of the gang to join them.

As Paddy shared out bread and cheese, they passed the beer keg from hand to hand, each swallowing a long cooling draught. Far below, the still-swollen stream swirled and eddied, as it raced towards the sea. The weeds and new grass spreading across the bare earth on either side of the massive stone pillars were lush and bright. But beneath the arch where the men rested, wet black dust trickled out from cracks in the mortar and fell like fine rain, darkening the fresh new growth beneath.

# Chapter Sixteen

'MR SANTANA, I am the traffic manager.' Clinton Warne's face was red with anger, and his chin jutted aggressively above his stiff collar. 'My decision was made after long and careful consideration, bearing in mind that the locomotive will, at different times, be required to pull both passenger carriages and goods wagons. The Evans locomotives are admirably suited to both.'

'Mr Warne—'

'No; having questioned my professional judgement, you must allow me to finish.'

James made a polite gesture of acquiescence, ignoring Harold Vane's smirk. The other directors carefully avoided looking at him. Instead they read or pretended to make notes on the agenda each had in front of him.

'There are several excellent reasons for choosing an engine that carries both fuel and water on top of its wheels.' Clinton Warne held up one hand and ostentatiously ticked them off. 'One, it does not require a separate tender. Two, it can be driven in either direction without being turned around which is an important advantage on journeys of relatively short distance. And three, the weight of fuel and water adds to the engine's own weight, providing valuable extra traction on gradients.' With a brisk nod of satisfaction at having proved his point, he settled back, looking around at his fellow directors who were also nodding.

Like mindless echoes, James thought. He took a breath. 'I know the design, and it is indeed an excellent one. However—'

'Enough!' Harold Vane slapped his hand down on the polished mahogany, causing Ingram Coles to jump and shoot him an irritated glance. 'Mr Santana, this matter was investigated, and a decision made before you joined the company. So as well as wasting valuable time you are also calling into question the competence of a valued member of the board.'

'Neither was intended, Mr Vane. But it appears both are unavoidable, as I would be failing in my professional duty if I did not reiterate my concern.' Switching his gaze to the traffic manager, James continued, 'Mr Warne, I assure you, my only reservation is over the weight.' Vane was right, he was indeed wasting his time. None of them would look at him. Except the solicitor, whose small eyes glittered with malevolent pleasure.

'Then might I suggest, Mr Santana, that instead of criticizing Mr Warne, you devote your attention to ensuring the track is laid correctly? That is *your* responsibility. And if you attend to it properly then the weight of the locomotive becomes irrelevant. Now, with the chairman's permission, I move that we turn to the matter of the guest list.' Murmurs of agreement and a general quickening of interest greeted his suggestion.

James sat back, outwardly calm, inwardly seething with anger and frustration. He had said what needed saying. He had sent a gang to check potential weak spots. What more could he do?

'I am negotiating hire of a single first-class carriage from Great Western,' Clinton Warne announced importantly, 'which will accommodate between fifteen and twenty guests, depending on the number of ladies in the party. Their gowns do require rather a lot of space.'

'So,' Ingram Coles, beamed around the table, 'who should we include? Ourselves, obviously. And I would suggest a journalist?' This time the murmurs of agreement were louder, and anticipation sharpened the atmosphere.

Victor Tyzack raised a finger. 'I move we invite Sir Gerald Radclyff. Obviously acceptance will depend on his state of health. But Dr Treloar assures me this is improving daily.'

'A capital idea!' Ingram Coles nodded enthusiastically. 'If Sir Gerald is paid the compliment of being one of the first to ride the line, he might well be persuaded to increase his investment.'

Catching Gilbert Mabey's eye, James glimpsed a reflection of his own weary cynicism and concurred with a barely perceptible shake of his head.

'It's possible,' the deputy chairman agreed. 'But I suspect an additional incentive will be required.'

'A directorship?' Ingram Coles suggested, looking around the table. 'And of course Lady Radclyff's presence will ensure the interest of other ladies.'

'Not only the ladies.' Harold Vane and Clinton Warne spoke simultaneously.

Carefully expressionless, James glanced up, but neither man was looking at him. Clearly the comment had been a general observation rather than an accusation directed specifically at him. Common sense said he should be relieved that his relationship with Chioe was still a secret known only to the two of them. But he loathed the deceit, hated the subterfuge.

As the debate continued amid growing animation, the rest of the agenda faded into insignificance. Tired, heartsick and anxious, aware of Gilbert Mabey's silent sympathy, and glad not to be entirely friendless, James stared blindly at the paper in front of him.

'There is nothing to discuss.' Sir Gerald Radclyff's tone, eminently reasonable, defied argument. Bathed, shaved, and fully dressed, his only concession to his condition was a blanket over his knees. 'I will soon be completely well again, and everything will be as it was.'

Chloe turned reluctantly from the window. She dreaded saying the things that had to be said. She wished she were outside in the sunshine, breathing the fresh scents of spring. The drawing-room felt over-warm and stuffy. Though he had refused to remain in bed, 'playing the invalid' as he'd put it, Gerald had heeded the doctor's warning against taking a chill, and a fire burned in every room.

'I am glad you are so much better.' She meant it. 'Everyone is amazed at the speed of your recovery.'

Her husband grunted. 'I can't imagine why. I'm not old, and I'm rarely ill.'

Chloe sat down carefully. It was the chair the doctor had occupied less than an hour ago. Greeting him with frosty politeness she had left the two men together, not returning until he'd gone.

'A seizure is not quite the same as ordinary illness. And the circumstances—'

'I know you heard me, Chloe, and I know I made myself quite clear: the matter is closed.'

'No, Gerald. It's not.' Her throat was tight, and she felt her heart thump against her ribs. 'I knew our marriage was different from others, but I never realized—'

'Have I not always treated you well?' he demanded.

'Indeed you have. Very well. And I have always appreciated your generosity.' Chloe swallowed. 'But that is not the point. You used me, Gerald. I was a disguise to secure your own safety. And in doing that you deliberately denied me the love—'

'Love?' he barked. 'What else would you call what I have done for you? I have cared for you and protected you. We have shared a companionship and happiness few couples could match. I have ensured your feminine delicacy was never burdened with the demands to which other, less fortunate, women are forced to submit.'

'Are you saying I should be *grateful*?'

'Indeed I am. This is real life, my dear. Not some fatuous and overheated romantic novel that bears no resemblance to the way real men and women behave.'

Forcing herself to remain seated, though every muscle craved the release of movement, she held herself stiff and straight, hands clasped tightly in her lap.

'And is our marriage typical of the way *real* men and women behave?' Watching his face, she wondered which had surprised him more: her directness, or the fact that for the first time in their life together she was challenging him.

He studied her thoughtfully. 'Tell me, my dear, what has brought about this sudden dissatisfaction?'

*Sudden* dissatisfaction? A swift rush of anger made her skin prickle. 'Gerald, you have in the past paid tribute to my intelligence. Did it never occur to you that sooner or later I would start to wonder about . . . about the lack of . . . of intimacy between us? Of course, there was no one in the household I could ask. Their loyalty to you is unswerving. Even my personal maid. Even *Polly*.' After a moment's fight for control, she lifted her head again.

'However, the married ladies of our social circle are not so reticent. They are not in the least reluctant to talk of intimate matters, though their opinion of their husbands' behaviour in the bedroom is anything but flattering. Their curiosity about us, and about the fact that after four years of marriage I am still childless, has caused me considerable discomfort. But my fear of appearing ignorant, and of their ridicule, ensured I always presented our marriage as *happy in every respect*.' She couldn't hide the depth of her hurt.

'Chloe, it should not be necessary to remind you that, as my wife, you have access to the highest levels of society, and a lifestyle to match. *I* have not changed. I am the same man to whom you made your wedding vows. The only difference is that, through unfortunate circumstances, you have become aware of a certain situation. As for children: if it means so much to you I will arrange an adoption.' He regarded her with an indulgent smile. 'Have I not always granted your every wish?'

She couldn't believe what she was hearing. He would buy her a *child*, in the same way that he had bought her a horse, or a new wardrobe of dresses? 'No, Gerald, you don't un—'

'In return,' he continued with a steely smoothness designed to crush any hint of resistance, 'I shall expect you to continue your portrayal of a loving and dutiful wife.' He looked intently at her. 'Do you hate me, Chloe?'

'No. I don't hate you.' The discovery of her husband's true nature had shaken her to the core. But that deceit did not erase his kindness and generosity over the years.

'Then what you have learned need make no difference.'

'But it does, Gerald,' she blurted. 'You say you have not changed. But I *have*. It's not just because of – the other evening. Gerald, I'm not a child any longer.'

'I see.' He was quiet for a moment. 'Then I must make myself absolutely clear: as my wife, certain standards of behaviour are expected of you. Thus far you have proved yourself equal to them, and to the honour of being Lady Radclyff. And I have taken enormous pleasure in your achievements. However. . .' – the word hung on the air and seemed to resound with dark threat – 'should you even *contemplate* any action that might jeopardize your spotless reputation I will divorce you. Divorcees are not received in society. You would lose wealth, position, friends, in fact everything to which you have become so happily accustomed. And this time there would be no rescue. For any young man having the temerity to challenge the proper order would very quickly find himself without friends or career.'

Chloe knew a moment's icy terror. *Did he know about James?* Sitting frozen and silent, she forced herself to stay calm. What was there to know? All they had actually done, apart from one exquisite, breathtaking kiss, was to talk. If Gerald had suspected anything untoward he would surely have said so sooner. Therefore his threats had been made in response to her declaration that she had changed. He was warning her about the future, not threatening her over the past.

Nothing he had said was new to her. She had already made these same points to James. But hearing the threats – for there was no doubt that was what they were – from Gerald himself brought home the terrible truth. She was trapped.

'Don't look so stricken, Chloe.' Her husband's smile was gentle. 'You have a life many would envy.' She flinched as he unwittingly repeated what the doctor had said. 'You say you are no longer a child. Then show you are a woman of strength and fortitude. Put this behind you. Look to the future. As soon as I am well enough – perhaps next week? – I will begin making enquiries about a suitable child. I want you to be happy, my dear. You do know that, don't you?'

A cold, smothering blanket of despair settled over her. 'Yes, Gerald.'

The following day as he rode up the drive towards Trewartha, James hoped, prayed, *willed* that Sir Gerald Radclyff was still confined, if not to his bed, then at least to his room. But the instant Hawkins opened the door James's hopes were dashed.

Following the butler across the hall he pushed his disappointment deep. If the baronet was already well enough to receive visitors, James knew he could not afford – for Chloe's sake – to relax his guard for an instant.

'Mr Santana,' Sir Gerald smiled, but there was an acerbic edge to his voice. 'To what do we owe this pleasure? No, sit down, Chloe.'

'I – I thought, if you had business to discuss—'

'I want you to stay.' He smiled, but it was an order. James felt a chill creep along his veins.

'Good morning, Sir Gerald, Lady Radclyff.' He inclined his head politely at Chloe, who looked down at the needlework lying in her lap. 'The directors asked me to invite you both to be their special guests on the train which will make the inaugural journey from Penryn to the mid-point of the line, which will be followed by a champagne lunch.'

'How very kind of them,' Sir Gerald said drily. 'Don't you think so, my dear?'

'Yes, indeed.'

Though he didn't dare look at her, afraid he might not be able to maintain the impassive façade of which he had always been so proud, and all too aware that the older man was very much on his guard, James knew something was terribly wrong.

'I must say I'm rather surprised you have come to issue the invitation in person,' the baronet said. 'I would have thought you had more important matters to attend to.'

'You're right, sir, I do. But the directors considered the importance of the occasion warranted both prompt delivery and my personal attention.' Taking the thick creamy envelope containing the deckle-edged card from his pocket, James laid it on the nearest side-table, noting that he had not been invited to sit down.

'Aren't you going to congratulate me on my swift recovery?'

'Indeed, sir, I was about to do so.'

The baronet's smile reminded James of a shark. It contained many more teeth than he remembered. 'It is all due to excellent care and loving attention.' Leaning across he patted Chloe's hand.

'It has made me appreciate even more my good fortune in having such a devoted wife.' His gaze snapped up at James who, acutely aware of undercurrents in the room and on his guard, met it evenly. 'You should marry. A young man of ambition needs the comfort of a wife and the prospect of sons to follow him. In fact,' – his smile was slow and lizard-like – 'my own dear Chloe and I hope to add to our family in the near future.'

Feeling as if he'd been punched hard in the stomach, James's glance flicked involuntarily to Chloe. He glimpsed wretched despair before she bent her head once more.

'C–congratulations to you both.' He forced the words past stiff lips. *What was going on?*

'Thank you.' Reaching out, the baronet tugged the braided bellpull. 'Well,' he sighed briskly, 'we mustn't detain you any longer. Hawkins will show you out.'

James swallowed his fury. 'And your reply, sir? May I tell the directors you will be joining them?'

'I suppose so. Yes, why not? It will be most interesting. Tell them we accept with pleasure. Ah, Hawkins, Mr Santana is leaving now.'

Thus dismissed, James was left with no alternative. With a brief bow, he preceded the butler into the hall and heard him close the door, shutting Chloe in and himself out.

'Mr Santana seemed somewhat on edge. Did you not think so,

my dear?'

It was like walking on ice, Chloe thought. Very thin ice: all that lay between her and drowning. She made a stitch, pricking her finger as she pushed the needle through the fine cloth, too nervous even to flinch.

'He did say he is very busy, particularly so since the contractor's sudden departure.'

'You could be right. Though my impression was that he seemed somewhat startled by our good news. Why would that be do you think?'

Was this some sort of test? Or was he simply playing? *Like a cat with a mouse.* Chloe adjusted her needlework so the tiny bright crimson patch was hidden in a fold. 'Mr Santana came on a business matter. The topics of marriage and a family are very personal. Perhaps they came as a surprise.'

'Really? Oh well.' Sir Gerald Radclyff's eyes were half-closed, his mouth satisfied. 'It does no harm to shake people's expectations occasionally. It ensures they talk. I would not want my business acquaintances thinking my illness has left me incapacitated in any way. Shall we have some tea?'

'There we are, ma'am. All done.' Polly stood back, wiping the residue of scented pomade from her hands onto a small towel kept for the purpose.

Opening her eyes, Chloe looked at her reflection in the dressing-table mirror. She turned her head and the morning sunlight gilded her hair, drawn back from a centre parting into a complicated chignon.

'Thank you, Polly.'

'You decided which it's to be then, ma'am?' Neatly replacing the silver-backed brushes and comb, Polly held the padded velvet boudoir chair as Chloe discarded her lacy peignoir.

She could feel a pulse throbbing in her temples. 'The blue.' Beneath her chemise, corset and petticoats, her skin was damp with perspiration yet her arms as she hugged them across her aching stomach felt icy. She stood still while Polly fastened the ties of her crinoline and ensured the hoops hung correctly. Then a silk scarf was laid lightly over her face and hair before Polly lifted the silk and taffeta dress carefully over her head. The band around her skull tightened.

'I can't,' she whispered.

Polly paused in her buttoning. 'Beg pardon, ma'am?'

'I can't go on the train.'

The maid's eyes met hers. 'I know, ma'am,' she said softly. 'Do you want me to tell the master?'

Chloe swallowed the tightness in her throat. 'No, Polly. I'll tell him myself.' After all, what could he actually *do*?

'Anyone could see you aren't well, ma'am.'

Chloe looked quickly at her maid, not sure whether to laugh or cry. Outside the breakfast-room she paused for a moment to flex painfully stiff shoulders. Then, steadying herself with a deep breath, she went in.

He was still at the table. The plates containing the remains of his breakfast had been pushed aside. A cup half full of coffee sat close to hand. But a wrinkled skin on the surface suggested it had been forgotten. Two newspapers lay to one side folded with a carelessness alien to her fastidious husband. He was still intent on the third.

She cleared her throat. 'Good morning, Gerald.'

Turning a page he gave the paper a quick shake and resumed reading without even glancing in her direction. His only response a preoccupied ' 'Morning, my dear.'

She sat down and shook her head as Hawkins approached with the coffee pot.

'Would you care for tea instead, madam?'

'No – yes. Yes, I would, Hawkins. Thank you.'

'I'll fetch it directly, madam.'

As the door closed behind him, Chloe leaned forward. 'Gerald? I'm very sorry, but I'm afraid I won't be able to go with you on the train. I have a terrible headache.' She waited, rigid with tension, for the questions.

He lowered the newspaper and studied her silently.

Her lips were paper dry. 'I'm very disappointed. But to attend the celebrations feeling as I do would be selfish and unfair, and I have no desire to spoil the party. I shall spend the day in my room.'

He nodded. 'You do not look your usual self. Perhaps a rest will restore the roses to your cheeks, and refresh your spirits.' Folding the paper he picked up the others and rose from the table. 'Naturally, I'm sorry you are unwell, but it is not the inconvenience it might otherwise have been. Some matters have arisen which require my urgent attention: business matters. So I shall be leaving earlier than planned.' He took out his watch. 'In fact. . . .' He glanced round as the butler came in with fresh tea. 'Hawkins, tell Robbins to bring the carriage at once, please.'

Ten minutes later, the clop of hooves and crunch of wheels had receded into the distance. Chloe sat alone in the breakfast-room sipping hot sweet tea. Gradually the knots in her stomach started to loosen.

The dining-room of the Royal Hotel was noisy and busy as people came and went. Waiters moved among the tables with loaded trays for those catching early coaches. Conversations ranged from excited arguments over various places of interest to be explored by those on holiday, to more intense discussions by men with important business to transact.

James sat alone at a small table in one corner toying with a spoon. He had spent a restless night: the little sleep he'd had filled with vivid fragments of dreams from which he had woken sweating and anxious. He had washed and shaved, barely conscious of doing so. And coming down to the bustle of the dining-room he had eaten knowing he needed fuel, but he'd tasted nothing.

Thinking of the day ahead he visualized the train ride. He had no idea if the directors had worked out a seating plan. But the arrangement of the carriage – which was really a combination of three wooden stagecoach bodies resting on an iron framework riding on eight iron-spoked wheels – meant that each pair of padded and buttoned seats facing one another would hold six to eight people.

If he were seated near Chloe there would be no opportunity for them to talk, and he desperately needed to find out what had happened. And if they were separated it would be even worse. To be in such close proximity and have to watch Sir Gerald claim ownership, when all three of them knew the marriage was a tissue of lies and deceit, would be intolerable. And as if that were not enough, he would be expected to make polite conversation, to join in the jollity and self-congratulation. How could he when he was utterly opposed to the whole idea?

He picked up the letter lying beside his plate. The thick creamy envelope was addressed to *Miss Vervan Polmear, c/o Mr James Santana*. Obviously from Edward Lumby, he hoped it confirmed her entitlement to the legacy. He would take it out to her. And,

while in the village, he would make sure the tally shop had sufficient food. He also needed to see the gangers, and to check all the
materials had arrived on-site. Together with a growing pile of
paperwork there was more than enough to keep him busy, *but
never enough to drive Chloe out of his thoughts.*

# Chapter Seventeen

'WILL you be requiring anything else, ma'am?'

Glancing up, Chloe replaced her cup carefully on the saucer. 'No, thank you, Hawkins. I'm not hungry.' She pushed back her chair and stood up. Her head still throbbed, but the crushing pressure had eased.

She had the day to herself, but what to do with it? Under Mrs Mudie's expert management the house ran like a well-oiled machine. In a couple of weeks' time it would crank up a gear for the annual spring-clean. Mattresses and carpets would be taken out and beaten, winter curtains changed for lighter summer ones, blankets and counterpanes would be washed, linen bleached, cupboards turned out, and furs and woollen clothes carefully laid by until required again in the autumn.

Claiming cleanliness, punctuality, order and method to be essential in a well-run house, Mrs Mudie was invaluable. Towards her mistress her manner was one of punctilious respect, but no warmth. Chloe had realized very quickly that in relation to the house her position resembled that of a ship's figurehead: decorative, but not really necessary.

In the morning-room, knowing she had to keep busy if she were to keep dangerous, tempting thoughts at bay, she went to her writing-table. Letters from various organizations of which she was a patron needed replies. Once they were done she would reward herself with a ride. Fresh air and physical activity would offer at least the *illusion* of escape. Might they also ease the tension that strained every nerve and muscle so painfully tight?

A brisk knock made her look up as the door opened and the housekeeper entered carrying two ledgers.

'Excuse me, madam, but I wonder if now would be a convenient

time for you to look at the accounts. I have checked the tradesmen's bills. They are all correct.'

No tradesman who valued Trewartha custom would dare over-
charge. Mrs Mudie had an encyclopaedic memory for prices.
About to suggest leaving it for a day or two, Chloe didn't get the
chance.

'I didn't like to ask while Sir Gerald was ill. But he has always
been most particular about prompt settlement. And we are now
over a week into the new month.'

Too drained to argue, Chloe nodded. 'Leave the books with me,
Mrs Mudie. I'll look at them directly.'

'Thank you, madam. I'm much obliged. Perhaps though, if it is
not too much trouble, I could have the money now? I'm going into
Penryn to do some shopping. I could pay the tradesmen at the same
time.'

Aware from previous experience that the housekeeper wouldn't
leave until she got what she wanted, Chloe stood up. 'I'll fetch it at
once.'

With Mrs Mudie following two paces behind, Chloe went down
the hall to her husband's study. Turning the doorknob, she paused.
Gerald had told her where he kept the cash tin. He'd said it was
important she knew in case of an emergency. But he had made it
clear that the rule of respecting each other's privacy also applied to
his study. She never entered without an invitation. And invitations
were extremely rare. To have the housekeeper watching would
make her feel even more of an intruder.

'I'm sure you have things to do before you leave for town, Mrs
Mudie. Why don't you come to the morning-room in fifteen minutes? I'll have the money ready for you.'

As the housekeeper hovered, obviously reluctant, Chloe went
into the study and closed the door behind her. It was a small,
almost petty victory, but to Chloe it was significant. She was
changing.

Standing by the door she looked around the decidedly masculine room, as if the deep glowing colours, the Persian carpet, the
glass-fronted bookcases, the leather button-back armchair with its
attendant side table beside the fireplace, might somehow help her
understand the man to whom she was married. They didn't. She
crossed to the large roll-top desk that stood at right angles to the
window. The lid was open, the leather-framed blotter almost hid-

den by copies of *The Times* and the *Western Morning News* all of which were folded to pages showing share prices and financial reports.

Inside the desk were two tiers of small drawers, and above them a row of slots contained folded papers, opened letters, and other documents she assumed related to business and the running of the estate.

Wary of disturbing anything, she crouched, her dress billowing around her, and opened the deep drawer on the right-hand side. Placing the cash tin on top of a leading article headed *Bankers' concern* she opened it. There was no key. It wasn't necessary. Theft was unheard of at Trewartha. No one who valued their job here would take so much as a biscuit without permission.

The tin contained several slim bundles of folded paper held by narrow red or blue strips of ribbon and, on top of these, a wad of banknotes secured by a silver clip. As she lifted out the clip it caught one of the red ribbons and pulled a package with it.

Disentangling the ribbon, Chloe lay the package on the newspaper while she extracted five notes. Setting the notes aside she picked up the package. About to replace it on top of the others, she noticed the handwriting. It seemed oddly familiar. She tilted her head to look more closely and, with a shock, recognized her father's flamboyant signature.

Easing out the folded sheet, she opened it. It was an IOU for 200 guineas. She gazed at it, nonplussed, then extracted another sheet. It was another IOU, this time for 400 guineas. There were no dates on the papers, and no names, other than her father's. Then they were no longer for money, but for parcels of land belonging to the Polglaze estate, and last of all, for the house itself. Why would Gerald have her father's IOUs? Unless ... had he, out of some sense of moral obligation, redeemed them on her father's behalf? That would mean *he* now owned. . . . But if that was the case why hadn't he told her? Because it would have been a cruel reminder of her father's hopeless addiction to gambling? Because he hadn't wanted to belabour her indebtedness to him?

The clock on the mantelpiece chimed. Mrs Mudie would be waiting. Quickly folding the sheets and replacing the ribbon, Chloe returned the package and the rest of the money to the tin.

After the housekeeper had gone, Chloe turned once more to her letter writing but found it impossible to concentrate. Leaving the writing-table, she hurried upstairs. She couldn't stay inside a moment longer.

In the dressing-room, surrounded by Chloe's winter dresses, skirts and jackets, Polly was examining hems, trimmings, and buttons, and making minor repairs before brushing and folding the garments, and storing them away for the summer in the huge cedar chests that would protect them from moths.

'I'd like my riding habit, please.' Chloe was already unfastening her cuffs and bodice.

'Yes, ma'am. Do you want me—?'

'No, you carry on here. I won't be leaving the grounds.'

'If you're sure, ma'am.' Polly's tone contained a hint of relief.

'Quite sure.' Chloe was firm. 'You have more than enough to do. I need some fresh air and will be perfectly content by myself.'

Half an hour later, having also refused Nathan's offer to accompany her, she set off along the drive, inhaling the scents of spring: the lingering perfume of bluebells, now almost over, and the sharp fragrance of young grass. It had never occurred to her before how rarely she ever did anything alone. In the house, out riding, paying calls, or at her charity work, there was always someone with her. Yet, despite constant company – or maybe because of it as, more often than not, she was accompanied by a servant – she had always felt slightly *apart*. She hadn't recognized it as loneliness. Not then. But since meeting James. . . .

After a short walk to warm and loosen the mare's muscles, she turned off the drive onto the grass and clicked her tongue. The mare broke into an easy canter. She hadn't been ridden for a few days and was alert and full of energy. Gathering the reins, Chloe gave a single kick with her heel. Ears pricked, the mare leapt forward and set off across the rolling parkland at a gallop. The sun was warm and the combination of speed and the crisp breeze made Chloe's eyes water. It was like riding the wind.

James held out the letter. 'A messenger brought it to the hotel late yesterday afternoon.'

Aware of Queenie watching with avid curiosity from the shanty doorway, Veryan wiped her hands on the torn shirt tied around her waist to protect her dress.

'Thank you.' Taking the envelope she turned it over, looking at her name and the address penned in flowing script and purple ink.

'Silly, isn't it?' She darted him a nervous smile. 'I'm afraid to open it.'

His brows rose. 'You? Afraid? I can't believe that. Look at it this way, whatever it says you'll be no worse off.'

He was right. She tore open the flap, holding her breath as she unfolded and scanned the letter. She looked up at him 'The family has accepted my claim.'

'I'm really pleased for you. Though it's no more than you deserve.'

'Mr Lumby—' she held the letter out to James. 'Here, you read it.'

'Well, well. He apologizes for having appeared to doubt you. And would be delighted to provide any legal or financial advice you may require.' He glanced up, his expression mocking.

'At a price,' Veryan sniffed. 'No thanks.'

He handed back the letter. 'So, what are your plans?'

Veryan hugged her arms across her body. 'I'm – I don't know. I dreamed about this, about getting off the line. But I never really thought – and now – I'm not sure where to go or what to do.'

He nodded, and she saw sympathy in his eyes. 'It's possible someone I know might be able to help. Would you like me to find out?'

Guessing who he meant and suppressing the twinge of envy, she nodded. 'Thank you.' She saw him tense and lift his head as the sound of a train whistle was carried towards them on the breeze.

'Paddy!' Tom's shout rebounded off the steep hillsides at either end of the viaduct. 'Over 'ere a minute. Look.' He frowned at the crack snaking through the stone chippings. 'We filled that in a couple of days ago. He shouldn' 'ave opened up again like that.'

'Why would you be thinking it's the same one?' Paddy prodded the crack with his iron bar.

'Well, if it isn't, they're opening up faster than we can fill them, and that can't be right.'

'It'll be all that rain, so it will.' Paddy sighed and shook his head. 'We can't spend any more time on this bloody viaduct. We've checked it twice now.' He peered across the narrow valley. 'They're finished on the far side. Well, so have we.' He turned to the rest of the gang. 'All right, lads. That'll do. We're skilled men, not a bloody maintenance crew. Ah, there's the boy. Sure, he's done well to be back so soon.'

'He's a good lad,' Tom agreed.

Paddy hammered the bar down twice more. 'It's solid enough. Fill it in.' A shout made both men glance round.

Davy was coming across the viaduct riding one of the tip-head horses and leading two others. The shout had made him look back.

'Will you be getting a move on, boy,' Paddy yelled. 'The train'll be along any time.'

Even as his shout died away they heard the shrill warning blast of the whistle. Davy kicked his horse into a trot, hauling on the halter ropes attached to the other two.

Another bellow echoed around them, and Tom saw one of the navvies on the far side, weaving after the animals, flailing his arms. He tripped and fell. Tom watched him stagger to his feet.

At both ends of the viaduct, navvies gathered their tools and moved to the side of the line.

'What was all that about?' Tom squinted up at Davy. Dangling against the animal's shaggy coat the boy's skinny legs were mottled with bruises.

'Da wanted a ride back.'

Tom and Paddy exchanged a brief glance. Paddy rubbed the blaze on the horse's forehead. 'Their hooves all sound? No cracks?'

Davy shook his head. 'Shoes went on a treat.'

'Get them over to the side of the track,' Tom urged. 'You'd best get off and hold them on a short rein until the train's gone by.'

In the distance Chloe heard the whistle blast. She reined in and the mare danced restlessly, reluctant to stop. There was a second blast, clearer this time. She pictured her husband sitting with some of the directors, a cynical smile hovering about his lips as they tried to persuade him to invest more money in the company. Was James sitting with them? Or was he among the other guests? Was he missing her? Did he understand why she had not been able to face being there?

She wheeled the mare and urged her forward. They flew down over the undulating grass, passing the brown scar of the embankment, heading for the bottom of the park from where she would be able to see the train come over the viaduct.

As the huge locomotive steamed slowly and majestically over the viaduct, Tom saw William Thomas lurch forward as the carriage passed, his arms raised. *What was he doing?* Then, seeing the man's leg swing wildly out to one side, Tom realized. Determined to get a ride back, Davy's father had jumped onto the buffers and was hanging onto the back of the coach.

The locomotive was barely twenty feet away, a gleaming black monster hissing steam, when it seemed to shiver. Tom blinked. A distortion of the air caused by heat rising from the stone ballast? Then a sharp crack like a gunshot made him start. It was followed by a low ominous rumble. He looked round quickly, but saw nothing untoward as, towering above him, the massive engine, came closer, snorting like some primeval beast, iron wheels grinding on iron rail.

This was no mirage. He could feel the ground vibrating beneath his feet. It was a strange sensation, unnerving. He gazed up as it drew level, deafened by the screeching and hiss of high-pressure steam. Glimpsing movement from the corner of his eye he glanced from the leviathan back towards the viaduct.

A block of stone from the rampart wall edging the supported track toppled slowly inward. It missed the rail, falling onto the outer edge of a sleeper. Then, as he watched, the ballast beneath the rails at the centre of the viaduct suddenly disappeared. For a split second Tom didn't believe what he was seeing. Then, as the noise reached him like distant rolling thunder, he realized the central arch had collapsed, crumbling into the valley far beneath.

He stared, speechless with horror as the other arches began to follow.

The monster steamed slowly past, unaware of the yawning chasm opening up behind as the rest of the viaduct began to break apart faster than the train was moving. The air was filled with yells and shouts as the other navvies registered what was happening. Tom saw Yorky and Nipper waving wildly at the driver.

'*No!*' he roared, too late. 'Keep going! Don't stop!' But the locomotive was already slowing. By the time it stopped, brakes shrieking like souls in torment, and clouds of steam billowing around the huge driving wheels, the locomotive was out of danger, but the rear end of the carriage was still on the supporting pillar built partly into the valley side.

There was another grating rumble. Then, with a long groan, the rails beneath the carriage began to twist as the pillar gave way and subsided in a tumbling avalanche of wood and stone and mud.

'Mother o' God,' Paddy gasped as the carriage tilted backward at an angle and stopped with a jerk, attached to the locomotive only by the coupling chains. Stricken faces peered through the windows. But the directors and their guests were not yet fully aware of the peril they were in.

A wail of terror rose to a scream as William Thomas slipped from his precarious perch on the buffers. Even as Tom darted forward towards the rear of the carriage, automatically reaching for the arm that clawed desperately for a handhold, William lost his grip and pitched headlong into the void. Tom stopped abruptly, closing his eyes as he heard the body land.

Behind him, Paddy clambered up the side of the locomotive to shove the wide-eyed, trembling driver back onto the footplate. 'Blow the whistle! Keep blowing the whistle!'

Chloe stared in disbelief at the empty space where the viaduct had been, her mouth dust-dry with shock. The sound of the whistle, short shrill blasts, galvanized her. *James was in the carriage.* So too was Gerald. She slammed her heel into the mare's side, leaning forward to urge her on. As they flew down the slope at breakneck speed she saw a gang of navvies swarming round the front part of the carriage. The door nearest the locomotive was opened and slowly, *too slowly*, figures began to emerge. But they were too far away for her to identify.

As the final rumble died away, Veryan looked at James. 'I thought . . . the men said you'd finished dynamiting.'

'We have.' His forehead creased in a puzzled frown. 'It can't be the quarry. Tomorrow's their day—' The train whistle cut him short. At the third urgent blast James turned towards the sound. Veryan watched the colour drain from his face. 'Oh no,' he whispered. 'Please, no.' He spun round, already running for his horse.

She raced after him. Paddy's gang was working on the viaduct. *Tom.* 'Take me with you,' she begged. 'Davy took horses to be shod this morning. He'll be on his way back. If anything's happened . . . I'm strong. I can help.'

All around them, women were emerging from the shanties. The younger ones were merely curious. The older ones, more experienced, were anxious. Seeing James they started forward.

'What's all the noise for?'

'What's going on?'

'That's what I'm going to find out.' Quickly astride his horse he kicked free of the stirrup to give Veryan a foothold and, seizing her elbow, hauled her up behind him. She barely had time to grab hold before they were hurtling out of the village.

Ashen and trembling, the directors and their guests were helped down onto the track, urged on by cries of, 'Don't you worry, that ol' carriage idn going nowhere till you're all out, safe and sound. Cmon now, we won't let 'e fall. Jump, my 'andsome. T'idn as far as it looks.' They were glad now of the grimy calloused hands belonging to men who, a few months ago, they had denounced as drunken heathens, unfit to live in decent society.

Amid the noise and mêlée, Tom glimpsed Davy who was losing his battle to hang onto the three horses. Terrified by the whistle blasts and gushing steam, their eyes rolled wildly, and each jerk of their heads threatened to wrench his arms out of their sockets. Still he hung on, leaning back as they skittered and tugged, dragging him over the stone ballast.

Ripping off his shirt as he ran towards the boy, Tom caught the material between his teeth and tore it into rough strips. 'All right, my 'andsome. You hang on now.' The horses twisted violently, pulling the ropes through Davy's small palms. His face screwed up and with a cry of pain he clutched his seared hands to his chest. Tom grabbed the ropes and tugged hard, yanking the animals' heads down.

'Here, lad.' He passed over the strips. 'Tie 'em over their eyes. They'll soon calm down.'

Wiping his nose on his sleeve, the boy did as he was told.

Tom talked soothingly to the horses, stroking and patting them. But all the time he was watching Davy. Had the boy seen his father fall?

Reaching the bottom of the long slope about fifty yards from the locomotive, Chloe jumped off the sweating mare. Her legs felt weak and shaky as she looped the reins over a post. *Please let him be safe.* She would let him go, never see him again, and do her best to be a good wife to Gerald. She would never ask for anything else. *Just let him be unharmed.*

Then, heedless of decorum, she clambered over the new wooden fence that separated the track from Trewartha land. Stumbling over the rough ballast stones, she hurried towards the milling knot of people. Two ladies had fainted. Lying in bright puddles of frilled and beribboned taffeta at the side of the track they looked like collapsed balloons. Anxious husbands knelt beside them, helpless and embarrassed. Catching sight of her, they both reached out like drowning men for a lifebelt.

'Lady Radclyff, thank Heaven. Please. . . .'

'Of course.' She forced a quick smile that was meant to be reassuring. 'Just one moment.' She scanned the faces, desperate to find James. 'I must first make sure my husband is—'

'Your husband?' Ingram Coles glanced up, perplexed, still patting his wife's limp hand. 'But . . . Lady Radclyff, Sir Gerald isn't with us.'

Chloe swivelled round. '*What?*'

'I received a message this morning. Sir Gerald regretted that, due to unforeseen circumstances, he would not be able to join us. I thought – we all thought – his illness – we were most concerned.'

'No, no, he's much better,' Chloe replied automatically. She opened her mouth, then closed it again. The chairman had not seen Gerald this morning. *So where was he?* He'd said nothing at breakfast about changing his plans. Had something happened *after* he left home? Or had he never intended to join the party? Just then, to Chloe's immense relief, Ingram Coles's wife moaned. He immediately turned to her.

'There, there, my dear. Are you recovered now?'

Eleanor Coles's eyes fluttered open and she raised one hand to her forehead.

At the sound of thundering hooves Chloe glanced round. Her heart leapt to her throat and she swayed, momentarily dizzy, as James reined his mount to a halt. She saw his gaze sweep the crowd, and find her. Their eyes locked. Then it hit her. *He hadn't been on the train either.*

Throwing his leg over the front of the saddle, he jumped down and strode towards her. Veryan Polmear slid from the saddle and ran to the other side of the track, her face intent, her eyes searching.

'Lady Radclyff.' Catching her hand James raised it briefly to his lips. Only Chloe knew how tightly he clasped her fingers. 'I am relieved to see you unharmed.'

'Mr Santana.' Relief left her weak. 'I didn't – I couldn't—' She swallowed hard, forcing a smile. 'I was not on the train . . . a minor indisposition. . . . I was riding when I saw . . . and I have just learned . . . it appears my husband did not join the train either.'

'Lady Radclyff,' Ingram Coles cried out plaintively. 'My wife needs—'

'Mr Santana,' Paddy shouted, running towards them.

'I'll see you later,' James whispered.

She gave a brief nod. As he strode away with the ganger, she clapped her hands, wincing as the whistle blew again. 'Ladies and gentlemen, could I have your attention? You are all most welcome to rest at Trewartha while carriages are prepared to return you to Falmouth. If you will follow me up through the park. . . .'

Veryan pushed anxiously through the throng. All around her the rough accents of navvies mingled with the refined tones of the directors. In other circumstances it might have amused her. But under what other circumstances would it have happened?

'Davy?' she shouted, craning to see over the heads around her.

'Over here.'

Turning, she saw Tom and was shaken by the strength of her relief. He beckoned and, as she started towards him she glimpsed heavily muscled shoulders and the dark curling hair on his chest and realized he was naked to the waist. Heat flushed her upper body. For goodness sake, there was nothing new about half-naked men. She saw them every day in and around the shanty. *He was different.* When she looked at him she felt strange: sort of shivery inside, as though she couldn't quite catch her breath. *He was just another navvy.* She couldn't . . . must not. . . .

A small body pushed though the people and hurled itself at her. Bending, she swept Davy up into her arms. He buried his face against her neck.

'It's all right,' she murmured, resting her cheek against his head. 'What happened to your hands?'

'Rope burns,' Tom answered, his eyes saying a lot more than his mouth. 'The whistle spooked the horses.' He jerked his head indicating the three animals, now docile under their blindfolds, being led away by Fen.

'That's your shirt.'

He shrugged.

'Is he dead?' Muffled against her neck, Davy's voice was thin and strained.

'What?' Veryan eased her head back to look at him. 'Is who dead?'

Placing his big hand on her shoulder, Tom drew her away to the side of the track. 'The boy's father jumped on the back of the coach as it came across the viaduct,' he murmured, then stood back so she could see the twisted and broken rails hanging out over empty space. He pointed down.

Veryan bit her lip. She had loathed and despised William Thomas, and though he deserved to suffer for his cruelty, that wasn't the type of death she would wish on anyone.

'Is he? Is he dead?' Davy pulled his head back, gazing at her.

She glanced at Tom and saw him nod.

'Yes, Davy. No one could have survived a fall like that.' She didn't want to think of what the body looked like.

'You sure? He won't come back?'

She held him closer, rocking from side to side. 'No, my love, he won't come back.'

Sagging against her, Davy's small body shuddered violently. 'You never done it. It wasn't you. It was him. I saw him.'

# Chapter Eighteen

V ERYAN glanced uncertainly at Tom, who shrugged again.
'What are you talking about, Davy?'
'The gypsy.' He wriggled. 'I'm a'right now. You can put me down.'
Veryan released him without a word, understanding he was embarrassed and feared watchers would think him a baby.
Squatting, Tom grasped the boy's shoulders and gently turned him around. 'What about the gypsy, my 'andsome?'
'It wasn't Veryan. She never killed him. It was me da.'
Stunned, Veryan dropped to her knees beside Tom. 'Davy, do you realize what you're saying?'
Shifting from one foot to the other, the boy scrubbed the back of his bandaged hand across his nose. 'I aren't daft,' he protested, hurt and hostile.
'Of course you're not,' Veryan reassured. 'But how do you know it was your father?'
' 'Cos I seen him. The gypsy was on top of you and you was trying to fight him off.'
Veryan's stomach heaved and she rubbed her arms, her skin crawling as she felt again the weight of the gypsy's body and smelled his stinking breath. Tom put his hand on her shoulder. She couldn't look at him. About to shrug it off she remained still. He'd heard the gossip the day he'd arrived at the shanty. Yet it had made no difference. The men had warned him off, but he'd ignored them. In spite of what everyone – including herself – believed she had done, he had still wanted to know her. She looked up at him, the warm weight now a surprising comfort.
'Why?' she whispered.
He seemed to understand. 'It didn't matter,' he said simply. Then

he turned to the boy. 'Go on, Davy. What happened?'

'Veryan had dropped the knife and was trying to reach it. But Da grabbed it. He stuck it in the gypsy, and the gypsy fell on her. Then Queenie and the rest come out.'

'And all this time I thought . . .' Veryan whispered. She glanced up. 'Why didn't you tell me, Davy?'

He squirmed again, visibly uncomfortable. 'I wanted to but I couldn't. Da knew I was the only one who seen what really happened. He said if I ever told he'd. . . .' His lower lip quivered. 'He'd k-kill—'

'He'd kill you?' Veryan prompted quietly.

'No!' Davy cried. 'He said he'd kill *you*. Then you'd be dead an' it would be all my fault. So I couldn't say nothing, could I?'

Veryan's eyes filled and she covered her mouth. 'Oh, you poor little soul.'

The boy gave a little groan. 'I got to pee.'

Tom jerked his head. 'Go on, over by the hedge. No one's looking.' As Davy scampered off Tom muttered fiercely, 'It's a good job the bastard's dead or I'd kill him myself for making the both of you suffer like that.'

Tom's anger, all the more powerful for being so rarely shown, made Veryan shiver. 'But if he wasn't dead, I still wouldn't know what really happened. It's strange. I had to believe Queenie when she said I'd done it. But I never *felt* as if I had.'

'That's because you didn't.'

'Yes, but don't you see?' She looked up at him, agonized. 'It doesn't make any difference. Everyone else believes I did it. And sooner or later the body will be found.' She shuddered. 'Every day I expect someone to. . . . And the longer it goes on, the more I hope, and the worse it gets. And now William is dead he can't be brought to trial. Besides,' – she drew a deep hopeless sigh – 'everyone knows Davy likes to spend time with me. Just as they know his father used to beat him. They'd think he was making it up. Blaming it on his father to protect me.'

'You don't have to worry about the body. It'll never be found.'

'How can you know that?' She was both anguished and scornful, not daring to hope he might be right.

He brought his head close to hers. 'Because he isn't where he was dumped. I tipped him down an old mineshaft.'

Suddenly she remembered: the night he'd gone out and none of the men had known where: the state of his shirt the next day. He'd done that for her? Even though at that time he – along with the rest of the shanty – believed she had killed Gypsy Ned?

The lump in her throat was painful. 'I'll never be able to repay you.'

He straightened up, his face tight and hard. 'Did I ask you to? I'm no blackmailer.'

'No, I didn't mean—'

'I'm not after your money. I told you so you'd know you're safe. You can go whenever you like. There's nothing to hold you here.'

She flinched. *The prospect should fill her with pleasure. Why didn't it?* Reaching into the pocket of her dress she pulled out the folded letter and held it up with shaking fingers. 'Mr Santana brought this with him this morning.'

His face set like stone. 'Good news is it?'

'Yes, I—' *suppose so.* What was wrong with her? Of course it was good news: the best.

'No good showing me.' He shoved both hands into his trouser pockets, his aggression startling. 'Can't bleddy read, can I.'

'I didn't—' About to apologize for her thoughtlessness, she was swamped by sudden anger. Why was he so defensive? And why take it out on her? Hadn't she been helping him? Retreating into her shell, pretending unconcern, she waved the letter. 'The legacy is confirmed. I just have to go and collect it.'

He didn't move, yet she'd have sworn—

'That's it then.' Turning away he whistled to Davy. 'Here, boy, time you took they horses back.'

With a high-pitched toot, the little engine trundled towards them from the head of the line. The wagons, recently loaded with ballast and rails, now carried navvies responding to the emergency signal from the locomotive.

Veryan watched Tom lift Davy onto one of the horses, wanting to say something, but not knowing what: angry with him, and not sure why. Handing Davy the leading ropes for the other two, and pulling off their blindfolds, Tom murmured something to him before slapping Davy's mount on the rump. The boy set off along the line towards the village and, without even glancing in her direction, Tom joined the other men.

She might as well go. There was certainly nothing to keep her here. Yet still she hesitated, and heard James Santana detail a ganger and six men to work with the driver of the locomotive to tow the coach away from the overhang.

'Watch yourselves. I don't want it, or you, going over the edge.' As they moved away he turned to the others. Tom was among them. 'I need two men to recover William Thomas's body. The rest of you take your picks and crowbars and get down into the valley. The rubble and boulders have dammed the river. It's already beginning to flood the valley.'

Chloe moved about the room, ensuring everyone was provided with food and a hot drink. Hawkins supervised Henry and Ellen, the housemaid, who hurried in and out with fresh supplies of sandwiches, cakes, tea, coffee and hot chocolate. As shock began to recede, relief made the men more effusive than usual. Chloe caught snatches as they exchanged their own impressions of the event.

'A catastrophe.' Ingram Coles shook his head. 'Of course, we must rebuild. But the cost—'

'Not now, my dear.' His wife tugged his sleeve. 'For the moment let us be grateful that we escaped with our lives.'

'Indeed.' He patted her hand. 'You're right.'

'Clearly the fault lies with the contractor, and the navvies, of course,' Clinton Warne was saying to anyone who would listen. 'If the line had been properly constructed. . . .'

'We cannot possibly accept legal liability,' Harold Vane insisted to the deputy chairman. 'That must be borne by those responsible.'

Victor Tyzack pressed his fingertips to his forehead. 'But as directors I really don't see how we can avoid—'

'Madam?'

Chloe started. 'Yes, Hawkins?'

'The carriages are ready.'

'Thank you, Hawkins. Ladies and gentlemen?' It took a moment for the loud, brittle buzz of conversation to die away. 'I'm sure you are anxious to get home as quickly as possible. Transport is waiting at the front door to take you back to Falmouth. However, if you all wish to leave together, two gentlemen will be required to travel alongside the drivers. Of course, if that is not acceptable, you are most welcome to remain here until—'

'No, no,' several voices cried in unison.

'Most kind, but—'

'—generous hospitality—'

'—would not dream of imposing any longer.'

Twenty minutes later Chloe stood on the gravel, watching the last carriage disappear down the drive. Turning to go back into the house she heard the drumming of hooves and looked over her shoulder. A galloping horse, its hatless rider crouched low in the saddle, breasted the rise and jumped the wooden fence that separated the lawns from the park beyond.

As one hand instinctively went to her loosened hair, she glanced down at her dust-streaked riding habit. But her anxiety about her dishevelled appearance melted away as she realized suddenly *it wasn't important*. She walked slowly across the gravel, absorbing every detail of him, overwhelmed with relief and gratitude that he was unharmed. How could she bear never to see him again? Yet, if she truly loved him, how could she jeopardize his future? She pressed a hand to her midriff against the deep grinding ache of impending loss.

Reining in, James jumped down. 'Whoa there, steady now.' His gaze devoured her as the horse skittered and pranced, nostrils wide, sides heaving after the headlong dash up the long slope. He stroked the soft muzzle, and she blushed under his scrutiny.

The stable boy came running out of the yard. 'Sorry, ma'am, but with all the others gone—'

'It's all right, Billy. Take care of Mr Santana's horse, will you?'

'Yes, ma'am. I'll give 'un a good rub down.' Billy crooned softly to the sweating, foam-flecked animal as he led it towards the yard.

James watched her while she talked to the stable lad. He loved her gentleness, her unexpected strength, the way she tilted her head. And her damaged fingers moved him unbearably. As she turned back to him, her eyes – before the lashes fluttered down – held an almost fevered brightness. A heady mix of tenderness and desire raced along his veins. 'Are your guests still inside?'

'They've just left.' She gestured jerkily, then rubbed her hands, betraying her tension. 'I wasn't sure if we would have sufficient transport for all of them. But the coachman and grooms managed to find horses for the barouche, the phaeton and the post chaise. So fortunately no one had to wait behind for a cab to be sent from Penryn.' She stumbled on the long folds of her riding habit. He caught her instantly, cupping her elbow. 'I'm talking too much. It's just – James, *I saw it happen*. And I thought – I believed you were—'

'I know.' Reluctant, but only too aware that they might be under observation, he released her. Side by side, careful not to touch, they approached the wide porch. 'I thought *you* were on the train,' he confided, his voice low and intense. 'And when I heard the whistle blasting on and on, and realized. . . .' He shook his head. 'If anything had happened to you—'

'*Don't,*' she begged.

He stopped. God help him, he had to know. He had to hear it from her own lips. 'Chloe, is it true? You and . . . him? A child?'

He saw her flinch, sensed her inward recoil, watched her face lose what little colour it possessed as some inner battle tore her apart.

'Not. . . .' After an eternity she raised her eyes to his. 'I should lie to you,' she whispered. 'Then you would go away, and you'd be safe. But I can't. You are the only person who has ever been honest with me. I owe you the same.' He saw her throat work as if swallowing was painful. 'When I spoke to Gerald about his . . . about what I had learned, he reminded me of my good fortune and my privileged position in society. Of how I would be an outcast if I did not continue in my role of loving and dutiful wife. He said' – she swallowed again – 'that if all that is missing from our marriage is a child, he will buy me one.'

'*Buy?*' He was incredulous.

She gave a brief nod. 'So you see it was not quite as it appeared, or as he intended you to believe.'

'Dear God!' James hissed, swinging round and driving a hand through his hair in raging frustration. 'Buy a child? *All* that is missing?'

'Please, James. Listen to me.' She bit her lip. 'He also made it very clear that if any man should find himself . . . attracted to me, and dared to challenge this arrangement, he would quickly find himself without friends or career.' Her gaze was anguished. 'He would destroy you. I would sooner live with him than live with that.'

He clamped his mouth shut. To argue would only increase her torment. He drew a long, deep breath. 'Do you know why Sir Gerald was not on the train?'

Her features lost their sharp anxiety, relaxing in relief and gratitude. 'I've no idea. He hadn't mentioned not going. The first I knew of it was when Mr Coles told me he had received a note of apology citing unforeseen circumstances as the reason he wouldn't be joining them.'

'So you don't know where he might be?'

She shook her head. 'But it must be important. He is still weak from his illness.'

He followed her into the hall and watched her alter as the butler came towards them. The suffering vulnerable young woman withdrew behind the practised façade of charming and thoughtful hostess. As she turned to James with a gracious smile, her eyes betrayed her. But only he could see them. 'I expect you'd like to refresh yourself? Hawkins will show you.' She addressed the butler. 'Hawkins, ask Ellen to bring a pot of coffee and some sandwiches to the drawing-room, will you please?'

When he entered the drawing-room, Chloe was already seated, a tray on the table in front of her. She looked up quickly, her expression troubled.

'Close the door. There's something else. . . .' She picked up a slim package of folded papers tied with narrow red ribbon. 'I don't understand. . . . Will you tell me what you think?'

Puzzled, he took them from her and sat down. Scanning the IOUs his perplexity deepened. He went through them a second time, recalling his conversation over dinner with Gilbert Mabey, the rumours about Sir Gerald.

Mabey's voice echoed in his head. '. . . a gambler . . . nerves of iron . . . friend of Polglase's. . . .' *Richard Polglase was Chloe's father. Richard Polglase couldn't pay his debts and shot himself.* '. . . won his wife on the turn of a card.'

As he realized the significance of those small pieces of paper, he sprang from his seat and strode to the window, trembling as he stared out across the park.

'James? James, what is it?' Chloe's eyes were wide and anxious.

He returned to his seat, but reluctantly. This was no time for sitting down. He wanted her in his arms, close and protected, while he destroyed her remaining illusions. He longed to take her hand, but dared not in case someone should come in.

'Chloe.' Strain roughened his voice and he cleared his throat. 'It is my belief that your husband holds these IOUs because it was to him your father lost his money and his estate.' He watched as she tried to grasp the implications.

'But . . . but they were friends. Are you saying *Gerald deliberately* bankrupted my father?'

He remained silent.

'But that would mean. . . .' Her voice fell to a whisper. 'Gerald drove my father to suicide. No. No, I can't believe that. It can't be true. For if it was, why would my father have asked Gerald to take care of me?'

'Would you say your father was a man of honour, Chloe?' James asked gently.

'Of course. I know that in many ways he was weak.' Her chin rose and her eyes glittered with tears. 'But he was a true gentleman. . . .' Then, as she saw what he meant, she gave a small pitiful cry and her lips quivered uncontrollably as she forced herself to face the reality on which her marriage had been based. 'Honour demanded that if my father could not pay his debts, then he must take his own life. And honour demanded his *friend* take responsibility for the welfare of his only child.' The tears spilled over and ran unheeded down her cheeks, now as pale as candle wax. 'Surely he could not have known . . . James, was it planned? Did Gerald drive my father to his death for *me*?' Her expression betrayed her horror and revulsion. But she didn't wait for an answer, the words spilling out as she put the pieces together. 'I was young and naïve. Gerald knew that despite my father's dissolute way of life, *I* had been strictly brought up. My innocence was his protection. If I did not know, I could not question. And he surrounded me with people whose jobs depended on my continuing ignorance. He was so kind, so generous. And all the time. . . .' As she raised eyes haunted and desolate, James saw her remaining beliefs about her marriage crumble as surely as the viaduct had done. 'I had no idea.'

'Of course you didn't.' His bitter anger made him harsh. 'How could you? You were the one innocent in all this.' He leaned forward. 'Chloe, you cannot stay with him. Not now.'

'No,' she agreed, utterly drained. 'No, I must leave. And soon.'

'Please, Chloe, let me—'

'No.' She drew herself up. 'No, James. I know you want to spare me any unpleasantness, but I must do this myself. It was *my* father he . . . *my* inheritance he took. It is *me* he has used and cheated and lied to. So *I* will tell him it is over. You must not be seen to be involved. He would twist everything and try to blame you. In fact, it would be wiser if you left now. He could be back at any moment. And I need time to prepare myself.'

At the drawing-room door he prevented her opening it by placing his hand against one of the panels. 'I love you, Chloe. Nothing he does, or threatens to do, can change that. Nor will it keep us apart. If you want me, I'm yours; body and soul, for the rest of our lives.'

'*If?*' She choked, her eyes glistening, star-bright, as she smiled. 'How can you doubt it?' Reaching up she touched his cheek with her fingertips.

Catching her hand he pressed his lips to her palm. Then, unable to stop himself, heedless of the risk, he took her face in his hands and covered her mouth with his own. *Gently. Don't frighten her.* For an instant she was utterly still. Then her arms slipped shyly around him and her lips clung, warm and sweet, to his own. Her impassioned response filled him with a joy too great for words. He could only murmur her name as he brushed his lips as lightly as butterfly wings over her cheek and temple before returning to her mouth.

When he released her, drawing on will-power he didn't know he possessed, she looked as pink and dewy as a morning rose. She opened her eyes. Her slow smile held the radiance of a sunrise.

'I had no idea . . .' she whispered in awe.

James laid his palm along her face. 'Come to the hotel as soon as you can. I'll book a separate room. You will need peace and privacy to recover.'

She nodded and turned away, but not before he glimpsed the flicker of uncertainty and disappointment.

Amused and deeply touched, he reassured her. 'It is only temporary, my love. Until we decide where we're going. Meanwhile, we delay the gossip for as long as possible. But I will never be far from your side. And, believe me, every moment we are apart, I shall be suffering the torments of Hell.'

She smiled, secure again. But he would not have a moment's peace until she had left this place forever.

'Chloe—'

'Don't worry, James. I'll be fine.' Smoothing her hair, she took a deep breath, and opened the door.

After seeing James off, she turned to the butler. 'Hawkins, I want to be informed the moment my husband returns. Immediately, do you understand?'

'Yes, madam.' A twitch of surprise cracked the butler's customary impassivity, but Chloe was already on her way upstairs.

'Leave all that, Polly. I want a trunk packed.'

'What, *now*, ma'am?' Polly straightened up, the half-folded wool jacket forgotten.

'Yes, now.' Chloe picked up her silver-backed brush and comb from the dressing-table.

'But – but— Where are you going, ma'am?'

'Away. I'm leaving.'

'For *ever*?' Polly's voice rose to a squeak.

'Yes, for ever. Now will you please start packing? Use that one. It's not too heavy.' She pointed to a reinforced leather trunk presently half-filled with winter clothes. 'Tip what's in there onto the bed. I'll send for them later.'

'Beggin' your pardon, ma'am, and please don't take me wrong, but are you sure you know what you're doing?' Polly cried, taking an armful of underwear from Chloe and laying it carefully in the now-empty chest.

'Yes,' Chloe replied firmly, removing several dresses from the armoire. She turned, looking directly at her maid. 'And if I had known before what I know now, I would have done it a lot sooner.'

Polly's face flamed. 'Oh, ma'am,' she whispered. 'I'm some sorry.'

Laying the dresses down for Polly to fold, Chloe walked past briskly to fetch two jackets with matching skirts. 'A little late, don't you think?'

'I don't blame you for being mad at me. But, ma'am, I didn't 'ave no choice, not if I was to keep me job. And what with the doctor's bills and all for mother. . . . There's only me, see? I couldn't 'ave got pay like this anywhere else.'

*Thirty pieces of silver?* Chloe bit the words back. Polly had been a victim too.

'Please, ma'am,' Polly began tentatively after they had worked in silence for a while. 'I know I got no right to ask, and I wouldn't if it was just for meself, but I'll have to get another job and without a reference I got no chance of anything half-decent.'

Chloe paused. 'I'll need a little time to think about it.'

'Yes, ma'am.' As Polly continued packing, resignation bowed her shoulders. Yet, Chloe noted, she still took pains to ensure neat folds and minimal creasing. She had always taken pride in her work, and had asked for lessons in hairdressing so her mistress would always be up to date with the constantly changing fashions.

Within the limits set by Sir Gerald, Polly had been a great comfort, as well as an excellent lady's maid. Chloe had grown from a child into a woman in her care. It would not be easy to find a replacement. *Did she want to?*

'Now I think of it,' Chloe said, 'I do know of a position that might suit you. The wages are not as high but they would be sufficient to ensure your mother's care. You might well have to travel abroad. And the lady concerned would require absolute loyalty and total discretion as her circumstances are . . . unusual.'

'Ma'am, they couldn't be more unusual that they were under this roof. I promise the lady would never 'ave no cause for complaint.'

Chloe smiled. 'Then say hello to your new mistress.' But as Polly's eyes widened in realization and relief, Chloe heard a carriage on the drive. 'This will have to do for tonight.' She closed the lid. 'Go now and pack your own things. We'll be leaving as soon as I have spoken to Sir Gerald.'

Polly frowned anxiously at her mistress's dusty habit and the escaped wispy curls that framed her face. 'Do you want to change first, ma'am?'

'There isn't time. Besides, Sir Gerald's good opinion is no longer of importance to me.'

As Polly opened the bedroom door, a breathless Ellen arrived on the threshold. 'If you please, ma'am, Mr Hawkins said to tell you the master's back.'

# Chapter Nineteen

CHLOE entered the drawing-room as the butler set a glass of sherry on the small table beside her husband's chair.

'Dinner in twenty minutes, Hawkins.' Resting his head against the shiny leather, Sir Gerald Radclyff closed his eyes, his expression weary but triumphant.

'Sir.' The butler bowed. 'Ma'am,' he acknowledged Chloe in passing and withdrew, closing the door.

'Good evening, Gerald. Where have you been all day?'

'Really, my dear,' he remonstrated, eyes still closed. 'I should not have to remind you that it is not a wife's place to question her husband's movements.'

'And I think you would agree that it is not something I make a habit of,' Chloe responded. 'However, there was an accident today. Not here,' she added as he opened one eye. 'The viaduct collapsed just after the train had crossed. Fortunately no one was hurt. But I thought— I didn't know you weren't on it until Ingram Coles told me.'

His mouth twitched. 'Well, as you see, I am unharmed.' Turning his head, he smiled and closed his eyes again. 'As for the viaduct. . . .' He shrugged one shoulder. 'The company is doomed anyway.'

Reluctant, but drawn, Chloe moved to the chair opposite. 'What do you mean? Why?'

'There has been a run on the banks. One of the major finance houses in London has declared bankruptcy, and railway shares are tumbling. By tomorrow their value will have fallen by two-thirds. Already dozens of companies and contractors have folded. As far as Ingram Coles and his shareholders are concerned, they've lost everything they invested.'

Chloe's hand flew to her mouth, her concern less for the directors than for all the ordinary people who had been persuaded that their hard-earned money would be totally safe. She had read the brochures and heard the directors' speeches, promising a handsome dividend as well as the prestige of being part of an historic venture. Now those promises lay in the rubble at the bottom of the valley.

'I've spent the entire day at the telegraph office in contact with my brokers. I had a feeling about the market.' He sighed with satisfaction. 'My gambler's instinct. It never fails me.'

Chloe caught her breath sharply, pierced by his words. But he didn't notice and smugly continued. 'I managed to sell all my railway and other relevant shares before the real panic began.' He smiled at her. And despite a complexion grey and lined with fatigue, his eyes gleamed with satisfaction. 'The Radclyff fortune is undiminished.'

'I'm delighted for you, Gerald,' she said politely.

His eyes narrowed a fraction, but his tone remained light, almost bantering. 'Do I take it you are displeased with me for not telling you my change of plan? I did not see the necessity. Matters of finance are not your concern. And had the viaduct not collapsed you would never have known of my absence from the party.' His frown deepened. 'Is there a reason for your remarkably untidy appearance?'

'Yes,' Chloe answered calmly. She folded her hands, amazed at her *detachment*. Was she in shock? Or was it just that, having lived with such extremes of emotion over the past weeks, she had gone past feeling anything? 'After the accident I naturally offered hospitality to the directors, their wives and guests while carriages were made ready to take them back to Falmouth. They were here for quite some, time. When. . . .' She hesitated. She would not lie, but nor would she compromise James. 'When everyone had gone, I went upstairs to begin packing. In the light of all that has happened my appearance did not seem particularly important.'

'Not important? You astound me. In fact I cannot believe you are serious. Quite apart from the example I expect you to set— Packing?' He enquired sharply. 'What packing?'

'I'm leaving you, Gerald.' And there it was. The end of the charade: the severing of a marriage that should never have happened. The room seemed to hold its breath. The clock on the mantelpiece tocked loudly, matching her heartbeat.

Heaving a sigh he made a dismissive gesture. 'Chloe, I've had a difficult day and I'm tired. I am most certainly not in the mood for such nonsense.' Taking a large gulp of his drink, he rested his head once more. 'Now, kindly go and change.' He waved her away with a limp hand. 'I have no wish to eat dinner in the company of—'

Taking the IOUs from her pocket, Chloe tossed the bundle onto the low table between them. At the soft thud his eyes flew open. But as his gaze fell on the small, ribbon-wrapped package not a muscle twitched. Such total impassivity, she realized, was what made him such a good gambler, *and so dangerous.*

As he raised his eyes, the hairs on the back of her neck stood up. 'Rifling through my desk, Chloe?' he said softly. 'You disappoint me. What am I to think of someone who—?'

'Had you given me the money for Mrs Mudie to pay the tradesmen, I would never have entered your study, let alone looked in your desk. And I would never have known.'

'Known what?' His perplexed smile so convincingly innocent that for an instant she wavered. 'My dear girl, what have you been imagining?'

'No, Gerald. You explain them.'

He sighed once more. 'It's perfectly simple. I knew your father was in deep trouble financially, and because of it he was in danger of . . . well, shall we say, of doing something foolish. So I took it upon myself, as his friend, to pay off his debts. I did not want him to know it was I who had done it. But somehow he found out. And, being a proud man, a man of honour, he could not live with the shame.' He shook his head in sadness.

Chloe nodded slowly. Wanting to believe the best of him that was exactly how she had explained it to herself: the straw she had clutched at. Until James had outlined the alternative: that this man she had loved and respected had played cards with her father and, after gradually winning most of the Polglase estate, had set his sights on her.

She had been the ultimate prize, the perfect disguise. Married to her he was untouchable, the rumours proved groundless. And he could continue his double life secure in the knowledge that few would willingly believe such behaviour of a *married* man.

*She must not think of James now.* 'And you never thought it necessary to tell me?'

'My dear, how could I? Your father was dead, and by his own

hand. You were devastated. You needed care and the security that had been so lacking in your life. My only concern, as your father's friend, was to spare you further suffering.'

'So you married me?' Her incredulous laugh was perilously close to a sob.

'Come, Chloe, no bitterness. I promised to arrange—'

'It didn't occur to you that I might be interested in the fact that you had acquired my family home, and my father's estate?'

He spread one hand. 'No, my dear, it didn't. There was no reason for you to know.'

'But what if I had found out? As, indeed, I have.'

He moved one shoulder casually. 'Really, it's of no consequence. Given the difference in our ages I am sure to die before you, and as my wife you will inherit it all anyway. So, now you know, let us put it all aside and—'

'No, Gerald. Oh, you're so convincing. But then you always have been. I really believed you loved me.'

'I do love you.' His voice was unexpectedly hoarse. Seeing her wounded incredulity he added, 'In my own way. Chloe, I didn't choose to be as I am. Believe me, it has caused me more grief than you can ever comprehend. But none of us can help our nature. It is something we are born with.'

'Then why,' she cried, 'did you not stay with others of your kind? How can you say you love me, yet do what you did? What kind of love is it that lies and cheats—'

'You don't understand.' For the first time his mask of impassivity cracked and she saw his desperation. 'I had no choice. Chloe, I have wealth and status, a position in society. But in the eyes of the law I – and men like me – are beasts, loathsome and abominated. I could be sent to prison for doing – for being what nature *and God*,' he laughed harshly, 'made me.'

Gazing at him, seeing the depth of his torment, despite all her own suffering she felt a sharp twist of sympathy. 'I'm so sorry,' she whispered.

His expression changed: hope turning to quickly hidden triumph. 'Come, Chloe, we can—'

'No, Gerald.' She cut him short with quiet finality. 'I meant what I said: I'm leaving.'

'Have you thought, *really* thought, about this? I could cut you off without a penny.'

She nodded. 'Yes, you could. I expect you will. But before you do I want my father's house returned to me. Legally it may belong to you, but morally it's mine. I also want enough money to pay the navvies two weeks' wages so they won't starve while they look for other work.'

He stared at her in disbelief. Then caught himself. 'This has gone far enough.' He was brisk, impatient. 'You are being ridiculous.'

'It's a small price to pay for my silence, Gerald,' she said gently and saw the flicker of shock and realization in his eyes.

His knuckles gleamed white as he gripped the glass and swallowed the last of his drink. 'How could you?' he whispered. 'How can you hate me so much, after all I've given you?'

She resisted another pang of pity, recognizing his ploy. 'Indeed, I have learned a great deal in the past four years. I don't hate you, Gerald. I loved you.' She saw the quick leap of hope.

'Then—'

'I said *loved*.' Interrupting him was something she would not have dared to do a fortnight ago. 'I don't any more. But nor do I have the heart, or the strength, to hate you.'

His very lack of expression told her she had struck deep. He gestured in dismissal. 'Well, if you are determined to go I will not stop you. But at least have the common sense to wait until the morning. It could be dangerous on the roads. Particularly if the navvies—'

'Thank you, but I prefer to leave now.' Chloe knew she was in greater danger by remaining here than from the navvies. Knowledge was power, and she had too much. 'It's not yet dark, and Polly is coming with me. As soon as the financial arrangements are confirmed I will be leaving Cornwall for a while, so you will suffer minimal embarrassment and will be free to continue living as you always have.'

He stared at her as though she was a stranger he had never seen before. And, she realized, in a way he hadn't. She was no longer the grateful, eager-to-please child he had manipulated to suit himself. They had both been living a lie. But while he had done so deliberately, she had not even known.

Still wearing her riding habit Chloe clutched her small reticule between gloved hands and gazed out of the window as the barouche swayed and jolted down the drive. Her trunk and overnight case together with Polly's bulging carpetbag were piled on the seat opposite. The sun had set in a glory of crimson and gold, and streaks of high cloud glowed deep pink against the paling sky.

'Beg pardon, ma'am, but can I ask where we're going?' Polly settled her hat more firmly.

Chloe's reflection smiled back at her. 'The Royal Hotel at Falmouth.' She did not look back.

Two days later Tom stood in the queue with the rest of the gang moving slowly nearer to the table set up outside the shop. Sitting on a rickety old chair, the bank official looked hot and uncomfortable in his black suit and stiff white collar. His pale face glistened and his hair was slicked down and shiny with pomade. Next to him sat Mr Santana with Lady Radclyff alongside.

The engineer had made a little speech telling them it was only through Her Ladyship's kindness that they were getting paid at all. She had gone pink, and Tom thought he'd never seen her look prettier.

'Name?' The clerk dipped his pen in the squat ink bottle and carefully drew it across the edge to remove the excess.

'Tom Reskilly.'

The clerk looked at Bernard Timms, who ran a stubby finger down his list, then gave a brief nod.

'It's not that I don't trust them,' Tom had overheard the engineer explaining the lists and checks to Lady Radclyff, 'but navvies are coming and going all the time. Some gangs stick together for the duration of a job. Others change almost daily. In those cases no one recognizes anyone else, and a man's name is whatever he chooses to call himself. I want to make sure that everyone entitled to pay gets it, but only once.'

Tom had seen her nod and give the engineer a quick shy smile. It had been obvious from the first time he saw them together that Mr Santana admired Lady Radclyff. But now, though they were both so polite and proper, it was plain as day just from the way they looked at each other that there was something more between them.

Envy, rare and powerful, mocked him. Was he going to leave without even trying? Pride was a fine thing. But where he was going the winters were bitterly cold. Pride didn't warm a man's bed, or his heart. All right, so he didn't have much money, certainly not as much as her, but he could make it. He had enough for his fare and to get a start. And what he lacked in cash he made up for in a strong back, a hunger to learn, and determination to succeed. If he didn't ask, he'd never know. And if she turned him down. . . . He'd deal with that when the time came.

'Make your mark there,' the bank clerk pointed.

'I'll *sign*,' Tom said, not quite able to mask his pride. Taking the pen, he wrote his name with care.

With the cash in his pocket reassuringly heavy against his thigh, he crossed to the shanty, ducking his head automatically as he went through the doorway. Veryan stood at the table chopping vegetables. Davy sat by the fire, his chin on his knees.

Tom hesitated. He had hoped to find her alone.

Davy looked round. 'All right, Tom?' He tried to grin, and Tom saw his grubby face was tear-stained.

'I'm better for seeing you two.' Sticking his hands in his pockets he fingered the coins, awkward in his uncertainty. 'Where's Queenie then?'

Veryan glanced up. 'She said she was going in to see Davy's mother for a minute.' Indicating the boy with a sidelong glance she gave her head a tiny shake. 'Bessie isn't well.'

'She idn ill, she's drunk ' Davy said, hunching his shoulders. 'She wants my money. I know she's me ma, but I don't have to give it to her, do I, Tom? She'll only use it for more drink, then I won't 'ave nothing to buy food.'

'You earned it, boy. I reckon it's yours. You don't have to give it to no – *anyone*,' he corrected himself carefully. He took a step towards Veryan. Her cheeks were just as pink and pretty as Lady Radclyff's. He leaned forward, lowering his voice. 'Can I talk to you a minute?'

She nodded, and carried on chopping.

He hesitated again, pushed one hand through his hair, and rubbed his face. 'Dear life!' It was half laugh, half frustration.

She looked up quickly. 'What?'

'Me. I never been short of words before. Always had the gift. Known for it I am. It didn't matter then, see. It was just a bit of fun. But now . . . well, it's different. It's important. And I don't want to say it wrong.'

She had stopped chopping, but she wouldn't look at him. 'Well,' she said softly, 'why don't you just say it, whatever it is?'

'All right. I will.' He cleared a sudden thickness from his throat.

'You know I said I had ambitions? Well, I'm going to Canada.' He almost jumped as her head flew up.

'Canada?' She couldn't hide her shock.

He nodded. 'It's a big country, and they've only just started building their railways. They'll need thousands and thousands of miles of track. And they'll need contractors. Men like me. I've spent my life on the lines. I know the job.' He had to pass his tongue over his teeth to free his upper lip. Sweat trickled down his back and sides. 'But I'll need help with letters and accounts and stuff like that. Just till I get the 'ang of it. It's got to be someone I can trust. And I thought. . . .' He cleared his throat again and blurted, 'Want to come with me, do 'e? Look, I know it's a bit sudden. It's took me all me time to get up the nerve to ask. So you just think about it for a minute, all right? I'll' – he gestured towards Davy – 'I'll chat to the boy while—'

'Wait.' Veryan put out a hand to stop him. 'Wait. Listen. I've been thinking, too.' Her face crumpled in a wry smile. I haven't slept for thinking. But I just kept going round in circles. All right, I've got a little money, so I won't have to go on the tramp, or on the parish. But I'll never be accepted back into society, not after all the years I've spent on the lines.' She hesitated, and he saw her colour deepen. 'What happens after?'

He stared at her, bewildered. 'What d'e mean? After what?'

As she moistened her lips he realized she was just as nervous. Hope leapt in him. 'After you get the hang of it and you don't need my help any more.'

'Bleddy hell,' he breathed, his eyes rolling in relief and frustration as he leaned forward and grasped her shoulders. 'I'll always need you, girl. *Always.*'

She made a wry face. 'I vowed I would never be a navvy woman.'

'You won't be no navvy woman,' Tom retorted instantly. 'You'll be a contractor's wife. You'll have the respect you deserve.'

She studied his face. 'You're a kind, decent man, Tom Reskilly. Yes, I'll go with you.'

'You will?' Even though it was what he had so desperately wanted, he could hardly believe it. I'll give 'ee a good life, maid. That's a promise. While there's breath in my body you'll want for nothing.'

'Tom . . . what about Davy?' As he glanced from the boy back to her anxious face, his thoughts racing, she continued quietly, 'I thought, with William gone things would be better for him. But in some ways it's worse. He isn't being beaten any more, but Bessie is selling herself for drink, and he's left to fend for himself. I can't just walk away and leave him. What sort of a life will he have?'

'Bleddy awful. But she is his mother. He might not want to leave her. And what if she doesn't want to let him go? She'd have us for child stealing.'

'Tom, if she goes on the parish, they'll put him in the children's home. And what if she takes up with another navvy? What will happen to him then?' She straightened, facing him squarely. 'If he wants to come, will you take both of us? I'll pay our fares,' she added quickly. 'And I'll leave money with Bessie to cover his wages. Tom, I have to offer him the chance. Then it's up to him to choose.'

'You're 'andsome,' he murmured. ' 'Course he can come. I'd miss the little b—' He stopped just in time. '. . . Little tacker something awful.' The warmth in her eyes made his heart swell.

'You truly are a kind, decent man, Tom Reskilly.' Wiping her hands on a rag, she crouched beside the boy. 'You know everybody will be leaving here soon, Davy—'

He looked over his shoulder. 'Can I go with you?'

Tom and Veryan exchanged a glance. 'That would mean leaving your mother,' Tom pointed out.

The boy's head drooped like a flower too heavy for its stem. 'She won't care.' He wiped his nose on his sleeve. 'I don't want to stay 'ere no more.'

Veryan swept the child into her arms and Tom saw her blink back welling tears. 'We'd love you to come with us. Wouldn't we, Tom?'

Leaning forward, Tom ruffled the boy's hair. 'We're going a long way, boy. We're going to make a new life in a new country.'

Davy looked up at him, a smile lighting his tear-streaked face. 'Cor! When?'

'Now.' Tom glanced from the half-prepared meal to Veryan. 'You're not doing any more of this. Meet me back here as soon as you're ready. I'm going to fetch one of the horses before someone else gets them.'

Veryan pulled off her makeshift apron. 'Come on, Davy. Let's wash your face and hands, then you can help me pack.'

Twenty minutes later she left her little hut for the last time.

Seeing the horse tied up outside, Davy raced across to the shanty. Veryan followed, carrying her meagre belongings wrapped in a thin blanket protected by a piece of tarpaulin to keep everything dry. It wasn't a big bundle nor, despite the books, was it particularly heavy. She squared her shoulders. And that was just as it should be. They were going to make a new, better life and leave the past behind.

Holding her breath against the stench that gushed out as she opened Bessie's door, Veryan glanced round, relieved not to see Queenie. She placed the money wrapped in a twist of paper on the filthy pillow beside Bessie's matted head. She had thought about leaving a note, then realized the pointlessness. Bessie couldn't read. Unconscious and snoring loudly, Davy's mother didn't stir.

As she re-entered the big shanty she saw Davy sitting on the top bunk while Tom stuffed clothes into his pack. Davy looked both nervous and excited. She knew exactly how he felt.

'You pick up any clothes for the boy?' Tom asked.

She shook her head. 'There's nothing fit to take. We'll buy him some new things when we reach Penryn.'

Davy's eyes were huge and his grin reached almost to his ears. 'Cor! Can I have—?'

'What's that 'orse doing out there?' Queenie waddled in. 'And where you been, girl? The veg should be on cooking by now.' She dropped heavily into her chair. 'C'mon, girl. Move yourself. I've 'ad some terrible day—'

'Ready?' Tom grinned at Veryan as he lifted Davy down and slung the pack over his shoulder.

She nodded, reassured by his solid presence. He would never let her down. She held out her hand to Davy. 'Ready.'

' 'Ere,' Queenie shouted, as they reached the door. 'What's going on? Where d'you think you're going?'

Looking up at Tom, Veryan smiled. 'Canada.'

Outside in the sunshine, ignoring Queenie's shrieks of rage, Veryan watched Tom throw Davy and the bundles up onto the horse's back. Then, falling into step alongside him as he led the horse out of the shanty village, she slipped her hand into his.

Sir Gerald Radclyff stood at the window looking down across the park to the stranded locomotive lit by the late afternoon sun. He raised the crystal glass and swallowed a mouthful of fine wine. *A dead end in front, a broken bridge behind.* Tossing back the rest of the wine he tugged the bell-pull.

'Have the carriage brought round, Hawkins. I feel lucky to-night.'

Seated alongside Chloe in the cab, James leaned forward to look through the gates.

'No wonder he made me promise not to visit,' Chloe murmured. The drive was overgrown, the lawns unkempt, the flowerbeds full of weeds. The house itself was of pleasing design, but peeling paint-work and windows half-covered with ivy and Virginia creeper pro-claimed years of neglect.

James took her hand. 'Are you looking forward to moving back in?'

'I won't live there again. In fact, I've decided that as soon as the transfer of ownership to me has been completed, I shall sell it.'

'What if he reneges on the agreement?' James was thoughtful.

Chloe smiled. 'He won't. He gave me his word. Besides, he has too much to lose.'

'Are you sure you want to sell?'

Turning to him she nodded. 'Quite sure. It's funny, when I need-ed comfort or mental escape I used to think about this house. But I don't need that any more. In any case, if you're going to be work-ing abroad, then I want to be with you.'

'You don't want to have somewhere of your own to come back to?'

She smiled at him. 'Why would I want to come back? There's nothing for me here. My home is where you are.'

'Dearest Chloe.' Raising her hand to his lips, he tapped on the cab roof and when the little door opened, told the driver to take them back to Falmouth. After the flap closed, he turned to her again. 'We'll have dinner, then I think you should get an early night. The next few days will be very full if we are to finalize matters before we leave for Spain.'

She squeezed his hand. 'I'm so looking forward to it.' After looking out of the window for a moment she turned back to him. 'You know it's strange, but for weeks I felt quite ill. I suppose it was the strain. Yet though I've had no proper rest, and the last few days have been busier than ever, I. . . .' Her cheeks burned and though shyness forced her gaze down, she refused to let it stop her tongue. 'I'm really not at all tired.' There was a short silence.

'Chloe?' He tilted her chin, and what she saw in his eyes made her heart leap. 'Are you sure?'

She raised her eyes to his. And smiled. 'Yes, James. Quite sure.'